She neede
hire her, and
So sh

The most obvious place to start cleaning was the table, but since Citizen Belanger was there, she started with the bench beside the door.

"What are you doing?"

Brigitte jumped at the stern sound of his voice but straightened her shoulders. "It appears you do need a housekeeper. Look at the dust I wiped from this bench."

She turned to face him, then gulped. He clenched and unclenched his jaw as he stared down at her. Perhaps she'd been a little too hasty in coming inside.

But no. She couldn't let him frighten her. She had to protect her children first, and that meant gleaning information from the irate man before her. "You stand rather straight, Citizen Belanger. Tell me—have you ever been in the army?"

"My past is hardly your concern."

She sucked in a sharp breath. Did he see the way her hands trembled? Did her face look as cold as it felt?

And why could he not answer this one question?

Books by Naomi Rawlings

Love Inspired Historical

Sanctuary for a Lady
The Wyoming Heir
The Soldier's Secrets

NAOMI RAWLINGS

A mother of two young boys, Naomi Rawlings spends her days picking up, cleaning, playing and, of course, writing. Her husband pastors a small church in Michigan's rugged Upper Peninsula, where her family shares its ten wooded acres with black bears, wolves, coyotes, deer and bald eagles. Naomi and her family live only three miles from Lake Superior, and while the scenery is beautiful, the area averages two hundred inches of snow per winter. Naomi writes bold, dramatic stories containing passionate words and powerful journeys. If you enjoyed the novel, she would love to hear from you. You can write Naomi at P.O. Box 134, Ontonagon, MI 49953, or contact her via her website and blog, at www.naomirawlings.com.

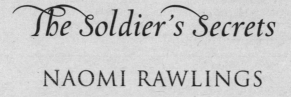

The Soldier's Secrets

NAOMI RAWLINGS

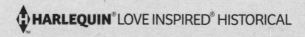

HARLEQUIN® LOVE INSPIRED® HISTORICAL

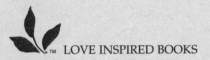 LOVE INSPIRED BOOKS

Recycling programs
for this product may
not exist in your area.

ISBN-13: 978-0-373-28260-9

THE SOLDIER'S SECRETS

www.Harlequin.com

Printed in U.S.A.

The integrity of the upright shall guide them: but the perverseness of transgressors shall destroy them.
—*Proverbs* 11:3

Pure religion and undefiled before God
and the Father is this,
To visit the fatherless and widows in their affliction,
[and] to keep himself unspotted from the world.
—*James* 1:27

To my parents, Marvin and Carolyn Montpetit.
Thank you for your love, guidance, and wisdom.
And thank you for the sacrifices you made to raise me
in a manner that honored God.

Acknowledgements

No book could ever make its way from my head to the story
in front of you without help from some amazing people.
First and foremost, I'd like to thank my husband, Brian. What
would I do without someone to cook dinner, watch the kids,
and love and encourage me through each and every book
I write? Second, I'd like to thank my critique partner,
Melissa Jagears. The longer I work with you, the more I come
to value your support for my stories as well as for everyday life.
My writing would suffer greatly without your brilliant mind,
and my heart would suffer greatly without your friendship.
Thank you for all the hours of critiquing you
poured into this story.

I'd also want to thank my agent, Natasha Kern, for teaching
me about writing and supporting me both professionally and
personally. Your love for writers and good stories shines
through all the hours you pour into Natasha Kern Literary
Agency. I deeply value your guidance and advice, as well as
your friendship. Thank you to my editor, Elizabeth Mazer,
for your helpful suggestions and enthusiasm about my stories—
and especially for your love of all things French.

Special thanks to Scott and Andrea Corpolongo Smith, owners
of Ontonagon, Michigan's Wintergreen Farms. Andrea read
over the farming portions of my novel to make sure I had all the
nettlesome details about blights, pests, and vegetables correct.
For more information about Wintergreen Farms, community
supported agriculture, organic vegetables, and yummy recipes,
visit their fabulous blog, wintergreen-farm.blogspot.com.

Beyond these people, numerous others have given me support
in one way or another—Sally Chambers, Glenn Haggerty,
Roseanna White, and Laurie Alice Eakes, to name a few.
Thank you all for your time and effort and helping me
to write the best books I possibly can.

Prologue

Calais, France, June 1795

Brigitte Dubois wrapped her arms about herself and trudged down the deserted street, darkness swallowing her every step. Night air toyed with the strands of hair hanging from beneath her mobcap, while mist from the sea nipped relentlessly at her ankles and a chill slithered up her spine.

It mattered not that it was summer, warm enough to sleep without a fire in the hearth, warm enough to draw beads of perspiration on her forehead, warm enough to attend her rendezvous with a shawl rather than a cloak. The cold came from inside, deep and frigid, a fear so terrifying she could hardly stay ahead of it. So her feet stumbled forward, over the cracked and chipping cobblestones, past the rows of houses shuttered tight against the darkness.

One night. One meeting. Then she could go home, gather her children and leave this wretched city.

Or so she hoped.

The breeze from the Channel swirled around her, ripe with the salty tang of sea and fish, while the clack of her wooden shoes against the street created the only sound in the deserted city besides the rhythmic lap of waves against the shore. The warehouse loomed before her at the end of the road, dark and menacing and ominously larger with each step she took toward its rusty iron doors.

Another shudder raced through her. Would this place become her tomb on this muggy summer night?

No, she'd not think such things. She had a house to return to, children to feed and a babe to tend. Alphonse wasn't going to kill her, not tonight. Her children were too important.

Which was why she had to get them away.

She slowed as she neared the warehouse, raising her hand to knock upon the small side door. But just as her knuckles would have met the cold iron, it swung inward.

"You're here." A guard hulked in the doorway, his voice loud against the empty street and tall stone houses.

"As I was told to be." She straightened her back, but not because she wanted to. No. Her shoulders ached to slump and her feet longed to slink into the shadows hovering beside the building, to creep back to her children and her house and the safety those four square walls offered.

But safety was a mere illusion. No one was ever truly safe from Alphonse Dubois.

"Come in." The planes and edges of the guard's face glinted hard in the dim light radiating from inside. He was huge, taller than her by nearly half a *mètre* and powerful enough to fell her with the club hanging at his side. Her eyes drifted down to the massive hand gripping the door, and she took a step back.

"That's the wrong direction, wench. And Alphonse doesn't like to wait." The guard's knuckles bulged around his club.

"Of course." She spoke easily, as though her body

wasn't trembling. As though her lungs didn't refuse to draw breath at the idea of stepping over the threshold.

"I said *move*." The man yanked her inside.

The door slammed behind her, its bang resonating through the packed warehouse. Gone was the grimy smell of coal smoke and familiar taste of the sea that permeated the streets of Calais. Aromas sweet like chocolate, tangy like salt and smooth like tobacco wrapped themselves around her.

Crates towered high, leaving only a narrow pathway through which to walk. Labels marked the sides of each and every box: silk from Lyons, and lace from Alençon and Arras, Dieppe and Le Puy. Tea from India, cocoa and cigars from the Caribbean. Sea salt from the Île de Ré, and more barrels of brandy than one could imagine. All sat stacked one atop the other in endless columns.

The contents of the single warehouse were worth a fortune in any land. But with France and England at war, Alphonse would reap even greater sums for his illegal French goods once his men smuggled them onto the English market. The trade materials like tea and chocolate and cigars would arrive on British shores under cover of darkness and away from the greedy eyes of the king's excise agents, bringing yet more profit to the smuggler.

And Alphonse had warehouses like this scattered through half of northern France.

"This way." A hot hand clamped around the back of her neck and shoved her forward, weaving her in an interminable maze toward the center of the warehouse.

When the crates finally stopped, she stood in a small open area in the middle of the warehouse.

With Alphonse Dubois looking on, seated dead in the center of his smuggling empire.

Heir to a *seigneury* by birth, he wielded more power

now than an inheritance ever would have given him. All of Calais knew his story, though she knew it better than most. He was a firstborn son who hadn't been content to accept the lands handed down for centuries, nor had he wanted to make do with his family's dwindling coffers. So rather than sitting in his chateau and watching as it crumbled about him while he ran through his precious few ancestral funds, he'd gone off and gotten himself rich.

Illegally.

Now Alphonse had as much money as England's king himself—and just as much power in a town such as Calais.

"Brigitte." The thin blade of his voice sliced through the air. "How pleasant to see you."

As though he'd given her a choice, as though earlier this afternoon he hadn't sent two of his henchmen to her house and summoned her while her children watched.

He studied her through eyes yellow with age, that putrid amber and the pale pink tint to his lips the only colors in a face otherwise gray as stone. "Sit."

It had come to this then, time for him to issue orders and her to defy him. Did he see the way her hands trembled? The fear that threatened to burst from her chest in a sob?

"I prefer to stand, *mer*—"

The guard shoved her forward, and she nearly toppled into the table. "A defiant one, she is. You can see it in her eyes." He planted both hands on her shoulders, forcing her down until she crumpled into the chair.

Alphonse's pink-tinged lips curved into a cruel smile. "You're dismissed, Gerard."

The guard moved back against the crates to stand beside another man, equally as muscular and thick of chest, and carrying another large club.

Alphonse took a sip of steaming liquid from a mug beside his hand, then reached for a sweet biscuit sitting on the table. He wore gray as always, the color matching his silver-tinted hair and aging skin. The monotonous color palate created an image more akin to a corpse then a living, breathing man.

"I hear you plan to leave Calais."

He'd found out.

She clutched her shawl against the base of her throat.

"Foolish woman." His eyes hardened into two frigid stones. "Did you think I'd let you steal my grandchildren away in the night?"

She hadn't a choice. He'd suck her children into the smuggling business if she didn't leave. Julien and Laurent were safe in the navy for now, but what of Danielle and Serge at home? How young did boys start running messages for Alphonse? Seven? Eight? Could Alphonse take Serge even now? And as for Danielle...

Brigitte swallowed, the type of work available to a girl in this industry too unbearable to imagine.

"No one leaves my employ without permission," he snapped.

"I'm not in your employ and never have been."

Something calculating and methodical moved behind his eyes. "No, you're family."

She cringed at the word. "My husband's dead. That eliminates any connection between you and I."

"It would, had I not five grandchildren whom you keep from me."

"With Henri dead, the children belong to me, and I'll not allow you to employ them in your wretched schemes. I'm not my husband."

"No, you most certainly are not." Alphonse ran his eyes slowly down her, his gazing lingering until revulsion flooded her body. "You claim you want to leave Calais, and let's say, just for the moment, that you have the money and means to do so. What do you intend to do? Where do you intend to go?"

To Reims. To my family.

She'd never be free of him if she said such things. He'd track her down and find her, taking her two oldest sons when they came home from the navy. Or he'd tell her she'd need to house his men and store his goods when one of his minions was in the area.

"Did you know, Brigitte, I have a rather marvelous memory?" He watched her through those hard, death-colored eyes. "It helps when one runs a business such as this."

A business? He spoke as though his smuggling success was some legitimate form of trade.

"For example, I seem to recall when you and my son first met. You were living in Reims, were you not? Acting as a governess?"

"I…" He couldn't remember where she came from and who her family was. Wouldn't use them as threats.

"I remember well, but every so often my mind fails me." He snapped his fingers, and one of the guards stepped forward, a sheaf of papers in hand. "I've learned to take excellent notes, you understand." He took the papers from the guard and flipped through them. "Ah, yes, everything is here. You're the niece of a *seigneur,* and your elder sister married a *seigneur*'s third son. Your father has passed on, but your mother apparently maintains good health and resides in your childhood home. I wonder how your mother and sister have fared, what with the *Révolution* and all."

She gripped the edge of the table, her nails digging into the aged wood. "How dare you."

"When my informants tell me you plan to leave Calais, that you hide away money and slowly pack your things, I ask myself, where might my dear daughter-in-law go? And why might she go there? And then it comes to me, where you hailed from, who your people are. Then just as I feel a spark of compassion and think that perhaps it's time for you to return to Reims, I remember my sweet grandchildren. Grandchildren who are useful to me."

"I won't let you touch them."

"I'd always intended for Henri to run my enterprise after I passed on." He continued on as though her words meant nothing. "'Twas a natural decision, you see, with him being my only son. But now that he's dead, one of your boys shall have to take over."

The breath whooshed out of her, and the air surrounding her grew thick and heavy. He couldn't get to the older boys. They were safe in the navy.

Weren't they?

"So which shall it be? Julien or Laurent? Julien would be advantageous in that—"

"What do you want?" She spit the words between them.

He winged an eyebrow up.

"That's why you brought me here, isn't it?" She toyed with the ends of the shawl lying in her lap. "To ask something in exchange for letting me move to Reims?"

He laughed, a soft, cruel sound. "Very astute, Brigitte. You always have been, you know. 'Twas why I was so in favor of Henri's marrying you from the first."

"I'd not have married him had I known he was a smuggler."

That cruel smile curved his lips yet again. "Which was why you made him such a perfect wife. You faithfully stayed home and bore his seed, not luring him away from his duties with words of love and flattery. *Oui,* you were perfect. Too dutiful to leave, yet too angry with his work to distract him."

"You're evil."

"It serves me well, does it not?" He took a sip of tea. "But let's begin negotiations. I have a certain task in mind, one that would perfectly suit a widow with three children to tend. You fulfill your assignment, and I let you and the children return to Reims. I'll even give you money to buy a house there. A nice little cottage near your sister, perhaps?"

She drew in a long, slow breath. Only one job, and then she and the children would be free. The proposition seemed almost too good to be believable. But then, he hadn't yet said what he wanted in exchange. "If I do your bidding, Julien and Laurent return to me in Reims when they reach port. They don't come to you."

"Of course."

"And I won't kill for you."

Alphonse's smile turned from cruel to dangerous. "Don't worry, *ma chère.* I seek only a spy. And justice. For the man who killed your husband."

Justice from a man like Alphonse? The very thought made her shiver. But what other choice had she?

Chapter One

Near Abbeville, France, July 1795

The children. She was doing this for the children.

Brigitte Dubois surveyed the countryside. The brilliant blue sky where two birds twittered and flirted with each other, the lush green forest to her right filled with a host of insect sounds, and the rolling fields stretching beyond the farmstead ahead and into the golden horizon.

Serene. Peaceful. A pleasant change from the grimy streets of Calais.

She must have the wrong house.

She'd never before given much thought to the soldier who had dragged her husband away in the night to execute him for his crimes. Had never wondered where he lived, what he did, if he had a family. But farming?

She forced her feet up the curving lane, climbing the little knoll to the cottage. A man stood near the stable, stuffing vegetables into an old wagon.

Her husband's alleged killer?

Surely killers didn't farm the pristine countryside or load vegetable wagons on sunny afternoons. They skulked about in the dead of night, meting out death and destruction.

"*Bonjour,* Citizen." She neared the stable where the vegetables waited, stacked neatly in crates and sacks.

The man's forearms bulged as he hefted another crate, his shirt straining against wide shoulders and a torso thick as a tree trunk. He would tower over Alphonse's guards, and he was so thick of chest her hands wouldn't touch if she wrapped her arms around him.

Powerful enough to drag a man like Henri from his bed. Strong enough to beat her dead if he learned what she was about.

"If you're wishing to buy food, I sell it at the market, not here." The man didn't stop his work but reached for another sack.

"I'm not in want of food, but a post." Not that she wanted to work for a possible murderer, but truly, Alphonse had left her little choice.

He turned to her and paused, his hands gripping a crate filled with turnips. Harshness radiated from his being, with eyes so dark and ominous they were nearly black, and hair the color of the sky at midnight. His chin jutted hard and strong beneath a chiseled face, and an angry scar curled and bunched around his right eyebrow.

She wet her suddenly parched lips.

"I haven't a job to offer you. I only employ tenant farmers, and I've three men waiting for plots next year already." He slid the crate onto the wagon bed, then turned and hefted another. "Have you tried in town? The butcher might be hiring, and we can always use another laundress or seamstress."

Brigitte glanced down at her lye-scarred hands, unlikely to recover after sixteen months of taking in laundry and mending. Besides, Abbeville was a small town, not like the bustling port of Calais. The people here probably had a favorite widow they took their mending to. "What about working as laundress here? You said you have tenants."

"Aye, and several of them have wives. There're women aplenty for doing women's work and older men to laze about. It's young men we've naught of."

Yes, she knew. Perhaps the war with the Netherlands had been settled, but France still warred with the Austrians in the east, the Italians in the south, and the English on the sea. Which meant the country sorely lacked young men…

Or rather, young, upstanding men. Her husband and the rest of Alphonse's smugglers had evaded enlistment.

As had the man before her.

That bore looking into. Why would a strong, healthy man be farming rather than serving his country?

Perhaps he'd gotten leave for some reason, or had already joined the army only to be injured and sent home.

But that still didn't explain how he had all his tenant positions filled and a waiting list of three farmers for next year.

And wondering these things would do little good unless she procured employment here and could seek answers. She forced her eyes back to the big brute of a man still loading the wagon. "What of you? Have you a wife to do your laundry and housework and cooking? I can bake bread and apple pies, cherry tarts and—"

"Non." The harsh word resonated through the air between them. "I've no wife, and no need of one."

Heat flooded her cheeks and she took a step back, even though the wagon already sat between them. "I wasn't asking for your hand, I was offering to hire my labor out."

She'd already tried to dig into his secrets from afar. She'd moved to Abbeville half a week ago, but talking to the townsfolk had gotten her nowhere. She had a meeting with Alphonse's man in three days' time, and nothing to report but the information Alphonse had already given her: officially, after Jean Paul Belanger's wife had died seven years ago, he'd gone to Paris and spent six years away from Abbeville, supposedly making furniture.

Furniture. In the middle of a revolution.

Did no one else think that odd?

Alphonse did. And Alphonse also thought Citizen Belanger the lead soldier that had found Henri and broken up a smuggling endeavor over a year ago, while going by a different surname. Now she was here to find proof and present it to Alphonse's man.

"Where did you say you were from?" The large man shoved another sack of grain onto the wagon and turned, his eyes studying her.

"Calais."

He frowned. "The port on the sea?"

"*Oui.* Have you been there? You can see England and its white cliffs from the shore. It's a beautiful city." Or it was if you lived in the proud stone houses set back from the sea and not in a shack near the harbor.

The man's eyes grew darker—which shouldn't have been possible, as they had started out the color of midnight.

He knew what she was about, he had to. She took an instinctive step back. If he flew at her—

"I've been there once, and it doesn't bear remembering."

Her breath puffed from her lips in shaky little bursts. It was as she'd told Alphonse, she'd be no good at this information gathering. If she couldn't look the man in the eye and ask him a simple question without giving herself away, how would she uncover his secrets?

If he had any secrets.

If he wasn't the wrong man entirely.

On the eve of Henri's capture, the sliver of moonlight trickling through the window had been so dim she could hardly make out her husband's form on the pallet beside her. But she'd felt his presence, the heat from his body, the tickle of his breath on her cheek. He was home, for once, not off on some smuggling errand for Alphonse, paying some strange woman for a place in her bed, or drinking himself through the wee hours until dawn. He'd eaten dinner with her and the children, kissed them and crawled into bed beside her as though they were a normal family.

Then the soldiers came. They didn't knock, just burst through the solid wooden door and shouted for Henri Dubois. One man yanked him from their bed. A big man, so broad of back and thick of chest his body eclipsed any light from the window.

Strange that she should recall that of all things, the way the soldier's body had been so large it obstructed the shadow of her husband's form being dragged to the door.

"Are you unwell?" Citizen Belanger watched her, his forehead wrinkling into deep furrows.

She shook her head, her throat too dry to speak.

"Citizen?" The farmer approached, stepping around the wagon and striding forward with a powerful gait.

"*Non,* I'm fine." She didn't want the hulking man beside her, innocent or not.

But he came, anyway, closer and closer until she stood in his shadow, those wide shoulders blocking the sun just as the soldier's body had blocked the light from the moon.

She pressed her eyes shut and ducked her head. What if this man *had* taken her husband? Would he drag her away to the guillotine, as well?

Her breaths grew quick and short, and the air squeezed from her lungs.

But nothing happened. She waited one moment, then two, before peeking an eyelid open. He stood beside her now, towering and strong, able to do anything he wished with those powerful hands and arms.

But concern cloaked his face rather than malice. "Are you ill? Need you sustenance?"

Sustenance? She wanted nothing from him—besides information, that was. She opened her mouth to proclaim herself well, except he stood so close she could only stare at his big, burly body.

"Here. Sit." He took her by the shoulder.

She lurched back, but his hands held her firm, leading her toward the house. Surely he didn't mean to take her inside, where 'twould be far more difficult for her to get away.

"Non." She planted her feet into the dirt. "I—I wish to stay in the sun."

He scowled, a look that had likely struck fear in many a heart. "Are you certain? Mayhap the sun's making you over warm. The house is cooler."

Her current state had nothing to do with the heat, but rather the opposite. Fear gripped her stomach and chest, an iciness that radiated from within and refused to release its hold. She'd felt it twice before. First when those soldiers had barged into their house and taken Henri away, and then the night Alphonse had given her this task.

Now she was in Abbeville, staring at the man she might well need to destroy and letting fear cripple her once again.

She's like Corinne. It was the only thing Jean Paul could think as he stared at the thin woman in his hold. She was tall yet slender, as his late wife had been, and had a quietly determined way about her. Unfortunately she also looked ready to faint.

He needed to get some food in her. He'd not have another woman starve in his hands, at least not when he had the means to prevent it.

"I should sit," she spoke quietly then slid from his grip, wilting against the stone and mud of the cottage wall before he could stop her.

"Are you unwell?" he asked again. A daft question, to be sure, with the way her face shone pale as stone.

She shook her head, a barely perceptible movement. "I simply…need a moment."

She needed more than a moment. Judging by the dark smudges beneath her eyes and hollowness in her face she needed a night of rest and a fortnight of sumptuous feasts.

"Come inside and lie down." He hunkered down and reached for her, wrapping one arm around her back and slipping another beneath her legs.

"Non!" The bloodcurdling scream rang across the fields, so loud his tenants likely heard it. "Remove your hands at once."

Stubborn woman. "If you'd simply let me…"

His voice trailed off as he met her eyes. They should have been clouded with pain, or mayhap in a temporary daze from nearly swooning. But fear raced through those deep brown orbs.

She was terrified.

Of him.

Why? He shifted back, giving her space enough to run if she so desired. The woman's chest heaved and her eyes turned wild, the stark anguish of fright and horror etched across her features.

"Let me get you a bit of water and bread." He rose and moved into the quiet sanctuary of his home. The cool air inside the dank daub walls wrapped around him, the familiar scents of rising bread and cold soup tugging him farther inside. But the surroundings didn't banish the woman's look of terror from his mind, nor the sound of her scream.

How many times had he heard screams like that? A woman's panic-filled cry, a child's voice saturated with fear?

And how many times had he been the cause?

Chapter Two

Jean Paul's hands shook, as they sometimes did when his memories from the Terror returned. He gritted his teeth and filled a mug with water, then grabbed the remaining loaf of bread and half a round of cheese, wrapping both in a bit of cloth.

The woman sitting outside his door couldn't know of his past, how he'd once evoked terror, how he'd turned his back on those in need for the glorious cause of the *Révolution*.

How their screams still haunted his dreams.

But she was wise to look at him with fear, as though she sensed the hideous things he'd done.

The walls of the house closed in on him, the air suddenly heavy and sour. He stalked toward the door. The woman had the right of it, much better to be in the sun than trapped inside a dark house.

He half expected her to have dragged herself into the woods. But she sat in the position he'd left her, with her back against the wall and her head slumped over her knees. Reddish-brown hair peeked from beneath her mobcap to dangle beside a gaunt cheek.

Too gaunt, too pale, too sickly. An image rose of a time long past. His wife lying on her pallet in the cottage they'd shared, her fingers and face naught but bones, her skin stark and pale, her body crumpled into a little ball as she struggled to suck air into her wheezing lungs.

He dropped to his knees and pressed the wooden mug to the stranger's lips.

"Drink," he commanded, perhaps a bit too forcefully. He attempted a half smile so as not to frighten her again, except the upward tilt to his lips felt rather stiff and foreign.

She took a gulp then slanted her gaze toward him, her eyes soft and dark rather than filled with fear. Mayhap his smile had worked?

"I'm better. Truly. I only needed a bit of rest."

Mayhap lack of food and water coupled with too much sun had caused her distress. He'd heard of people going mad after a day working the fields. Or then again, she might be with child. Swooning went along with bearing young, did it not?

She'd said she needed work. Her husband could be a soldier who'd left her with child and gone to the front. Or worse yet, her husband might have been killed in battle.

He opened his mouth to ask, but the woman braced her hands on the ground to push herself up. "*Merci,* Citizen, but I must away."

He shoved the water back in front of her face. "Drink more. I've brought you bread and cheese, as well. I'll not have you nearly swoon one moment and then be up and about the next."

She took the mug from his hands and swallowed. The wooden cup no sooner left her lips than he placed the bread before her. She nibbled at a crumb or two then wrinkled her nose, a ridiculous expression considering how ill she'd looked just minutes before.

But with the thick, dense state of the bread, he could hardly blame her. It tasted little better than mud, he knew.

He'd been making and eating the loaves since his mother's death last fall, and no matter what he tried, the heavy dough refused to rise.

The woman handed the bread back to him then rose unsteadily to her feet. "I'm fine, truly, and I've other business to attend now that I've an answer regarding a post here."

He stood with her. So they were back to discussing a post. Could the woman cook? Mayhap offering her work wouldn't be so terrible…

But no. He wasn't ready to have a woman about his house, not with the way Corinne's memories still rose up to grip his thoughts. "Try looking about town for work, and if you find naught there, then head to Saint-Valery. 'tis not more than a day's walk, and there's always work at the harbor."

Her chin tilted stubbornly into the air. "I thank you for your time, Citizen."

He held out a bundle of bread and cheese. "Here, I trust it keeps you until you find a post."

Her eyes softened. "You're too generous."

The woman didn't know the half of it. "Take it."

"Merci." She tucked the bundle beneath her arm. "I think I should have enjoyed a post here."

And with that she walked off. Head high, shoulders back, posture perfect, even if her gait was rather wobbly.

Brigitte settled the food in the overlarge pocket of her apron and hurried down the road. The children. She had to get to the children. They'd been alone in the woods for far too long while she'd sat in the shade like a child, drinking water and eating bread.

Of all the ways to prove herself a capable housekeeper to Citizen Belanger. She'd gone half-mad, nearly fainting and then screaming at a man who'd tried to help her.

Tried to help. How long since a man or woman had shown her kindness the way Jean Paul Belanger just had?

And here she was forced to spy on him. She swallowed the unease creeping up her throat and rushed forward, not slowing until the lane curved and the woods started, its towering trees and rambling brambles shielding her from the farmstead. At the first break in the brush, she veered into the forest.

"Danielle, Serge."

Only the song of insects and birds answered her.

"Serge," she called louder. "Danielle."

Somewhere ahead, a babe mewled. She stepped over a decaying log then skirted a pit of mud.

"Here we are." Serge sat on the forest floor beneath a tree, holding eight-month-old Victor in his lap. The babe's eyes landed on her, and he let out a piercing wail. Brigitte reached for her youngest son and settled onto the ground, then brought him forward to feed.

"Are you unwell, *Maman?*" Serge's vibrant brown eyes, humming with energy and life, searched hers.

Unwell? Was it possible to be anything but unwell with the orders Alphonse had given her and her failure to gain a post at the farm? How was she going to tend her children and feed her babe while working a job in town and spying on Citizen Belanger two *kilomètres* away?

If only Alphonse had given her money to live on while she carried out her assignment. But he'd been all too clear on that point: she'd receive funds only after she provided information.

Where were they going to live in the meantime?

"Maman?" Serge rose up on his knees and pressed his forehead to hers. "Why are you crying?"

She reached up and touched her cheek. Sure enough,

moisture trailed down her skin. "*Maman* had a hard day, is all. Nothing you need worry about."

Her six-year-old son sank back to the ground, a frown tugging his little lips downward, but he stayed quiet. She wiped the last of the tears from her face and leaned her head back against the tree trunk while Victor nursed.

The leaves swayed peacefully above as the soft songs of crickets, birds and toads twined around her. She sucked in a breath of moist air ripe with the scent of foliage. If only she could stay here with her children, shrouded by the forest and never worrying about money or Alphonse, or how to feed her sons and...

Daughter.

She jerked upright so quickly the babe howled. "Where's Danielle?"

Serge shrugged. "She went off to find some supper. Said she won't eat no more pulse."

A sinking sensation started in her chest and fell through to her stomach. "How long ago did she leave? I told her to watch you."

Serge shrugged again.

That girl. One would think an only daughter raised with four brothers would be a help to her mother, but not Danielle Dubois. Oh, no.

"Danielle," Brigitte called into the trees.

Nothing but the birds and frogs again.

"I'll find her!" Serge jumped to his feet, a patch of reddish brown hair flopping over his eyes.

"Non." She gripped his hand and pulled him down beside her. "Once Victor has finished eating we'll look together."

Serge scowled at his little brother. "Do we have to wait? Victor eats slow."

She smoothed her hand over the babe's head, the featherlike hairs separating between her fingers. "He doesn't take so very long, and he needs to eat. You were the same as a babe."

Serge poked out his bottom lip. "I suppose we can wait a bit before we look."

"What will you be looking for?" a young female voice asked from behind them.

Brigitte craned her head around and released a breath. "Danielle."

Her daughter of three and ten stood not a *mètre* from them, moving silently over the fallen leaves and underbrush. Her black hair tumbled freely about her shoulders and mud-streaked face, and thorns had tangled in the shoulder of her dress—one of only two she owned—to shred fabric about her upper arm.

"Danielle, come forward this instant." Brigitte stood and shifted Victor to her shoulder. "What were you thinking leaving your brothers alone in the woods?"

"I was looking for food." Danielle swiped a strand of hair away from her face. "But the rabbit got away."

"And a rabbit justifies you leaving your brothers?" She raised an eyebrow, hoping against hope that some semblance of guilt might flit through her daughter's head.

Danielle merely rolled her eyes.

"Aw, Danielle." Serge sprang to his feet. "You said you were going to catch one this time. I don't wanna eat no more pulse."

"I can try again."

"*Non. Non. Non.* There will be no more hunting expeditions, especially on land that belongs to another. And no one has to eat pulse tonight because I've bread and cheese." Brigitte reached into the pocket of her apron, fumbled to unwrap the food and broke the cheese into several sections.

"Is it from the land owner?" Danielle snatched a hunk of cheese and bit into it. "Did you get the post?"

"Non." And she had no one to blame but herself. What man would hire a woman who nearly fainted on his doorstep?

"So what are we going to do?" Serge stuffed his entire piece of cheese into his little mouth and chewed.

"I'll go back and request the post again."

Her cheese gone, Danielle reached for a piece of bread. "But if he already told you no—"

"I need to convince him, is all. He'll change his mind." He had to, because if she couldn't get a job with Citizen Belanger, then she had little means to fulfill Alphonse's task.

Danielle bit into her bread, barely chewing before she spat it out. "This tastes terrible."

Did the girl never stop? "Just a moment ago you were complaining about pulse."

"I wanted to replace the pulse with rabbit, not bread that tastes like dung."

"Hush now. It was a gift, and you ought be grateful, no matter how it tastes."

"Can I have another piece of cheese?" Serge asked.

Brigitte glanced at the little orange chunk of food remaining, then broke it in half and gave the pieces to her children. The taste of bread she'd had at Citizen Belanger's and some pulse later this evening would suffice for herself. She hefted Victor higher onto her shoulder, then took up their single valise. "Come, children. We'd best be off."

"Where are we going?" Serge gulped down the remainder of his bread, evidently not caring that the loaf was dense as a rock.

"Oui. You said we were done staying at the inn." Danielle scrambled to pick up the remaining food.

Indeed they were done with the inn. Remaining there

another night would take the last of their money. "We'll sleep in the forest tonight, and I'll go back to Citizen Belanger in the morn."

"Why do you have to work for him?" Danielle stuffed the leftover bread in her pocket. "Isn't there another job you can find?"

If only the child knew. "*Non.* There's no other job."

At least not one that would accomplish her purposes.

She lifted a tree branch out of her way and started back toward the road. Danielle didn't follow but stood rooted to the ground, her forehead drawn together.

Brigitte raised her eyes to the sky. Hopefully her daughter wouldn't figure out the true reason they were in Abbeville. Who could guess what trouble Danielle might attempt if she thought Citizen Belanger to be her father's killer? Goodness, the impulsive girl might sneak into the man's house at night and take a knife to his throat.

"Well, we don't need to sleep outside," Danielle declared. "I found a house."

Brigitte stilled. "A house?"

Danielle lifted a shoulder. "More like a shack, really."

"We can't stay in somebody else's house."

"It doesn't belong to anyone. It's abandoned."

"Someone still must own it."

"Not if the owner was killed in the Terror," Danielle shot back flippantly, as though the Terror was nothing more than a minor skirmish rather than ten blood-soaked months of the *Révolution.*

As though her own father hadn't been killed during those horror-filled days. To be sure, smuggling was a crime that would have left Henri imprisoned were he caught under any other government—but only the Terror dragged men out of their beds for justice via the guillotine.

Brigitte blew out a hard breath to push away the bitter memories.

'Twas unthinkable to live somewhere without paying. But then a house, even a dilapidated one, would offer shelter and protection. And if Danielle had found it, it must be nearby. Perchance all they needed was one night's stay. Hopefully with a little persistence on her part—plus a conversation where she managed not to faint—Citizen Belanger would hire her and offer shelter on his farm.

Not that she wanted to work for a suspected murderer.

But then, what other choice had she? "Show me the house, Danielle."

Chapter Three

Jean Paul yawned as he surveyed his beans, the green plants leafy and tall as they wove their way up the trellis. Though it was only the beginning of July, within another week or two his first batch of the tender pods would be ready to harvest.

He paused to pluck a weed, then went on to his tomatoes, squash, carrots and potatoes. The leaf lettuce and kale needed to be cut yet again, radishes waited to be picked and the summer squash would be ready about the same time as the beans and cucumbers. More food than he'd ever be able to consume, and just in the vegetable garden. His fields stretched beyond, filled with a mixture of wheat, turnips, barely and clover that he rotated yearly.

He drew in a breath of fresh morning air and looked out over his work. His land. His fields. Today he needed to weed the lower field and check the—

"Bonjour?" A voice called from up near the house.

He glanced at the sun, barely risen above the trees in the east, and hastened through the rows of radishes and tomatoes. Was there an emergency in town? A task for which the mayor needed him? Someone must have good reason for calling before the sun had been up an hour.

"Bonjour?" The voice echoed again, its light, feminine cadence accompanied by a pounding sound.

Who could it be? He frowned as he trudged around the side of the house.

And there she was, standing beside his cottage door as though she'd appeared from the mist. She wore the same threadbare dress and apron as yesterday, and her hair was once again tucked sloppily under her mobcap with stray auburn tresses hanging down to frame her cheeks. Her skin was paler than milk from a cow, and the features of her thin face sunken with weariness.

And yet she seemed beautiful somehow, in the delicate way only a woman could be beautiful when tired and hungry. He took a step forward, the urge to aid her twining through him. He'd hustle her inside where he could give her food and let her sleep. Offer her—

His movement must have given himself away because she turned to face him, then bit her lip.

"Citizen, forgive me. I thought you were…" Her eyes slid back to the door.

"Inside, hiding from you?"

Her cheeks pinked, a truly lovely shade, and a much better color than the deathly white that had stolen over her when last they'd spoken.

"Non, Citizen. I don't have a need to hide from women—or men. Farmers start their days early." He surveyed her again, her thin, willowy body and slender shoulders, the hollowness in her cheeks and her bonelike fingers. "As do you."

Her cheeks turned from soft pink to bright red, and she dipped her gaze to the ground. "I came to see about the post again. Perhaps you've changed your mind and are willing to hire me?"

"You need food, not a post."

"*Non.* I—"

"Wait here. I've soup you can take." He headed toward the well along the side of the yard and reeled the bucket up, his leftover food from yesterday's evening meal cool and fresh thanks to the water.

Footsteps padded on the earth behind him. "I didn't come for food. I came for a post."

He hefted the bucket out of the well and headed for the house. "And I told you yesterday, I've no need of a maid."

"The deplorable taste of your bread convinced me otherwise."

The side of his mouth twitched into that foreign feeling of a smile. The woman might be slight of body, but it took a speck of courage to tell him his food tasted horrid while he prepared yet another meal for her. "'Tis true, I've no knack for making bread. Though on days when I head to town, as I did yesterday, I purchase some."

He opened the door to his cottage, and rather than try to force her inside as he had yesterday, he left the door open and set the soup on the table. He ladled the thickened liquid from his bucket into a second pail, then reached for the loaf of bread from the baker's, tore it in half and wrapped it. The meal should suffice her for today, mayhap even tomorrow if she rationed it.

"I don't need your charity." She stood in the doorway, arms crossed over her slender chest.

He moved to her and held out the food. "You look as though you've not eaten for a month."

"I don't claim to eat well, but that's a situation I can remedy myself. *If* you hire me."

Having a woman in his home would be like salt on memories that were far too raw. Corinne's smile when he made her laugh, the shine of her hair in the lamplight, the taste of her lips beneath his and feel of her face in his hands. How many days had they toiled together, working side by side in the fields? How many nights had they spent in each others' arms in the little house at the back of his property? How many times had he come through the door, tired and dirty, to find a fresh meal and smiling wife awaiting his return...

"Citizen?" The woman in the doorway cleared her throat.

"*Non.* I can't hire you." He dipped his head toward the food he still held. "Now take this and make haste."

Her vulnerable gaze trapped him. She was so much like Corinne. Oh, her hair might be tinted with red and russet rather than blond, and her eyes might be a soft brown rather than blue. But she held herself the same—with strength and dignity.

Nothing good would come of having her about this house. Besides, if he did offer work, he hadn't any place to put the woman except for the cottage at the back of the property. The one he'd shared with Corinne.

He'd not darkened the door of that building since his wife's death, and he had no intentions to start now. The structure could sit and rot until it fell down for all he cared. Mayhap it already had fallen down. He didn't know, and he didn't plan to check.

"What about for bread?" the woman asked.

"What mean you, 'for bread'?"

"You could hire me to make your bread." She swallowed, her throat working too hard for such a simple action. "And I'll bring you a fresh loaf every morn."

He ran his eyes slowly down her. "How do I know you're not a worse baker than I?"

Her chin came up a defiant notch. "I assure you, Citizen, a slug could mix together some mud, bake it and create a more tasteful loaf than that which you shared yesterday."

He raised an eyebrow. "Tell me, did you compare your previous employer to a slug? It might explain why you're in need of a post."

Her face flushed, as though she hadn't fully realized what she'd been saying until he drew attention to her words. "Pardon me, but I'd best be on my way."

She turned, leaving the food in his hands.

"Wait."

She stopped just outside the door, the sun's tinted rays bouncing off the back of her mobcap and turning her skin a silky gold.

He thrust the food forward. "You're forgetting something."

"I told you I don't take charity." She kept her back to him. "I work for my food."

She wasn't like the other widows he offered food to, the ones with little mouths to feed and run-down cottages to keep. The ones that would burst into tears if he dared ask compensation for the goods he offered.

"Do you live near enough to bring me bread every morn? I'll not hire you if it means you must walk to and from town."

"I live quite close, *merci*."

His mind ran through the houses between his farm and Abbeville. Where could she possibly shelter? He'd not seen her until yesterday, so she couldn't live too near. But if she was at his door before the sun had fully risen, she couldn't live that far, either. 'Twas almost as though she'd been dropped off by the afternoon sun yesterday and planned to stay for the rest of her life.

But if her rigid posture was any indication—and the rather noticeable fact that she still showed him her back rather than her front—she wasn't going to volunteer where she stayed.

"Let's strike a bargain, shall we? You can bring me bread on the morrow, but only if you take my food today."

She turned slowly, her forehead drawn into a series of subtle furrows. "Have you flour, or am I to purchase some in town?"

"I farm wheat, remember?"

She licked her lips, dry and cracked yet somehow compelling. "I'll need oil and yeast, as well."

"Let me package some for you." He turned back toward the shelves that held his foodstuffs, trying to stop that unfamiliar smile from peeking out the corner of his mouth.

He failed.

Nothing. Thirty hours until her meeting with Alphonse's man, and still she had no information to offer.

Brigitte moved her tired feet along the overgrown path through the woods, her fingers clenched around the food from Citizen Belanger. She'd not expected to bake bread in exchange for food but at least her children would eat this day and she had reason to return to his house on the morrow.

And tomorrow she would ask again for a job. Hopefully the stubborn man would hire her.

A vision crept up from the corners of her mind, an aged memory of Mademoiselle Elise from years long past. The governess's eyes had been stern as she stared down at Brigitte, retching over a bush. *I told you one biscuit, but you ate most of the platter. Serves you right to be sick half the night. Be sure your sin will find you out.*

And then their strict old governess had walked off, leaving her to retch alone.

The same urge to retch twined through her again as it had years ago. What was she doing lying to a stranger like Citizen Belanger—a stranger who fed her, no less?

Would her sin find her out? Would Citizen Belanger discover the truth?

"Father, no! Please keep us safe." The frantic prayer burst from her lips before she could stop it.

She risked far more than a stomachache if she were caught this time.

The small hut Danielle had led them to last night emerged from the shadow of the woods. It looked as though it hadn't been used for a decade. Weeds grew up beside the door, and an empty darkness radiated from the cracks around the shutters. But it was sturdy, with heavy timbers pitched tightly together and a thick thatch roof promising warmth come winter.

Not that she planned to be here for winter. Alphonse would want her mission completed long before then.

The door to the little shack burst open. "Did you get the post, *Maman?*"

"*Non.* But I took a different job." Brigitte dipped her chin toward the bundle of ingredients she carried. "We've bread to bake for Citizen Belanger."

Danielle rolled her eyes. "How dull."

"'Tis work, daughter. We mustn't be particular."

"I don't understand. If this landowner is looking for a housekeeper, why won't he hire you?"

She slanted her eyes away from her daughter's gaze. Sometimes the girl was a touch too bright. "He's not looking for a housekeeper, exactly."

"But when we left the inn in Abbeville, you said—"

"Please trust me, Danielle." She pressed her free hand to her temple, already beginning to throb. "Perhaps I can't explain everything at the moment, but I have reasons for my actions."

Danielle scowled, black hair falling about her face in a riot of tangles.

"Good reasons," she added. Reasons that would grant them their freedom from Alphonse. But how to explain such things to a mere child?

"Then why are you doing all of this? Why are we using the name Moreau instead of Dubois? I don't like having a pretend name."

Brigitte's cheeks went cold, every last drop of heat leaving her face to pool in her toes. "I told you before we left Calais, we're using my family name now because I can't risk people here knowing our relationship to Alphonse."

Danielle propped her hands on her hips, a gesture far too mature for a girl of only three and ten. "You've never been ashamed of our name before."

"*Oui,* when we lived in Calais and everyone knew us. But not now." If Citizen Belanger truly was the solider responsible for her husband's death, her surname could give everything away. "We'll call ourselves Moreau in Reims, too, so accustom yourself to it." She nodded toward the door. "Now let's inside and see what progress you made on your studies."

Danielle flipped some hair over her shoulder and huffed. "I hate English."

Nothing unusual about that. Perchance she was pushing the studies a mite hard given their current living situation, but the girl found trouble too easily when she hadn't something to occupy her mind. Besides, English had been a most useful language living in Calais, and if the war fell in favor of the English, it might become even more necessary. "Did you finish your arithmetic and grammar?"

"I still have those, too," Danielle grumbled.

Brigitte pressed her hand to her temple again, the pounding growing ever harder, then moved into the little house.

"How do I tell the difference between a *b* and a *d*

again?" Serge sat at the table, scrunching his nose as he stared at the letters copied onto his slate.

She ignored the thick layer of dust caking everything from the wobbly table to the shelves to the pallet in the corner where Victor slept, and instead set the food on the table and peered over Serge's shoulder. "A *b* has a ball on the back of the stick, remember? And the *d* has the ball on the front.... Yes, like that. But I told Danielle to finish her studies before you started. What are you doing with the slate?"

Serge's piece of chalk clattered to the table while his eyes latched on to the soup and bread. "Did you bring food?"

She sighed. There went any chance of reviewing the alphabet or figuring out why Serge had the slate. "*Oui.* Citizen Belanger sent us some of his soup and bread from last night."

Serge was already off his chair and scrambling toward the shelves that held naught but two bowls, a motley collection of eating utensils and three plates—all seemingly left behind by the house's last inhabitants. "I'm hungry."

"Patience, son. I must heat it first." She crossed the small room to the aging pot on the hearth.

"I don't mind it cold." Serge set the bowls on the table.

"Me, neither," Danielle piped up.

She ran her eyes over her children's slender forms. Serge, with his too-short trousers and too-thin hips. And Danielle, with her gaunt face, bony shoulders and dress that would fit a girl who weighed half again as much as Danielle. Was she doing such a poor job of providing for her children that they clambered after cold, day-old soup?

Evidently.

She dished the hearty broth and vegetables out, and Danielle sank down onto the dirt floor with her bowl while Serge climbed back onto the single chair and gulped his food.

"Slow down, child. It won't run off on you."

But he finished his bowl in less than a dozen bites and pushed it toward her. "Can I have more?"

The bucket had seemed like so much food but it now stood half empty without enough sustenance to see herself and the children through the evening meal. Though she could hardly blame Citizen Belanger for shortage when the man assumed he fed one person rather than four.

"*Oui.* Serge, you can have a second helping, but we'll be eating pulse later tonight."

The boy nodded eagerly, and Danielle's dish appeared on the table beside his.

"May I have more, too?"

Her own stomach twisted with hunger, but she nodded at Danielle and divided her portion into two extra servings. Then she tore a piece of bread off the half loaf and chewed. At least the bread from the baker tasted palatable.

One mission for Alphonse, that's all she needed to complete. Then she wouldn't have to depend on the charity of a farmer for her children's food. She could purchase her own cottage much like this one and surround herself with friends and loved ones rather than hide in the woods.

If only she could manage to finish her mission without being discovered.

Jean Paul hunched over the table in his cottage, quill gripped tightly between his fingers as he thought back over the previous weeks while he prepared his monthly report. No strangers had passed through town—well, besides the woman baking him bread. But she was hardly worth reporting. Frail, thin women with lips the color of autumn apples and skin pale as the moon weren't a threat to the government.

And here he was, thinking of the woman again when he had business to tend. All day she had flitted through his mind, whether he be working the fields or meeting with Pierre or stocking food in the stable. Mayhap he should send her away for good on the morrow so he'd not be so distracted.

Either that, or he could hire her.

Something hard fisted around his chest. No. It mattered not how grateful he'd be for a meal he didn't cook for himself or how much dust collected inside his cottage walls.

He let out a low growl. He had a report to write, and here he was, completely distracted by that fool woman yet again.

He bent his head over the paper and forced his thoughts away from soft brown eyes and onto more important matters, like whether any suspiciously large wagons of smuggled English wool had made their way inland from the coast over the past month.

But he came up with nothing. Nor had he heard of any large shipments of French brandy, lace or the like headed toward the coast.

The tallow candle flickered shadows across the walls and table as he scratched his message onto the foolscap. The words seemed unimportant. Insignificant. But a certain representative in the National Convention named Joseph Fouché wrote him back every month, always thanking him for the information. Twice now, the local gendarmes had found army deserters due to his reports. And once a rather large shipment of brandy was discovered on the coast, only minutes away from being loaded onto a vessel bound for England.

The spies were a little harder to track. He wasn't certain he'd ever found one but he reported anyone with the slightest accent or less-than-fluent French.

A knock sounded on his door, soft and unhurried. He rose and glanced out the window. Darkness had long fallen, and only one type of person would knock so softly this far into the night. He took an extra blanket from the chest in the bedchamber, then made his way to the door.

He'd never met the man standing outside, would probably forget his unmemorable face if ever they chanced to meet again. But then, spies weren't supposed to be remembered.

The man silently held out a piece of paper. "Citizen Belanger?"

He barely glanced at the missive, the signature at the bottom standing out like a flame. He had a similar letter tucked away in his bedroom, all of Fouché's men did.

"Come. I've a bed for you in the stable, but I need you gone before the sun rises."

He asked not of the man's business as he led him to the pallet tucked into the stall beside his mare's. He had no desire to know the secret workings of his government, but if providing shelter for a night would aid his country's cause, then he'd house a hundred men. Because France was now a republic, a place where all people were citizens of equal value, where power and wealth were based upon one's actions rather than right of birth.

To keep the French First Republic alive, the Convention fought not only revolution from within, but enemies from without. He might not be able to dart off into battle with the farm and an old wound in his shoulder, but he could supply food to the gendarmerie post for a fair price, ship some of his extra to the soldiers, watch his hometown for any sign of upset, and give rest and sustenance to government agents when so needed.

As terrible as the actions in his past had been, his country's cause was just. He refused to shed more innocent blood in the name of liberty, but he'd found a way to keep serving France without the pain and horror.

Because France needed a government of the people rather than the tyranny of a king. And he would do whatever necessary to keep the Republic alive.

Including pushing all thoughts of his lovely bread baker to the side and getting back to work on his report.

Chapter Four

Morning sun slanted down over the fields, turning the earth a dark gold as Brigitte emerged from the woods. She drew in a breath and inhaled the soft scents of soil and dew and foliage, so different from the hard, tangy scent of the sea that saturated Calais.

The thatched roof of Citizen Belanger's house arose before her, a mere speck amid the rows of crops sprouting from the earth. Tomorrow she'd find a different way through the woods, one that led to the road so she approached the house from the drive rather than the fields. Citizen Belanger was already asking questions about where she lived. The man didn't need to know about their stay in the little cottage in the woods.

She yawned and moved her lagging feet along the edge of the field, wiping a strand of hair from her face. She shouldn't be so tired, not when she'd woken a mere hour ago. Yet weariness clung to her, growing worse with each passing day. She sighed and pressed her eyelids open wider.

Perchance she'd have time for a nap before she met Alphonse's man tonight. If she baked Citizen Belanger's bread in a timely manner, and the children behaved, and she didn't have to scrounge for food....

She was fooling herself. The nap wouldn't happen; they never did.

She gave the house a wide berth as she circled around, careful lest Citizen Belanger was already working in his garden or the stable. But alas, the house sat quiet and peaceful, like a cottage in a painting with the sun's warm fingers wrapped around it while fields dipped and swelled into the distance.

She raised her hand to the door, but it swung open before she knocked.

"Citizen Belanger." She jerked backward, stumbling over an uneven patch of dirt.

He reached out and gripped her arm with his big, solid hand. "Are you unwell?"

Heat flooded her face. On their first meeting, she'd nearly fainted, yesterday she'd accused him of making worse bread than a slug and today she'd almost fallen. The man must think her a dunce.

But he didn't look at her as though she were a dunce. No. His eyes were soft and dark, but more the color of the earth after a hard rain than midnight. And his hand still rested on her arm, warm and strong and…comforting?

How long since a man had touched her out of concern rather than force? Another wave of heat exploded onto her cheeks, and she ducked her head.

But he kept his grip on her, this gaze roving slowly over her as though looking for…

What? She peeked up at him. His face was a hard mixture of prominent bones and taut skin, firm planes and severe angles with that inexplicable scar twisting around his eyebrow. And he was far too big. His hair brushed the top of the doorjamb and his shoulders spanned wide enough to eclipse any view she might have of inside.

Yet his eyes were still soft, as was his touch. He couldn't

be all ominous terror, not when he provided her food and work. Not when he asked after her health.

He released her arm and took the bread from her hands. "You look ill."

She swallowed. 'Twasn't a very romantic thing to say after surveying her so closely—not that she wanted romance from the man she needed to spy on.

"I'm grateful for your concern, but I'm fine." Except for the dull thudding at the back of her head, the subtle aching in her joints and the weariness that beset her. But those were hardly severe enough to hinder her from her duties.

"Are you with child?"

"Pardon?" The word burst from her lips on a gust of air. How dare he inquire after such a thing?

But he seemed not the least embarrassed by his question. Instead, he raised a dark eyebrow at her. "Are you?"

"*Non.* Not that it's any of your concern."

His dark eyes travelled her body once more, from the top of her mobcap down her overlarge dress, pausing a moment at her stomach before drawing his gaze down to her ill-fitting shoes. Why he should have the need to examine her yet again, when all he'd done was stare at her since she'd arrived, she hardly knew.

Whatever he saw must have convinced him she spoke the truth, because his eyes moved back up to her face. "Did you eat the soup and bread I sent yesterday?"

"*Oui.*" And that wasn't a lie. He needn't know the food was gone already, or how little of it she'd consumed herself. "Have you thought more about hiring me as a maid?"

"The bread will suffice." He reached into the pocket of his trousers and pulled out two coins. "Here are two *livres* for your labor."

She took a step back. She needed money, yes, but not so much. Bread sold for perhaps one *livre* in town, maybe

less, as most of that price was tied into the cost of wheat—
something Citizen Belanger had much of. "Sixteen *sous*
should suffice, since you provided the flour."

He crossed his arms over his chest. "Look at you,
woman. You're nigh on starved, plus you've bruises beneath your eyes and tired lines at the edges of your mouth.
I might not know who you are or from whence you came,
but I can see you need two *livres,* not sixteen *sous.* Take
the coins, or don't bother returning with more bread on
the morrow."

The impossible man. Was he really going to make her
argue about getting paid *less?* "One *livre,* four *sous,* but
not two *livres.*"

His face remained hard. "'Tis not up for bargain."

She stared at the two *livres* nestled in his palm, their
value of twenty *sous* a piece easily worth twice the loaf of
bread she'd brought him. But if she didn't accept, where did
that leave her tomorrow? Or the day after that? The two
livres would allow her to purchase more pulse in town with
several *sous* left over. Perhaps she could even buy fabric
for Serge's trousers and Danielle's dress. "Fine, then. But
tomorrow I take one *livre* and four *sous.*"

"Only if you don't wish to return the next day. Wait
here."

She opened her mouth to ask what he was about, but
he disappeared into the house before she could speak, the
insufferable oaf.

She tapped her foot on the ground, peering through the
doorway to catch glimpses of him rummaging by the table.
But she wasn't going in to see what he was doing, no. He
probably expected that. He'd suck her into his house and
then…then…then…

She blew a breath upward, the gust fluttering the wisps
of hair hanging near her face. She didn't know what the

man would do if she went inside. Didn't know much of anything about him. Things weren't going according to plan. She had to meet Alphonse's man this evening, and at this precise moment, she was further away from getting the job she needed to spy on Citizen Belanger than she'd been when first they'd met.

The time for being polite was past. She needed to convince him to hire her, and she needed to do so now.

She walked inside. The most obvious place to start cleaning was the table, but since Citizen Belanger hulked there throwing food into another bundle, she started with the bench beside the door. She took up the folds of her apron and wiped the smooth wood. Her worn apron was hardly white to begin with, but after cleaning the bench, dark streaks of dust stained the fabric.

"What are you doing?"

She jumped at the stern sound of his voice but straightened her shoulders. "It appears you do need a housekeeper. Look at the dust I wiped from this bench."

She turned and held out her apron, then gulped. Citizen Belanger's jaw clenched and unclenched as he stared down at her, while muscles corded in tight ropes along his neck and arms. He looked ready to stride over and strangle her.

She took a step backward. Perhaps she'd been a little too hasty in coming inside.

But no. She couldn't let him frighten her. She had to protect her children first, and that meant gleaning information from the irate man before her—however unpleasant that prospect might be. "You stand rather straight, Citizen Belanger. Tell me. Have you ever been in the army?"

His hands tightened into fists around the bundle of food he held, and he stalked toward her.

She took another step back only to bump into the bench behind her.

"My past is hardly your concern."

Oh, no. He was supposed to see her work and decide to hire her, not get angry. He was supposed to answer her questions, not corner her against the wall. She licked her lips. "I was simply making conversation. You know I'm from Calais. Why can I not know whether you've been in the army? You've the bearing of a well-trained soldier."

"I have nothing of the sort. And I might know you're from Calais, but I hardly know why you're here, or where you're staying, or why you're suddenly so concerned with whether I was a soldier."

She sucked in a painfully sharp breath. Did he see the way her hands trembled? Did her face look as cold as it felt?

And why could he not answer this one question? He turned every situation around until she was the one under interrogation. About where she lived. How much she'd eaten. Whether she was sick. If she carried a child.

"Why are you so concerned with my past?" His eyes narrowed, as though they could bore through her flesh and clothes and see straight into her heart.

She pushed down the urge to curl like a babe against the wall and raised her chin. "I told you. I was making conversation."

"If you've such a penchant for conversation, you provide it. Where are you staying?"

She stared back at him. She couldn't tell this stranger, this possible murderer, where she and the children hid, no.

"I see you like being interrogated as little as I do." He thrust the bundle of food toward her stomach with such force she had little choice but to take it. "Here's more flour, yeast and oil."

She opened and closed her mouth before finally finding some words. "I've plenty yet left over from yesterday."

He frowned, which did nothing to soften his already austere face. "You should be nearly out of flour. I've been making bread for nigh on a year now. I know how much is needed."

"Oui, but you gave me two days' worth."

"Non. I gave you one day's…" His voice trailed off, and the furrows across his brow deepened along with his frown. "Made you no bread for yourself?"

"'Twas your ingredients I used. I'm no thief to take them for myself." Or she wasn't yet. She only prayed her task for Alphonse wouldn't turn her into one.

"Mayhap I gave you that amount so you could take a portion," he growled.

"Well, you neglected to inform me."

"I assumed it understood. You're thin as a corpse and pale as fresh snow."

"And you're large as a mountain and meaner than a bull, but I don't think such traits make you a thief."

She clamped her teeth into her tongue the instant the words flew out. Why, oh, why, must she blurt such things when she argued with him? First the comment about a slug and now this. She'd never had such trouble when she argued with Henri—though that might have been due to the fact she'd never really argued with her husband, just obeyed.

Yet no emotion flitted across Citizen Belanger's face as the words settled between them, not even a registering of the insult. If anything, his demeanor grew harder, more like stone and less like flesh and blood. "Sustenance is nothing about which to jest. People die from lack thereof. Have you any soup remaining from yesterday?"

"I'm not starving." And she wasn't. She managed to eat every day, even if it was less than the little Serge consumed. "If you would simply hire me as your maid, you'd see the ridiculousness of your concerns."

"I asked if you have any soup left. Answer me, woman."

She pressed her lips firmly together. Let him take that as her answer.

"Wait here." He tromped back to the shelves beside the table, mad at her for some inexplicable reason. She was taking his food and eating it, was she not? Why should he grow angry?

When he returned, he clutched a bundle of salt fish. "Take this. And I've raspberries in the stable. Follow me."

He shoved past her and strode outside.

Wrong. Wrong. Wrong. Everything kept growing worse rather than better. Here he was plying her with food when she needed a chance to search his property.

She headed to the stable to find a wagon already laden with produce waiting just inside the doors. "As I've told you before, I don't need your charity. I need a post."

"And as *I've* told *you* before, I've no post for you." He walked around the wagon and plucked a crate of raspberries from the back.

"And then you hired me to make bread, which only proves you could use my labor but are too stubborn to admit thus."

A shadow crossed his face, dark and brooding, transforming him from the oversize person that had given her food into the dangerous menace that had stared at her inside when she'd asked whether he'd been in the military. The man before her now could hurt her without a flicker of emotion crossing his granite face.

The man before her now might well have killed Henri.

He came forward and held out a small crate of raspberries. "Things aren't as simple as they appear. Now be off with you. I've a trip to make to town and fields to tend thereafter. I'll expect my bread the same time tomorrow. And make two loaves for yourself this day."

He turned and went farther into the stable, leading an aging gray horse out of its stall and guiding the beast toward the front of the wagon.

Brigitte tightened her grip on the food and watched him, his face still hard and void of expression as he hooked the horse to the cart.

He was likely going to town to sell his vegetables, and he'd be gone at least two hours, if not half the day. She'd already tried asking about his past and cleaning his house. So if she couldn't ask questions and she couldn't snoop under the guise of being his housekeeper, that left sneaking.

Could she do such a thing? Break into another person's house while the owner was gone?

The moisture leached from her mouth. But if she wanted evidence of Citizen Belanger's past before she met with Alphonse's man, then she'd have one chance to get it. Later this morning, after he left for town.

Jean Paul watched her stomp from the stable, back straight and head high. Women, they were naught but a sore trial, and this one more than most. How many times must he refuse her before she understood he wouldn't hire her?

A dozen? Two dozen? A hundred?

He scowled, and Sylvie—a mare too old for the army to bother confiscating—snorted back at him.

The confounding woman would likely keep asking for as long as she brought him bread. What made her so set on working for him? Had she heard stories of the others he'd helped?

But the others lived elsewhere and didn't come to his house each day. He saw some once a week and others once a month, a few only when rent was due on the property he let. He didn't have to open his home to them.

His heart gave a solid, painful beat inside his chest. The woman with the bread would get the same answer each time she asked about a post.

He couldn't have someone else about the place when he harbored such terrible secrets from his past. When he still longed for his wife.

And he doubted he'd ever be ready to open his home, or his heart, to another.

Chapter Five

She was a miscrcant. A traitor. An utter and complete hypocrite.

Showing up on Citizen Belanger's doorstep to ask for a job two days ago had seemed like a sound plan. So how had she ended up here, sneaking through his front door, about to become a criminal?

And all so she could do Alphonse's bidding. She'd hated Henri's illegal activities, but once she stepped inside Jean Paul's house, how was she any different than Henri?

Because she was trying to save her family? That answer felt hollow. A wisp of truth cloaked in a lie. She was breaking into a person's house because she feared her father-in-law, and that fear was pushing her into the dark world she'd despised for so long. Wasn't there some verse in the Bible about such things? Not the one about her sin finding her out that her governess had been so fond of, but another. One that the priest used to quote at mass. Something about…about…about…

Reaping what you sowed. Yes, that was it. From Galatians chapter 6. *"Be not deceived; God is not mocked: for whatsoever a man soweth, that shall he also reap. For he that soweth to his flesh shall of the flesh reap corruption;*

*but he that soweth to the Spirit shall of the Spirit reap life
everlasting."*

She grimaced at the door in front of her. Well, she certainly wouldn't reap life everlasting by sneaking about.
But she needed information.

She tucked her perpetually errant strand of hair back
up under her mobcap and gave a final look about the
yard.

Empty. Not so much as a bird overhead to watch her.

Though the wagon was gone from the stable, she
knocked and waited one moment, then another, to be certain no one tarried within.

Everything lay still and quiet.

She slowly lifted the latch and let herself inside, heading straight toward the shelves lining the far wall. But she
stopped when her gaze fell to his table. It was beautiful, a
masterpiece fit only for a king or some royal relative. She'd
been too far away to notice the details earlier that morn,
but cornucopias had been carefully carved along the edge
of the table, the generous cones overflowing with grapes
and squash and apples. The fruit spilled down the side of
the table, etched onto the legs with what must have been
painfully accurate carving skills.

When Citizen Belanger had left Abbeville before the
Révolution, he'd supposedly gone to Paris to make furniture. Perhaps there was a grain of truth in the tale, after
all. Citizen Belanger must have made the table and matching chairs himself, for a farmer could hardly afford to purchase something so exquisite.

She trailed a finger over a cornucopia carved on the
top of a chair, then forced her gaze away from the furniture and toward the shelves beside the hearth. She had an
entire house to search and hadn't time to tarry, regardless
of how beautiful the furniture.

* * *

"You're late."

Jean Paul barely glanced at the gendarme as he pulled his wagon to a stop in front of the gendarmerie post. He hopped down and scanned the yard for Captain Monfort, but the gendarme glowering from beneath his black bicorn hat was the only one out of doors.

"I've been waiting for over a quarter hour."

"My previous stop took longer than I planned." As had the talk with his mysterious bread maker that morn. He hefted a crate of lettuce and carried it toward the entrance to the kitchen. "My apologies."

Gravel crunched behind him, then came the gendarme's morose voice. "A contract to supply the gendarmerie with food is hardly a trivial matter. I daresay if you continue to be late, we'll have to look elsewhere for our food."

Jean Paul rolled his eyes. Who was this whelp of a soldier? If the man wanted to be intimidating, he needed to stand straighter and give a hard gaze rather than shift away from one. But either way, his dourness had naught to do with Jean Paul's late arrival. The man had helped unload deliveries for the past three weeks and had been ill tempered each time.

Jean Paul nudged open the door to the empty kitchen and set his crate down with a thud before heading back to the wagon. "I'll try to be more punctual next week."

He set the flour and remaining crates of vegetables by the side of the road and hopped back atop his wagon. If the gendarme was going to be so friendly, he could carry the rest of the food back to the kitchen himself.

"Where are you going?" the other man barked.

Jean Paul took up Sylvie's reigns as the gendarme hastened toward him. "Away. You have your food. Two sacks of flour, four crates of produce. 'Tis settled."

And he had little tolerance for ill-mannered men in uniform.

"'Tis hardly settled. You've more turnips left, and raspberries." The gendarme stalked to the back of the wagon and reached in for the final crate of berries.

Jean Paul jumped down, clamping his hand about the other man's arm. "You've raspberries aplenty. What remains is for Widow Arnaud."

"You hardly gave us enough raspberries to keep the gendarmerie two days, let alone a week," the other man sputtered, his cheeks dark with red.

"'Twill have to suffice. My contract is for four crates of produce. I decide what that produce entails."

"The widow won't know they were coming, and thus won't miss them."

Jean Paul crossed his arms over his chest and glared. "The widow has three boys and a daughter who delight in berries. Furthermore, she's a widow because her husband died in the Batavian campaign. I should think a soldier like yourself would be respectful of such sacrifice."

"Are you implying I've a lack of respect?" The gendarme moved his hand to the hilt of his sword.

Jean Paul drew in a small breath. He must tread carefully. 'Twas a reason he sold food to the gendarmerie. Doing so kept him in their good graces, and they therefore asked no questions about his staying in Abbeville—though with his shoulder injury mostly recovered, he could manage as a soldier in one of the military campaigns. They also didn't question why he'd suddenly returned to Abbeville a year ago, nor did they wonder where he'd gotten the money to purchase the land surrounding his farm.

They simply bought his food.

True, his contacts in Paris could quash any resistance the gendarmerie post gave him, but he'd rather not go that route. Too many townsfolk would raise their brows if Paris got involved.

Yet he wasn't about to let widows starve while the waists of the gendarmes expanded, either. One person, one gift, one act of generosity when Corinne was ill, and she might be alive today. "The raspberries go to the Widow Arnaud, and if that's a problem, I can start taking my raspberries to market instead of here. I'll get a better price than you give me."

The gendarme curled his lips until his teeth showed, but his mouth held nothing of a smile. "You wouldn't dare."

"'Tis my food until you put money in my hand. I can sell it wherever I wish."

"We might visit your farm in the night and raid your food stores."

"Try it, and see how long Abbeville retains a gendarmerie post."

A murderous look flitted across the soldier's face.

"Does your captain know the threats you make?" Jean Paul growled.

The man just glared.

"Perhaps you should make yourself scarce next week when I deliver the foodstuffs, or I might find an urge to speak with your superior."

"Jean Paul!" a voice bellowed. "I didn't know you were here."

He recognized the speaker before he turned.

Mayor Narcise waddled down the steps of the post, a smile wreathing his flabby face. "I've been meaning to talk to you, my boy."

"*Bonjour,* Jean Paul." Captain Monfort followed the mayor down the steps, his eyes surveying the near-empty wagon. "Our chef was saying to me earlier this week how much he appreciates your deliveries. Did he tell you such?"

"The kitchen was empty when I arrived."

"Ah, I forgot he ran to the market. I trust Gilles here helped you unload?"

"In a manner of speaking." Jean Paul slanted a glance at the gendarme, who was steadily backing away from the group with two of the crates.

The captain gave a curt nod and straightened the lapels on his coat. "Good. You're dismissed, Gilles."

The scrap of a soldier headed toward the kitchen at a brisk clip.

"Well, then." The mayor gave Jean Paul a hearty slap on the back. "My sister's been wanting you over to sup. Nagging me about it for nigh on a week now, but I haven't seen hide nor hair of you."

Supper again. Jean Paul stuck a finger into the collar of his shirt and tugged. He'd been to four meals in town during the past year, each painfully awkward. Everyone sat around the table staring at him, praising him for the day he stumbled upon Citizen Benoit and her daughter being set upon by three army deserters. He'd done nothing special, only what any man of character would have when he chased off two of the scoundrels and dragged the other one before the magistrate.

He hadn't realized Citizen Benoit was the mayor's sister.

Or that he would be hailed as a hero for his deed.

"Well, what say you to supper on the morrow?" The mayor slapped him on the back again, then gave Captain Monfort a wink. "We'll even invite the captain here."

Jean Paul shook off the mayor's flaccid arm. "'Tis a busy week with the first vegetables coming on."

"Make time, boy. You've tasted the food my sister serves. The finest in all of Picardy."

"*Oui.* 'Tis so," Captain Monfort agreed.

Jean Paul glanced between the two men, Captain Monfort with his pristine uniform and the glimmer of respect twinkling in his eyes, and the mayor with his protruding stomach and hopeful expression.

He swallowed hard. He was the last person to deserve such respect and reverence. But then, the mayor and captain didn't understand the innocent blood that lay on his hands from the six years he'd spent away from Abbeville. He'd thought he'd been serving his country, but countless other men served France without ever spilling blood the way he had.

"I accept." His throat tightened on the words, but he forced them out. He could manage one more night of hero worship.

If only he didn't feel like a fraud.

Nothing. There was nothing here. Brigitte peeked under the bed one last time, just to be certain. What had she missed? No hidden journal of Citizen Belanger's military days sat stuffed beneath his pillow. No tattered and stained National Guard coat was secreted away in his chest of drawers. And no mysterious trunk lay under this bed, nor under any of the three others inside the chamber.

Oh, the beds themselves were beautiful, just as breathtaking as the table and chairs had been. One had leaves and acorns carved on it while another had the same cornucopias as the dining set. But after an hour spent scouring every centimeter of the two-room house, she still had no information about where he'd been in April of 1794, when Henri was killed.

What was she going to tell Alphonse's man? That Citizen Belanger had beautiful furniture? She bit her lip and stared at the empty space under the bed, willing a trunk or secret crate to suddenly appear. Then all she need do was look inside and find proof of Citizen Belanger's...

Innocence? Guilt? What did she hope to find?

Citizen Belanger was big, like the man who had stolen Henri from their bed. And by his own admission, he'd been to Calais before. Yet Alphonse had said Citizen Belanger disappeared to Paris at the beginning of the *Révolution,* and she'd found nothing indicative of Paris in his house. Nothing indicative he'd been gone any length of time at all.

Perhaps he was innocent. The man had given her family three meals now and paid her two *livres* for a loaf of bread. Murderers didn't care for the poor or search for excuses to give away money.

Did they?

She sighed and wiped a strand of hair from her face. She'd best go search the stable before she left. Perchance he'd something hidden away there.

"Ho, Sylvie." A masculine voice resonated through the house, followed by the telltale creak of a wagon.

She stilled, blood rushing in her ears and her palms suddenly damp. Citizen Belanger couldn't be back so quickly. She'd barely been here an hour.

Or had it been two?

She glanced out the bedroom window, its shutters thrown open to let in the warm summer air. The sun was high against the blue tapestry of sky, much higher than it should be had she only been working an hour.

The outer door to the house squeaked open and then thudded shut. She looked frantically about the room, then dove beneath the bed.

Chapter Six

Jean Paul scratched the back of his neck as he surveyed the main chamber of his house. Strange. He could have sworn he'd put Sylvie's blanket in the stable yesterday's eve, but the stable held no sign of it. The only other place it might be was inside the house. Yet no blanket lay in a haphazard pile on the table or hastily thrown over the rocking chair.

What had happened to it? A blanket didn't simply up and disappear.

Or did it?

Mayhap he was losing his mind. There'd been a missing chicken yesterday, an absent mug this morn at breakfast and now his mare's...

He looked around his cottage one more time. 'Twas more than a misplaced blanket or cup gone afoot. The entire house seemed wrong. The Bible lay at an odd angle on the mantle, the bench by the table was absent of dust, and the quilt on the rocker was folded a bit too neatly.

His heart quickened in his chest. Someone had been here. In his house. In his things.

He stood still, forcing his heart to slow and his blood to cease racing. Forcing the return of his old, familiar calm that had stayed him through all manner of horrors and deeds during the Terror.

He looked around a third time, assessing every centimeter of his house. Who had been here, and why?

Someone who knew of his past? Someone searching for him? Someone who wanted vengeance?

It couldn't be. He'd moved back home over a year ago, and no one had since found him. Why would a person come looking now?

Or perhaps someone had learned of his letters to the Convention every month, of the men he sometimes sheltered in his stable. A hiding royalist that had escaped the terror, or a spy for the English that had sniffed him out. Then again, the man he'd harbored last night could well have been a spy selling information to the English while only pretending to work for the French.

No, no, no. It couldn't be. His imagination was running amuck with strange and alarming possibilities while he missed the likeliest culprits: thieves. Or maybe a pair of deserters who had happened upon an empty house.

But while many things were slightly disturbed, nothing of worth was missing. A thief would have taken…

What? He kept little of value in the house, had learned long ago to hide the things he cherished. His gaze landed on the mantle above the hearth. His knife. That was gone.

He moved stealthily toward the bedchamber, footsteps soft, ears open for the slightest of sounds.

If an attacker had tarried, he'd likely be hidden in the bedchamber and would strike the moment Jean Paul opened the door. He glanced again at the empty spot where his knife usually rested, and his gut twisted. He reached for the kitchen knife hanging on a hook against the wall and held it at the ready.

He drew in a breath, then flung the bedchamber door open. It flew backward to bang against the wall.

Empty. The room held no one. But a person had been there. The dusty dirt floor bore fresh marks by all three of the unused beds, and the drawers of his dresser all fit perfectly into place. When was the last time he'd bothered to close the drawers properly?

A person had been here, and not some army deserter or thief looking for easy loot. A person had searched his house, and there could only be one reason for such actions:

Someone knew of his past.

Brigitte curled herself tighter against the wall and stared at the booted feet visible from beneath the bed. Did he know someone had been in his house, or was he merely retrieving something from the bedchamber?

She swallowed past a throat tight with fear. What if he sensed something amiss?

Would he hurt her if he found her? Take her to the magistrate for snooping about?

No, no. Surely not. This man had been kind to her, given her food and work, asked after her health. He wouldn't hurt her.

Unless the kindness was all a farce, some odd sort of disguise for his past deeds. If he was indeed the man who had killed Henri and he found her hiding here, perhaps he would kill her, too. Kill her and bury her on the farm, where no one would ever discover—

The dusty boots turned suddenly and strode out of the chamber. A moment later the outside door banged shut.

Brigitte clasped a hand over her heart and willed its frantic pace to slow, willed the roaring in her ears to stop and the dampness to leave her hands and forehead. She was safe.

Well, mostly safe. She still had to climb out the bed-chamber window and escape through the garden without being noticed. And then she needed to meet Alphonse's man tonight and explain why she had no new evidence regarding Jean Paul Belanger.

She closed her eyes and let her head fall back against the cool dirt floor. 'Twould be astonishing if her heart survived this assignment.

Brigitte turned her back against the setting sun and moved her leaden feet along the clover field, skirting the trees that lined the edge. Had she really argued with Citizen Belanger over the price of her bread and snuck into his house earlier that day? The events seemed so distant, they might have occurred a week ago.

Her weariness was growing worse. Her joints ached as she trudged through the green countryside. Sweat slicked her hands and beaded on her forehead, and her head pounded with each step she took.

Surely she felt ill because of the meeting and what lay ahead at the rendezvous location, not because she was getting sick. She couldn't get sick right now.

"*Bonjour,* Citizen," a voice called from the field.

She stilled, her pulse thudding sluggishly against her throat. Had Alphonse's man already found her? No one was supposed to know she was here besides the person she needed to meet—whomever that was.

"*Bonjour?*" she answered tentatively.

A man emerged from the midst of the cows grazing in the field, his clothing smeared with mud and hands crusted with dirt.

Or rather, his *hand* was crusted with dirt. He only had one. His other arm stopped somewhere beneath his elbow, leaving the remainder of his sleeve to hang free.

"Oh." She took a step back. This couldn't be the man Alphonse had sent.

"I've yet to meet you, Citizen." The man dipped his head at her, his young face tanned beneath the uncocked hat he wore. "I'm Pierre Dufort, one of Jean Paul Belanger's tenants."

Well, that certainly explained his presence in the field. Her eyes slid to the gaping hole at the end of his shirtsleeve. How did a farmer work with only one hand?

"I lost it in the Batavian campaign."

She jerked her eyes up to meet his and found herself staring once again into that terribly young face, a face not much older than Julien's or Laurent's.

'Twas almost worse than looking at the amputated arm.

"I'm sorry. I shouldn't have stared. My name is Brigitte Moreau and I'm—" She licked her lips. How to describe why she was here near Abbeville, let alone cutting through a field? "Living in the area for a bit. I trust Citizen Belanger won't mind my travelling through his land?"

"Jean Paul's hardly the type to bother with a person crossing his field now and then."

She only hoped he was right, but then, he hadn't been cowering under a bed in fear of Jean Paul Belanger eight hours earlier.

"And no need to apologize about staring. 'Tis hardly a secret." He raised his arm, drawing attention to the incomplete limb. "I lost my hand. Everyone can see as much."

But he was so young to face the rest of his days maimed. Had he a mother who sent him off to fight? A wife? Did he blame whoever had sent him into the army for the injury he'd suffered? She swallowed hard, then glanced away.

"*Adieu,* then. I must be…"

"I have two sons…"

The both spoke at the same time then fell silent.

"You were saying?" The subtle lines around Pierre's eyes creased with curiosity.

"In the navy." She cleared her throat. "I have two sons in the navy." She wasn't sure why she told him, save that he might understand something she couldn't. Might be able to name the aching sorrow that filled her chest every night as she lay down to sleep and longed for her oldest children. And if he couldn't name it, he'd assuredly felt it before. One would have to after losing an arm on the battlefield.

"Good seamen, are they? That's noble of you, now, sending your boys off to serve their country."

But it didn't feel very noble, not at moments like this when she simply wanted them home. "I hope…" Her eyes drifted down to his empty sleeve again. "That is, I want…"

"Don't worry yourself." Pierre smiled softly. "Your boys'll fare fine. Battle at sea's a mite different then battle on land. I've nary met a sailor who lost his arm."

Yes. Battle at sea certainly was different, because if either Laurent's or Julien's frigate was captured, her boys wouldn't face the mere loss of a hand—they would be killed, thrown into a gaol or impressed onto a British warship. Was she mad for thinking the loss of an arm seemed the better consequence? What kind of mother sent her children into the navy at all?

The kind who wanted to help her country fight against its tyrannical neighbor.

The kind who wanted to keep them away from Alphonse Dubois.

"They're only fifteen."

Pierre put his hand on her shoulder, a gentle touch like one Laurent or Julien might use to comfort her were they here in Abbeville. "Citizen Moreau, Brigitte, why don't you come home and sup with me and my wife tonight? Looks like you need a little cheer to lift your spirits."

She looked up into Pierre's face, kindness and hospitality emanating from a young man who had every reason to be angry at life.

"That's a kind offer, but I must make haste. I've three younger children back at the house." And she was already late for her rendezvous.

"Some other time, then. I've got a wee babe I like to show off, and my wife will be pleased to meet another woman. She and Citizen Fortier are the only two women on Jean Paul's land, you know."

No. She didn't know and hadn't given much thought to who Citizen Belanger's tenants were, whether they were married or widowed, whether they had all their hands or feet or ears. Though Jean Paul had told her there were women around to work as laundresses, and most farmers had wives and children to help bear the work.

"*Au revoir,* for I hope we meet again, Citizen Moreau." He gave her a little wave.

"*Au revoir.*" She turned and took two steps away, then looked back. Pierre made his way along the edge of the field, his gaping sleeve hanging comfortably at his side.

"Did Citizen Belanger hire you after he learned of your arm?" The question exploded from her lips.

Pierre turned, a slow smile spreading across his face. "*Oui.* And I'd not have found work save for him. My father is the butcher, you see. There's little one can do around a butcher shop when missing a hand. But I'm not the only one he saved from such dire straits. Citizen Courtemanche limps, and Citizen Fortier lost her farm after her husband's death. Then there's Citizen…"

She held up a hand to stem his words. "I understand."

And she did. Pierre could likely go on for a quarter hour listing Citizen Belanger's tenants and why each of them needed an extra bit of help. It certainly explained how he had three men waiting to become tenants in a country where all able-bodied men were off at war.

What murderer hired one-armed men, cripples and widows?

What murderer helped needy people with food?

She turned back toward the path that ran along the edge of the field. Maybe now she had evidence enough to give Alphonse's man.

Chapter Seven

Jean Paul bent over the green-and-amber-tinted field and fingered the stalks of wheat. No orange or yellow stripes on the leaves, no powdery mildew coating the plant, no holes where aphids, worms or flies had chewed through the leaves. It was completely, utterly healthy.

Or it should be. But the stalks were only half the size of those in the field behind it. And the hulls growing on each plant considerably fewer than the number on the stalks in the neighboring field.

He shouldn't have planted wheat here again, not after he'd grown it last year. He'd known as much when he'd tilled the soil and plowed this spring. The field was due for barley, then turnips and clover. His father had started using that crop rotation a decade back, and it had served the little farm well. The soil seemed attached to growing plants in that order, though he could hardly explain why.

But France needed wheat, and squeezing an extra year of grain out of this field had seemed like a good idea. But now it looked as though the plot of land would yield only half as much as his two other wheat fields.

He raised his eyes to the heavens. Was it too much to ask for two straight seasons of wheat?

Mayhap if he spread manure on the field this wheat might begin to thrive. That certainly worked for his vegetable patch, and this parcel was nearly the same size. On the morrow, he'd scrounge up some manure from his tenants who kept animals. 'Twas worth the attempt, though he probably should have tried the manure before now if he expected to see much difference come harvest.

And as for this field, next year it would get barley. Then turnips. Then clover. At least until he could figure out why his crops insisted on growing only in that order. Maybe if he understood why, he'd then be able to coax two straight years of wheat from the ground.

He straightened and surveyed his land beneath the setting sun. Farming might be frustrating at times, when his crops refused to grow or developed blights, when weather harmed them or pests descended. But nothing else on earth could replace the joy of seeing a field planted in spring and harvested in fall. Of taking a parcel of dark soil and cultivating life from it. Of watching the day and night, sun and rain, move in an endless cycle that drew his crops from the ground.

He'd been daft for ever turning his back on the land and going to Paris.

Something bright flashed along the edge of the field, followed by a sudden flurry of movement. The unease from earlier that afternoon flooded back. First his house, now his field. Something was definitely amiss.

Crouching low, he moved stealthily toward the disturbance. Had the silvery flash been the sun glinting off a knife? His own blade he'd kept above the hearth? He reached down to grip the hilt of his garden knife. 'Twas too rusted and dull to do much damage, but he was taller and broader of chest than most. If he surprised his enemy, he might well win the match.

He slowed as he neared the edge of the field and peered through the gilded stalks. Something moved again, a glimpse of black and green and white. He paused and sucked in a breath to still his thudding heart.

Not a man. Not an enemy at all, but a girl.

Or at least he assumed the creature was a girl since the frame was too small to belong to a woman fully grown, and she wore a faded green dress and apron. But with her hair falling in wild tangles about her shoulders, and dirt streaking her face, one could hardly be certain.

She paused for a moment, standing with hands on her hips as she stared at the ground, then she raised a knife above her head and—

"Halt!" He sprang from the field.

The girl whirled, took one look at him then loosed a scream fit to warn all the province of her whereabouts.

"Don't come any closer," she rasped, clutching the knife—his missing knife from above the hearth—to her chest in an awkward grip.

'Twas one thing to have the imp sneak into his cottage and steal his blade. 'Twas another entirely to see she knew not how to use it. "Has no one shown you how to wield a knife, child?"

Her gaze skittered down his body, stopping at his hand, which clutched his oversize garden knife. *Fool!* He'd forgotten about the thing. He slipped it back into the loop on his belt and raised his hands innocently. "I mean you no harm."

Her knuckles remained white as chalk around the hilt of his blade. "Then turn yourself around and go back from where you came."

"'Tis my property. Mayhap you should be the one hastening away." Not that he intended to let her go without first accounting for herself.

"Fine, then. You stay, and I'll make haste." She took a small step backward, then another, her movements revealing what her skirt had hidden when he'd first happened upon her.

One of his chickens lay half strangled at her feet. "Not so fast. I've a question or two first. Like how you got hold of my knife, and what you're doing on my land? Why you've taken one of my chickens, and how you intend to compensate for it?"

She glanced wildly around the woods then took another step back.

She was scared now. 'Twould be but a moment before—

She turned and ran.

He glanced at the twitching chicken still on the ground, then at the girl tearing through the woods. She must have realized the knife would do little to thwart a man three times her size—especially when she knew not how to hold the thing.

But she deserved credit enough for being brave. It took courage to spar with a man such as him, knife or no knife.

He hastened after her. She ran fast for one so small. At first, he'd have guessed her ten years of age, but she dashed around saplings and leaped over fallen branches too agilely for a child. She was likely a budding woman, one short of stature, but mature enough of body to run smartly through the brush and brambles.

He squinted into the gloom as he raced forward, darkness snaking its shadowy fingers through the woods. Were it not for the white apron strings trailing behind her, he'd have lost her when she darted into a thick stand of trees.

Then she turned to look back at him. A fatal mistake, that. Her foot caught on a gnarled root, and she sprawled forward, landing face down on the forest floor. She scrambled furiously to heave herself up. But not fast enough. He reached down and hauled her up by her shoulders.

"You're a quick one," he rasped through the heavy rise and fall of his chest.

She crossed her arms over her slender chest and glared at him.

He nearly laughed—would have, had she not stolen two chickens, a blanket, a mug and his favorite knife over the past several days. "Who is your father, child? I've need to speak with him."

"He's dead," she spewed flatly.

Of course he was. What father would let his child traipse about the countryside stealing blankets and chickens and the like? "Your mother, then?"

"You should know. She brought you bread this morn."

Jean Paul narrowed his eyes. *That* was her mother? The woman who had shown up at his doorstep for the past three days?

With hair so black it gleamed and eyes as blue and clear as ice, the girl didn't appear to be related. But there was something about her face, about the subtle curve of her cheek as it sloped into her jaw, the gentle cheekbones and straight little nose. She hadn't her mother's hair and eyes, but they shared the same face.

Why had the woman never mentioned she had a child? He'd have provided more soup and salt fish and…

The realization crashed through his head. 'Twas why the woman still seemed so thin and weak after the three meals he'd supplied. She was likely giving her food to the child and going without herself.

"Does your mother know you've been snooping about my house? That you've stolen my knife and chicken?"

The girl stared evenly back at him, her blue eyes firm with determination.

"I'm missing a horse blanket, as well. And I had another chicken disappear yesterday." It was all starting to make sense now, the eerie feeling he'd had in his house earlier, the things that had disappeared from his property.

She remained sullenly silent, her chin jutting into the air.

"*Non.* I suppose if your mother knew what you were about, you'd not be here. Stand, child." He jerked her up by her shoulder. "We're going to visit your home."

"You're late," a man's dark voice snarled.

Brigitte stepped around a tree and peered into the thickening shadows of the forest. Her blood pounded against her temples, and the trees blurred into a solid, hazy mass for a moment before righting themselves. "A tenant saw me headed here. I was detained."

"I didn't ask for excuses."

A chill trickled down her spine at the harsh edge to his voice, but she took another step forward.

"Have you proof?"

She whirled around, causing her head to spin. The voice that had seemed in front of her now came from behind, but shadows still shrouded the man, whomever he was. Sweat beaded on her forehead and slicked her palms, yet she straightened her shoulders. Strong, she was going to act strong, not like some frightened child. "Proof of what? Citizen Belanger is innocent."

The man laughed, a cruel, taunting sound. "Citizen Belanger is innocent of nothing, and it's your job to prove thus."

"*Non.* It's my job to prove the truth, and the man you speak of is innocent."

A form emerged from the shadows, not as tall or thick of chest as Citizen Belanger, but then, few men were. The fading light filtered through the leafy trees above, barely illuminating his bicorn hat and…

She gasped as her eyes fell on his uniform, the crisp blue coat edged in red trim, the tan breeches and black boots. "You're a gendarme."

His gray eyes gleamed hard in the darkness. "That I am."

"But…" Her mouth opened and closed, then opened again. Alphonse had said she'd meet one of his men near Abbeville, but he'd not mentioned that the man worked for the military police. That the man would possess the power to throw her into prison with a single word.

"You didn't think your father-in-law employed merely seamen, did you?"

Her mouth stayed open, her jaw seemingly frozen in the undignified position. She'd never given much thought to who Alphonse employed or why. She'd only known he was too powerful for her to thwart.

The gendarme raised an eyebrow at her, sand-colored hair curling out from beneath his hat. "Service in the gendarmerie pays very little. I find your father-in-law to be a rather generous employer."

"And Alphonse benefits from having a man in the gendarmerie," she whispered. Yes, the benefits to both parties were far too clear. A man in the gendarmerie could see that certain shipments of wool, brandy and the like were overlooked while the smuggled goods traveled to and from the coast.

The gendarme smiled at her, a chilling half curve of lips. "*Oui,* you understand perfectly."

She raised her chin—hopefully he didn't notice the way it trembled—and glared at the gendarme. "Jean Paul Belanger is innocent. I've done what I came to do. I demand I be compensated for my work and released. So if you'd kindly pay me, Citizen, I shall be on my way come morning."

"Not before you offer proof of his innocence."

Brigitte thrust her hand in the direction of the farm. "Look at his land. Need you proof beyond that? He feeds the hungry and lets land to widows and one-armed tenants. Since when do murderers feed babes?"

"Feeding babes isn't proof." The gendarme gripped her upper arm, his fingers digging into the flesh beneath her sleeve. "He was gone from Abbeville for six years, and no one knows what he did in his absence."

"All the town knows that. He went to Paris and made furniture. I've been inside his house, and the furniture is beautiful, exquisite even. He could easily have made furniture in Paris."

With one hand still holding her arm, the gendarme rested his other hand on the hilt of his sword. "Have you learned nothing in the days you've been here?"

Of course she'd learned something. That she was on some ridiculous fool's errand. That the man she'd been sent to spy on was kind and generous and not a murderer, regardless of when or why he'd been in Paris—if he'd even gone there in the first place and hadn't spent his years away from Abbeville in some other city.

"If you're so certain he's the man, why not..." She couldn't force the words past her tongue. The person they discussed had offered her food and work, after all. But why was Alphonse so hesitant to murder the man he suspected of killing his son? She swallowed and attempted the words again. "Why is Alphonse being so careful with Citizen Belanger when he's killed men before for simply being in his way?"

The gendarme's breath puffed hot against her cheek and the silver of his eyes seared into her. "If you've not yet determined that, then you're worse at this job than I suspected."

Heat crept through her, whether from embarrassment over the gendarme's words or her own sick body, she couldn't tell. Her muscles ached, and her feet smarted inside her shoes. What she wouldn't give to be back at the cottage, lying on the old pallet and resting her tired body. "I am not 'worse' at this job. I've gotten into his house. I've scoured every box and crate and corner, and I found nothing to suggest the man was ever in the military. Do you not think that proof of his innocence?"

"He was in Paris for the start of the *Révolution*. Then last year he returns with unfathomable money, buys up land surrounding his farm, hires tenants who can barely manage half a day's work, distributes food to the needy and goes about the countryside rescuing women."

Rescuing women? She nodded her head as though she knew of what the gendarme spoke.

"Where did the money come from?" he pressed. "And why return to Abbeville just as the Terror leaves?"

"Perhaps he made the money making furniture, as he claims."

The guard released her arm with a sudden thrust. "You're a fool, wench. He didn't make that fancy furniture, his brother did. And where, for that matter, is his brother? Have you asked that of Citizen Belanger yet? Michel Belanger disappeared more than a year ago, never to be heard from again."

The gendarme paced in front of her with short, tense strides. "Something's not right. And if Alphonse Dubois could kill Belanger without the entire town crying in outrage, he would. A man rescues two ninnies from a couple army deserters and the entire town hails him as a hero."

Apparently she wasn't the only woman Citizen Belanger

tried rescuing, but that hardly explained why Alphonse feared killing him. "I see."

"Though accidents can happen, even to heroes. A fire, perhaps, that burns his house during the night? Or maybe the axel on his wagon breaks, causing our dear Citizen Belanger to careen into a tree."

Brigitte's chest grew so tight her heart struggled to beat. *"Non."*

"Are you defending him?" The gendarme whirled back toward her, his face etched with hatred and malice. "The man who murdered your husband? Don't you want justice for killers?"

"This isn't justice."

She didn't see the slap coming. One moment the gendarme paced before her, and the next his hand struck her cheek, her skin burning at the contact.

She lurched back. "How dare you?"

"Mind yourself, wench. You know naught of justice."

Maybe so, but Henri had been tried before he went to the guillotine, tried and found very guilty of crimes he'd committed. Didn't justice involve a trial? "This is revenge."

The guard raised his hand again. She lunged out of reach, though her quick movements set off the pounding in her head once more.

"The snake deserves to pay," the gendarme growled.

"You're not even certain Citizen Belanger is the man you seek."

The man spit onto the damp forest floor. "They're all the same, aren't they? Men like Belanger getting rich while the poor still work for him. We have ourselves a *Révolution,* and a man like Belanger comes up with all kinds of money to buy land and make himself another lord over us."

"You've probably been watching him for a year, and

you've not found any more evidence than I. Otherwise Citizen Belanger would be dead."

"A man like Belanger, he's hiding something. I'll give you one week, and if you still bring me no evidence, I'll have you escorted back to Dubois."

She froze at those words, terror sinking it's claws into her heart. She couldn't allow her children to go back there, not ever.

The man ran his eyes down her then laughed. "I advise you to school your features, Citizen Dubois. Your face gives your thoughts away."

"Moreau," she croaked. "It's Citizen Moreau."

He paused a moment. "Citizen Moreau? You've managed to do something right, at least."

And then he turned, stalking off through the trees and leaving her to stare after him.

Lovely. Just lovely. The one thing she'd done "right" in all of this had been a lie.

Chapter Eight

Jean Paul stared ahead at the familiar stand of trees—trees he hadn't seen in over six years—and a cold sweat broke out over his forehead. "Where did you say you lived?"

The girl beside him didn't speak, not that he was surprised. She hadn't uttered a single word since he yanked her off the forest floor a quarter hour ago and demanded to see her mother. But she didn't need to speak for him to recognize the overgrown trail or the thick stand of fir trees toward which they walked.

No. It couldn't be. His feet stumbled, though the ground beneath him was flat and even. "How long have you been living here?"

The girl worked her jaw back and forth, as if debating whether he was worthy of an answer before opening her mouth. "You don't yet know where I'm taking you."

If only she was wrong. "'Tis but one house on this path."

She crossed her arms. "And how would you know such?"

"Because it's my property. We might have been walking for over a quarter hour, but we've not yet left my land, and you've taken a rather roundabout way home."

Her eyes snapped defiantly, but she kept her mouth clamped tight.

"I assume you're taking me to the hut up the trail? The one with the timbered sides, a thatched roof and the hearth against the far wall? Windows facing south and west?"

The one he'd taken Corinne to after their wedding nine years ago and had shared with his beloved wife for two brief years before her death.

The girl's gaze darted frantically about, as though searching for some excuse that might appease him.

"How long?"

"I don't know what you're talking about."

The liar. He sucked in a breath, long and hard and hopefully calming. It didn't work. If anything, the anger bubbled hotter inside him. How dare strangers come onto his land and invade his house? How dare they use his bed and table and hearth? Sully the place he'd once shared with his beloved? "I'll not ask you again. How long have you been living in my house?"

The girl licked her lips and stared at the overgrown trail in front of her. "The house doesn't belong to you. It can't. It's an abandoned hut, grown thick with weeds on the outside and coated by dust within. The owner's dead."

"Dead?" The word echoed furiously through his head. He hastened ahead of her, his long-legged strides making quick work of the ground. Past the large maple to his left and the saplings on his right. Past the sunny spot where Corinne had planted her garden and the shaded place where she'd done the wash.

The familiar cottage loomed before him, made of the very logs he'd hewn with his father and brother, the very sheaves of wheat he'd bound together for the roof. He burst through the door, panting as he surveyed the long-abandoned structure.

Dim orange light from the waning sun cast shadows against the far wall, while little motes of dust shimmered through the air. The dishes, the few he'd not bothered to take with him when he left Abbeville, sat precisely in their places on the shelf, next to two loaves of bread—one of which would come to him in the morn. The hearth stood dark but held ashes from a recent fire, and the bed lay in the corner, the tick an uncomfortable mess of straw and dried leaves laying on one of the early bed frames his brother had made. He pressed his eyes shut, but he could still see Corinne's form huddled on the bed, still hear the coughs wracking her pale body and smell death haunting the corners of the room.

A rustling sounded from the direction of the tick, and he forced his eyes open. A boy sat up and rubbed his face, then jerked straight.

"Where's *Maman?* What have you done with her?" His eyes lit with terror and he scooted back against the wall, leaving a smaller bundle still sleeping in the middle of the bed. A babe.

Jean Paul stared for a moment, his heart beating wildly against his ribs as he sucked in great gulps of air. There were more children?

"You can't take my maman." A fat tear rolled down the boy's cheek. "You have to give her back."

More moisture coursed down the child's thin cheeks, and something hard fisted in his chest. First the sister, now the boy. He was doing it again, meting out Terror. And he didn't even have a uniform or sword or orders from the representative-on-mission to blame for their reactions. He seemed to terrify people just as he was. He'd certainly frightened their mother when first they met.

"I haven't taken your mother. I'm in search of her."

"Then where is she?" The urchin's chin trembled so hard 'twas surprising his teeth didn't clatter together.

"That's what I'm trying to find out." He glanced about the house for a second time, but the single room afforded no place for the woman to hide.

"She had a meeting in town." The girl slipped inside from behind him, almost as though she'd been waiting for that precise moment to enter.

Jean Paul narrowed his eyes at her, and pink rose in her cheeks. 'Twas exactly what she'd done.

"*Maman* left us?" A fresh bout of tears streaked down the boy's face.

The girl shrugged. "You were asleep with Victor, so *Maman* left me in charge."

"Then why were you in my lower field butchering a chicken when you had children to tend?" Jean Paul turned on her.

"I was getting supper, and Serge didn't know I was gone, did you, Serge?" She gave the boy a look so fierce it might well bring the admiral of Britain's navy to his knees. "Because you were sleeping."

The child solemnly nodded before moving his hand to his thin stomach. "What did you bring us?"

"Nothing."

"Does that mean we have to eat pulse?"

"I'll go find a squirrel or something."

She headed for the door but Jean Paul reached out and gripped her arm before she could slip outside. "I have some questions before you go darting off across the countryside trying to slay my animals. How long have you been living in my house?"

"Three days." The boy rolled off the pallet, mindful not to bump the babe. "Danielle found it because the inn was too expensive. Can she go catch the squirrel now?"

"No." Jean Paul released the girl but shut the door behind him and leaned his back solidly against the exit. "No one's going anywhere until your mother returns."

"But that means we'll have to eat pulse."

"Then mayhap your sister should fix some."

The girl glowered at him but stalked to the hearth to poke at the ashes.

Jean Paul pulled the room's single chair beside the door and settled in. Otherwise the girl just might run out of the house the instant he turned his back. "In the meantime, Serge, why don't you tell me how many brothers and sisters you have?"

And then the boy could tell him their names—he still didn't know what to call his bread woman—followed by what his family was doing in Abbeville. And if the boy still felt like talking after that, Jean Paul could think of a half dozen more questions. He was going to find some answers, even if he needed to stay half the night to do so.

The path swayed before her, a twisting line of trampled foliage barely visible in the pressing dark. Brigitte stumbled forward, her muscles aching while her head pounded relentlessly with the gendarme's warning. One week. Only seven days to dig up evidence against Jean Paul Belanger, and if she wasn't successful, she'd be sent back to Alphonse.

Because despite all her adamant claims Citizen Belanger was innocent, she still didn't know for certain. The gendarme had been right. Giving work to injured men and food to widows didn't mean Citizen Belanger had never been a soldier.

She had to think up another way to spy. Her current efforts weren't working, and the one time she'd been daring enough to steal into his house, he'd nearly happened upon her.

Her stomach churned violently and the woods around her blurred, then began to sway. Her foot snagged on a tree root and she stumbled, sprawling forward until her knees dug into the moist dirt and her hands fisted on a bit of moss.

Oh, Father, what have I done? I'm only trying to protect my children, but what if I lose them instead?

There were Bible verses about reaping what you sowed. Pierre had sowed clover in the spring and now his cattle grazed on a clover field. She sowed deceit by lying to Citizen Belanger and then spying on him, so would she reap deceit or betrayal in turn?

I haven't a choice, God. Remember?

But did she? Certainly working for Alphonse was the easiest choice, the best choice to get her and the children away from his influence, but was it God's choice?

She stared at the dirt as her stomach heaved and retched sickeningly into the base of the tree.

She was sick with fever. She had to be. She'd not felt so wretched in years, but she remembered well the misery a fever wrought. The way her joints and muscles pained her as she lay shivering beneath layers of blankets. The way night blurred into day and day into night as she stayed curled on her bed. The way Henri had continued with his smuggling business as always, leaving her home to tend their young twins.

But she couldn't be sick right now. She had to get up. Go back to the house and see that the children were safe. Feed Victor and make some pulse for Serge and Danielle. Deliver Citizen Belanger's bread on the morrow.

She slowly pushed her body up. As though intent on proving its point, her stomach gave another sickening lurch. She sank back to the ground and curled into a ball. The last rays of sun had vanished, and slivers of gray sky appeared through the dense leaves while a chorus of night toads and insects surrounded her. But she had to drag her body off the ground. The house wasn't far…at least she didn't think so.

Not that she knew quite where she was.

How long since her meeting with the gendarme? A quarter hour, or two? She groaned and tried to heft herself up, only to have her arms and legs start shaking. She fell back to the ground and retched yet again.

"Maman?" A voice called, though she could hardly hear it between her heaves.

"Maman?" Cool fingers smoothed away the hair that clung to her cheek. Then a slender body pressed itself against her back. "Are you unwell?"

"Danielle," she whispered through her sickness. "You're here. You're safe."

"Of course I'm here and safe. Where else would I be?"

Tears streamed down Brigitte's face to mix with her retching. Her stomach emptied itself of its contents until it felt as though she'd spewed forth the very life from her body. Then she rolled away from the refuse and rested against the base of the tree trunk.

"Your brothers," she croaked. "Where are your brothers?"

"At the house." Danielle held a hand to her forehead. "Awaiting your return."

Brigitte closed her eyes. A moment more of rest, then she would rise and walk back to the house.

"Citizen Belanger found where we're staying. It's his house, *Maman,* and he's waiting to talk to you."

Citizen Belanger? His house? How could that be? Brigitte pressed her eyelids tighter together and groaned.

'Twas a good quarter hour of walking to get from the farmstead to the hut. And it didn't seem possible a man could own so much property, especially with the *Révolution* ravaging the country.

"Is he angry?"

"Um, I don't think he's mad about the house. Exactly. But I sort of, maybe, took some things that we needed from around his property."

Brigitte leaned her head back against the tree. This could not be happening. Not with her so sick and Alphonse's mission still unfulfilled. "What did you take?"

Danielle's cool fingers touched her face and then tucked some hair behind her ear. "Fret not, *Maman*. We need to get you home. Once Citizen Belanger sees you're unwell, he'll leave and come back in the morn."

If only she could be so sure. But she'd been found squatting in the man's house while her daughter stole his things, and just that morning he'd generously paid her two *livres* for bread worth only half that. He had every right to be furious. "We'd best hasten."

"You're worrying too much. Citizen Belanger acts all mean and has that terrible stare, but he wasn't upset...well, except about the chickens and knife. But once he got to the house and saw Victor and Serge, he acted more concerned than angry."

"We need to go." And she'd pray her target, turned employer, turned landlord, would have mercy on her once she reached the house.

"Do you need help getting up?"

She nodded—a mistake, since her world tilted precariously, and her stomach churned again.

Danielle slipped a hand beneath her back, and Brigitte gripped the tree bark to pull herself up. Iciness flooded her skin and her legs weighed heavy as granite.

"Are you sure you can walk, *Maman?*"

"Quite sure." But with her first step away from the tree, her world faded into blackness.

Chapter Nine

Jean Paul sucked in a deep breath as he stared at the cottage sitting innocently in the morning light.

He could go in.

The roof wouldn't fall down on him, the sky wouldn't crash around him and the world wouldn't end if he simply stepped through that door. He'd done it last night when he was too angry with Danielle to think about where he went. And he'd done it a second time when he'd carried Brigitte to her bed after she'd collapsed. Nothing unspeakable had happened either time.

So why did the thought of going in this morn make his skin crawl and sweat bead on the back of his neck?

The situation was too familiar. The last woman who'd lain sick in that cottage had died. Now another woman lay in the very spot where Corinne had—only this woman had three younglings and no husband.

What would he do with the children should she die?

He took one step toward the cottage, then another. It rested peacefully amid the trees and brambles, no screams or signs of distress emanating from within. Surely the children didn't need him. Danielle seemed competent enough to care for her mother—provided the girl didn't dart off to steal his chickens, that was.

He should turn around. He had fields to tend and tenants to see to, more food to deliver and a stop to make in town. No need to go inside. He'd come to check, and the children didn't require his help. In fact, Brigitte was probably up and around, her fever gone as she busily tended her family.

A shriek rang from inside. "Victor, *non!*"

Then a crash followed, accompanied by a babe's wail and more shouts.

Jean Paul covered the five remaining strides to the door and thrust it open. Chaos filled the little space before him. The dishes from the bottom shelf had all come crashing to the floor, and the babe sat in the middle of the mess, moisture quickly collecting in his eyes.

"I told you to watch him," Danielle shouted at Serge, her hair a wild tangle of ebony-colored waves.

Serge sank down onto the floor beside his brother and slung his hands over his knees. "I thought he just wanted to stand up. How was I to know he would pull the dishes down?"

A groan sounded from the bed. Jean Paul turned toward the dim corner of the room and the very spot his wife had once occupied.

Ice, rather than blood, filtered through his veins.

"Look at that, Serge. You went and woke *Maman* up because you weren't watching Victor." Danielle left off yelling and turned to Brigitte, plopping down on the mattress and stroking damp hair back from her mother's face.

"What's wrong with her?" Jean Paul croaked, then cursed the fear that saturated his voice.

All three sets of eyes turned to him.

"She has a fever." Danielle laid her wrist against her mother's forehead.

"Does she need a physician?"

"Just rest. Which she doesn't seem to be getting with Serge and Victor around."

Damp hair clung to Brigitte's porcelain face, and her brown eyes were closed and sunken into her head. She slept restlessly, her arm occasionally twitching and head jerking from side to side. He took a step forward, would have reached out and felt the hot skin of her face, but Danielle scowled at him.

"I said she's fine."

His throat felt as though a liter of sand had been poured down it. "She hardly looks fine."

He growled at himself. Of course she wasn't "fine." The sick woman had nothing. Literally nothing. She slept with his horse blanket and the only food was a bit of pulse and the bread from last night—half a loaf of which had already been eaten. He was supposed to stop people from dying due to want of food, not watch it happen on his very property. "I'm going for the physician."

"I said she'll be all right. Don't trouble yourself."

"Is she oft ill?"

The girl's gaze fell to the floor. "Never."

Something tugged on the bottom of his shirt, and he looked down to find the little boy, his eyes wide.

"Is she going to die like *Papa?*"

"Non." At least he hoped not. "I'll return with the physician."

Danielle sprang to her feet. "But we can't afford—"

"Don't worry about what you can afford." His words came out rough and hard, and Serge skittered back to his place beside the babe. "The important thing is that your mother grows well."

He turned toward the door and yanked it open.

"Jean Paul! There you are." Pierre wiped perspiration

from his forehead with his shirtsleeve as he headed up the path with Samuel. "When you weren't in the south field, I grew worried."

Indeed, the man must have searched half the land before finding him tucked away back here.

Pierre stopped and craned his neck, trying to see into the house. "I didn't realize you were letting this place out."

Neither had he, but until he figured out precisely what he was going to do with Brigitte Moreau and her children, he didn't want people nosing about. He took a step forward, which forced the other two men back, then closed the door behind him. "Well, what is it you want?"

"I've a question about the dam on the lower field. Then I found Samuel here stomping through the fields hollering for you." Pierre nudged the small, wiry clerk from the mayor's office.

Samuel cleared his throat. "Mayor Narcise would like to see you this morn. Something about adding another widow to the food distribution. And then there's this letter."

Jean Paul reached out and took the missive sealed with the mayor's insignia, likely about that wretched dinner he was supposed to attend tonight. As if he didn't have enough to worry about. Why did the entire town seem to need him when he could hardly manage affairs on his own farm?

A crash, a shout, a flash of color followed by the timbre of a whisper. Brigitte struggled through her hazy, dreamlike state. Her children were here and well, that much she could discern through the commotion. But she was far from well herself. Her body ached, and her mind moved sluggishly over the chaotic sounds. She struggled to open an eyelid, but her head throbbed with the sudden light.

"*Maman?* Are you awake?"

Slender hands, likely Danielle's, eased her up until she

was half sitting. Then a mug touched her lips. She attempted to swallow, but her throat rebelled against the reflex and the cool stream of water slid down the side of her face and neck.

"Oh, *Maman,* please swallow. You'll never get better otherwise."

She reached a hand out to touch her daughter, to soothe away the worry in the girl's voice. But her arm weighed like lead, and she could barely lift it off the tick before it thudded down.

"Fine," she mumbled. She was fine. Danielle need not worry.

But her word must not have come out as she'd intended, because Danielle's hands were on her again, moving frantically over her body. "Don't fret. Everything's all settled. Citizen Belanger has gone for the physician, and Serge and Victor are playing in the corner. You fed Victor earlier. Do you remember? He wanted to eat and…"

No. She didn't remember, but if her little son could find nourishment from her body despite its sickened state, then so be it.

"We're going to have you up and about in no time. Please don't get any sicker. We need you here, with us. *Maman?* Can you hear me? We need you."

Brigitte tried to move her hand again, but as before, her limb weighed too heavily. She moaned something in response, yet her attempt at comfort hardly placated Danielle. Instead, a soft, warm lump rested on her stomach and quiet sobs filtered to her ears.

She slid her hand slowly along the blanket, forcing her wretched arm to move though doing so drained her last bit of strength. Finally her fingers touched the dense tangles that could only be Danielle's hair. She stroked gently while her daughter cried.

This was wrong. All wrong. Danielle shouldn't be crying on her stomach. She was the one who should worry, not her daughter. She was the one who only had a week to please Alphonse and had now fallen sick.

God, please heal me, she prayed against Danielle's sobs. *Please make me...* But her thoughts drifted into darkness before she finished the prayer.

For the second time that day, Jean Paul hastened through the twisting path that led to the cottage. He'd sent the physician on nearly an hour ago then stayed and listened to the mayor natter about everything from the cost of bread to another widow to supper later that night. The more he attempted to excuse himself from conversation, the more the mayor babbled.

He let himself into the somber cottage to find the physician bent over his patient while Danielle looked over the man's shoulder. The two boys played quietly in front of the cold hearth, the oldest using an array of spoons and forks as toy soldiers, and the youngest chewing on one such spoon—er, soldier.

"What's wrong with her?" He stepped nearer Brigitte, her skin so pale a part of him longed to lean down and hold his cheek over her nose and mouth to make certain she still breathed.

The physician pushed his spectacles higher on his face and scratched the balding spot at the back of his head. "Nothing that can't be fixed, Citizen, though I'm glad you sent for me. A fever this severe shouldn't be left untended."

"You can save her?"

The physician nodded, and Jean Paul blew out a long, slow breath.

A faint smile whispered across Danielle's mouth, and she turned grateful eyes to Physician Trudeau. *"Merci."*

"I merely need a few instruments from my bag." The older man pushed to his feet and moved his heavy girth to the table. "Citizen Belanger, would you please position the chair by the pallet, next to Citizen Moreau's arm."

Position the...? Ah, he meant to bleed her. Jean Paul glanced at the deathly pale woman, then hefted the chair. Bleeding had done nothing to cure Corinne, but she'd been far gone by the time he'd found money to summon the physician. Perhaps letting a person's blood earlier in the illness would be of more aid. He set the chair down with a thud.

"Yes, very good." Physician Trudeau closed his bag and lumbered back toward his patient.

"What are you doing with that knife and rope?" Danielle stared at the instruments in the physician's hand, her face as pale as her mother's.

Physician Trudeau furrowed scruffy gray eyebrows at her. "Move away from the patient, child. I need to treat her."

"Treat her? With a knife and rope? How will those help her?" She threw herself onto the bed, positioning her body between the physician and her mother. Red stained the cheeks that had been pale just moments ago, and she turned her glare on him. "Is this how you mean to help my mother, Citizen Belanger? By letting some stranger tie her to a post and take a knife to her arm?"

Jean Paul opened his mouth, but no words came.

"Now see here, Jean Paul." Anger mottled Physician Trudeau's face. "Remove this child, or I'll refuse to practice here and this woman's death will be on your hands."

Another death on his hands? He swallowed. "Step aside, Danielle. The physician only means to help."

"He means to use that knife on my mother." Her voice grew high-pitched and panicked.

Serge dropped one of his fork-soldiers and came to his

sister's side. "You're going to cut my *maman?* I thought you were a physician."

Physician Trudeau drew up his flaccid chest. "It's called bloodletting, and it's an established medical practice. Now I'll not let a bunch of younglings tell me how best to treat my patients. Jean Paul, what's it to be? My services or the whims of these children?"

Serge flung himself forward, his fists clenching the front of Jean Paul's shirt so tight they'd likely never let go. "*Non!* Tell him *non.* Don't let him hurt *Maman!*"

Jean Paul glanced at the tick where Brigitte lay. He couldn't let the woman die. What would happen to her children? They'd already suffered enough loss with their father.

But if the physician let her blood and Brigitte passed, anyway, how would he explain that to her children? What children wouldn't be upset by the idea of cutting their sick mother? Danielle might be just a child, but in some ways, she was a woman already. This was a choice for Brigitte's family, not some stranger who had met them only yesterday.

"Thank you for your service, Physician Trudeau, but we're not going to let Brigitte's blood."

The physician turned as quickly as his heavy form would allow and stalked to his bag. "Then don't come asking for my services on the morrow, or any day after that. When this woman lies dead in a cold grave, remember you were the one that killed her, not me." He thrust the knife, rope and bowl back into his bag, clasped it shut and hastened to the door. The entire house shook as the solid wood slammed behind him.

"And good riddance. As though I would let some stranger cut my mother while she sleeps." Danielle crossed her arms, her gaze still riveted on the shut door.

Serge tugged on Jean Paul's shirt again, his chin trembling. "B-but what if the man's right? What if we just killed *Maman?*"

"We didn't." Danielle sounded so confident. So sure.

But what if she was wrong? What if the boy and physician were right and Brigitte lay in the earth a week hence? Jean Paul stared down at his hands, large and scarred and capable of so much harm. It seemed no matter what he did, how hard he tried to help, he could do naught but hurt people.

Chapter Ten

Jean Paul trudged through the wooded path, no longer overgrown with weeds as it had been after half a week of use, but trampled and defined. His shoulders ached, his lower back throbbed, dirt caked his hands and sweat streaked the side of his face. What he wouldn't give for a quick dip in the stream, a hearty meal and a long night's rest.

Yet he couldn't force himself to go home without first checking on her.

The delirious fever had clung to Brigitte Moreau for the past three days. If it wasn't gone on the morrow, he'd start making arrangements for the children. Corinne's illness had tarried a month, but after the first week, she'd been gone from him in every way but body. He couldn't allow Brigitte's children to watch death slowly claim her. Bad enough that he'd have to see it, himself. The last time had robbed the very life from his soul.

Not that watching the woman currently in his little hut die would rob his life. He didn't know her, and hardly cared what happened.

Or rather, he shouldn't care.

So why did he tromp to the forgotten house every night

to see if she improved? Because of the children? Because she had that same quiet determination that Corinne had once possessed? Because she'd come to him tired and hungry, and he hadn't met her needs?

Sickness plagued the countryside constantly, and with the Terror last year plus the wars France fought against Britain and Austria, Prussia, Italy and Spain, the loss of one more life should hardly matter.

At least that's what he told himself. Now if only he could get his heart to believe it.

He stopped in front of the cottage and knocked on the door. A child wailed from inside, followed by the sound of Danielle's sharp tongue.

He let himself in and surveyed the commotion with a single glance. The raspberries and salt pork he'd brought the children yesterday's eve were scattered across the floor, the babe happily sticking the dirt-laden berries into his mouth. Meanwhile Serge cowered in a corner and Danielle stood above him, hands on hips, and a torrent of words pouring from her mouth.

"Why can you never do as I request? Don't you want *Maman* to get better? If she's ever to improve, we need—"

"Halt," Jean Paul barked.

"Merci." A quiet voice whispered from the corner.

A fragile hope kindled in his chest, like warm embers buried under layers of ash. He turned to find Brigitte sitting propped against the bed's headboard, her hair a drenched mess of dark auburn and her brown eyes a touch too bright with fever.

But she was awake.

"I'm sorry you got woken, *Maman*." Danielle hurried to her mother's side. "It's Serge's fault. I told him to watch Victor…"

Brigitte held up a slim hand to stop the rush of words, but her daughter paid no heed.

"Serge was playing instead and…"

"Stop talking, Danielle." Could the girl not see how her mother moved her hand to her temple and rubbed under the endless chatter?

Danielle's words ceased for a moment, then started up again. "Am I upsetting you? Because it should be Serge who—"

"I said enough." He stopped his teeth from grinding together. Barely. Brigitte's eyes fluttered closed, and a faint wince appeared across her forehead. The woman needed calm and quiet if she was going to regain her strength— not something she was likely to have with three younglings about. "Danielle, take the children out of doors."

"But supper—"

"Listen to Citizen Belanger," Brigitte rasped, her voice far too quiet for the way her chest heaved as she spoke.

Jean Paul scooped the babe off the floor and plopped him into Danielle's arms. "I'll see to supper later."

Danielle's eyes darted between him and Brigitte. "Why do you want us to leave? So you can interrogate her?"

Jean Paul ran his eyes over Brigitte's slender frame, her white skin, tangled hair and moist forehead. Interrogate her? He wanted merely to touch her. To make certain with his own hands that her condition had improved, that she wouldn't be buried in a grave beside Corinne a week hence.

"Obey," Brigitte commanded before sinking back onto the tick, her eyes closed.

Danielle sent him a dark look, then propped the babe on her hip and stalked through the door in a swish of skirts while Serge scrambled after her.

He closed the door and moved to the bed. "You're better."

She peeked a weary eyelid open. "The fever broke this morn, or so Danielle tells me."

He crouched beside her and pressed a hand to her cheek. Still warm, but the raging heat that had emanated from her skin when he'd brushed her face last night was gone. *Thank You, Father.* He'd been so certain Physician Trudeau had been right, that he'd have yet another death on his hands.

But it seemed as though Brigitte would recover.

Brigitte smiled at the man hunched beside her, or tried to. Her face felt too tired to work properly. Citizen Belanger still looked a touch terrifying, with his black hair and dark eyes and the odd scar that bunched around his eyebrow. But there was nothing terrifying in his bent position, or in the way his eyes brimmed with concern as they ran over her.

Hadn't Danielle told her as much? Her daughter had said something about Citizen Belanger acting more concerned than angry. Or at least she thought that's what Danielle had said, but she could hardly be certain of anything after enduring such a fever.

"I see you found where the children and I were staying." Her vocal cords, stiff from disuse, grated against each other as she spoke. "I thought it might be your property. I'd hoped not, but still I wondered."

He scowled. "You should have told me about the children, about where you were living."

She shrugged slightly and attempted to shift farther up on the pallet before falling back again, exhausted. Her fever may have broken, but her strength had yet to return. And the tiredness that had plagued her before her illness still clung to every pore of her body.

"Let me help." Strong arms braced her back, and Citizen Belanger's powerful body lifted her higher in the bed. Then he eased the two flimsy pillows behind her back.

"Merci."

His face hovered a mere breath away from hers. This close, his eyes were no longer hard and dark, but that deep, warm shade of soil after a good rain.

He stayed in his position a moment longer than he ought, one arm still wrapped about her shoulders, his body leaning over hers. His gaze flitted across her face, settling on her lips for the briefest of instants.

Something inside her turned warm and soft, and then a wave of ice swept through her. What was she doing, lying here so close to the man she should be spying on? Staring into his eyes instead of wheedling some information about his past? She shifted away and cleared her throat. "I asked you for a post. Have you changed your mind?"

He leaned back, his gaze no longer resting on her dry, cracked lips. "I would have changed my mind long ago, had I known you had three children with whom you shared my food, or that you hadn't money for the inn."

She looked away. "My children were hardly your concern."

And she hadn't known whether she could trust him.

Yet he'd found where they lived and hadn't kicked them out. From the mess of salt pork and raspberries on the floor, she could surmise he continued to feed them. And he was here with her now, was he not? Touching her face and asking how she fared, concern radiating from his gargantuan form. She might know little of his past, but he'd cared for her and her children rather than cast them out.

"A family living on my land is my concern. A family starving when I have food aplenty is my concern. A family—"

She held up her hand. "We were hardly starving. I have

three children in my care, Citizen. I'm careful with whom I trust."

He lurched back as if slapped, though she'd hardly the energy to lift her hand and attempt such a thing.

"'Tis nothing against you." Though having Alphonse suspect him of killing Henri surely didn't help matters. "I'm careful of everyone."

"I understand," he growled, his face an unreadable mask of dark features and angry lines.

"Do you? Have you any children of your own?"

"I had a wife once...we shared this very cottage. 'Twas why my family built it, for Corinne and I, but she died before she bore any babes." His chest rose and fell with suddenly heavy breathing, and his eyes shifted away from her.

"I'm sorry," she whispered. And she was. "I meant not to upset you."

"I'm not upset." Iron crusted his words.

She merely reached out and rested her hand atop his. A muscle in his jaw methodically twitched back and forth, but after another moment, he sighed and turned his own work-roughened hand over to squeeze hers.

"I lost my husband a year past. 'Tis a hardship I'd never wish on another."

"Do you still love him? Even though he's dead, do you still think of him as though he's here...? Wish for him at odd times, like when you're working in the fields or lying down at night?"

Brigitte swallowed and glanced down at her hands. 'Twould almost be easier to spout a falsehood and bring the man a bit of comfort by sharing the sorrow he still obviously felt. But she couldn't lie, not about something as sacred as the love between a husband and wife. "I don't think it's wrong if you still love your wife. But Henri and I...we weren't like that. I stopped loving him years ago, if

I ever loved him at all. The man had a golden tongue, but after we married, he didn't treat me well."

"You have three children to care for by yourself. Do you not miss him for that?"

She raised one side of her lips up into a half smile. "Five children. I've two twin boys in the navy."

He sank back onto his knees, his gaze traveling slowly over her face. "I'd not have guessed you old enough to have sons in the navy."

"I was young when I married Henri, and the twins followed soon after." Heat stained her cheeks and she cleared her throat. "Quite soon after."

"You're blessed to have the children. You can't understand how many times I've wished that Corinne, before she died…" His voice trailed off and he swallowed tightly.

"I'm sorry she died so young."

He gave a slight nod but his eyes turned dark and distant, as though imagining another time, a happier time. A time when dreams still existed.

She nestled farther back against the pillows and yawned. The weariness was creeping back. Another few minutes, and she'd not have the strength to remember his words. "Speaking of children, you seem to have done an admirable job caring for mine. Thank you. I trust they are well?"

"As well as can be expected, if you don't mind shouting voices and broken dishes and…" He glanced at the mess of food in front of the hearth. "Spilled food. I've put Danielle to work baking bread in your stead."

"Danielle? Housework?"

"She gave me that very look." He reached down and trailed a thumb over the wrinkles in her forehead.

She found herself moving toward him, the heat of his skin, the silent strength of his body. "She hates housework."

Was she a fool for taking pleasure in the moment? Here she was, lying abed, her hair and clothing damp with sweat, her body reeking of sickness, and all she wanted was to roll closer to the man. To take comfort in the feel of strong arms around her and another heart beating beside hers.

"Danielle's, ah, growing more accustomed to the work," he whispered. "She tends the children well enough, if you don't mind the shouting. Her bread might not taste like yours, but it's better than mine. And she doesn't argue when I pay her two *livres*."

Her eyes drifted half closed. "Two *livres* for a loaf of bread in which you supply the ingredients. Foolish child."

"I think her rather smart."

Brigitte would have smiled, but a bout of shivers overtook her, and she burrowed deeper beneath the blanket.

"Are you cold? 'Tis summer and the air hot."

"The fever still hasn't left, though it fades. Perchance I'll awake well on the morrow."

"Let me help." He leaned over and tucked the blanket around her, so tightly she had little hope of freeing her hands.

"Warmer?" Softness laced his usually gruff voice.

She nodded and huddled into a ball beneath the covers.

"Have you another blanket?" He looked around the bare cottage.

"Non." She yawned, her eyelids drifting farther closed. "Danielle found this one somewhere. We brought none with us."

"It's my mare's."

She forced her eyes open at that. "Your what?"

He brushed a strand of hair back from her face, a wry twist to his lips. "Hush now. You need sleep."

"But Danielle said she found this blanket."

"Ah, yes, I think your eldest daughter uses the word

found a bit loosely. But 'tis a matter for another time. Sleep first."

She blinked, so tired and yet with so many duties left to tend. "The children are still outside. They've yet to eat and—"

A calloused hand clamped over her mouth. "Do you always fret so? I wonder not why you took fever."

He was right, she'd probably brought the fever on herself with her business and worrying and lack of food.

He kept his hand firmly over his mouth. He was too close again, his body leaning over hers and his large, rough hands touching her face. But she'd hardly the strength to protest, so she closed her eyes as commanded.

The pallet beneath her faded away, along with the walls of the cottage and mess on the floor. Instead, she travelled to a soft place, a place where there was comfort and love, support and caring. A place where she didn't have to work for Alphonse or fear he would come for her children. A place where she found solace in the arms of a good man.

What a shame such a place existed only in her dreams.

Jean Paul stared at Brigitte's still form, her eyelashes fanned against her soft cheeks and her slender body curled up on the tick. He shifted his hand from her mouth where he'd been shushing her to stroke the side of her face. She turned into his touch.

If only he had true comfort to offer rather than horrid memories and nighttime terrors.

He'd not asked a single question he'd intended. He needed to know her story. Of all the places she could go for work, all the people she could seek for help, how had she come to his yard just over a week ago? Her presence here, in his life and in his forgotten hut, made no sense.

Unless God Himself had wrapped her up like a pretty

package and dropped her under his nose. Someone to help. Someone to care for. Someone to love.

But he didn't love Brigitte Moreau. He hardly knew her.

He stroked a strand of damp hair away from her face. Mayhap he didn't love her, but he'd been caring for her needs since first they met. Even when he'd thought she had her own dwelling, he'd given her food and money.

How was that different than caring for a wife?

And with her children, God almost seemed to foist upon him the family he might have had if Corinne still lived.

But he didn't deserve such a gift, not after the things he'd done. The Moreau family's presence was probably some cruel type of jest, punishing him for his past deeds. God would give him Brigitte and the children for a time only to rip them away again.

It had happened with Corinne; it could happen again.

Jean Paul pulled his hand back from her face and stood.

Best to let Danielle take care of the woman and keep his distance. Best not to get any more involved than he already was.

He headed for the door, yanked it open then closed it tight behind him. Three children, caked head to toe with mud, stared back at him.

"What have you been doing?" He'd told them to play outside, not slather themselves in dirt and water.

Serge shrugged, the movement causing a blob of muck to slide down his cheek and land on the ground. "Victor threw some at me, so I threw some back."

"Except he hit me instead." Danielle's face was murderous. Thick clumps of mud twined with her hair and stained the front of her dress and apron.

Propped on Danielle's hip, Victor grinned. Mire covered his gown and coated his hands and feet. He reached one of those muddy little hands up and patted his sister's cheek, leaving a nice, fresh smear.

Jean Paul rolled his eyes toward the heavens. Why him? Why these younglings? Why after a long day of working in the fields?

And why, more than anything, after he'd decided to leave Brigitte alone?

"Is dinner ready?" Serge asked.

"Ah…" Had he promised to prepare some food? He couldn't quite remember, but then, he'd have likely told the children they could set fire to the farmstead if it would give him a couple minutes alone with Brigitte.

Or rather, that had been his thought before he'd decided to stay away from her.

"Where is it?" Serge patted his stomach. "I'm hungry."

"Oh, be quiet, Serge." Danielle shifted the babe higher on her hip. "You ought be asking after *Maman,* not dinner."

"Your mother's asleep," Jean Paul muttered as he stared at the children. What was he going to do with them? He could hardly let the filthy hooligans tromp back inside and soil their house. Besides, they'd wake their mother.

Not that he cared. Because he didn't. No. Not him. He definitely cared not whether Brigitte slept long enough to restore a creamy hue to her cheeks or put that glint of quiet determination back in her eyes.

And blast it all! What was he doing thinking about the woman's hair and eyes when he'd just sworn off her?

"I want to see *Maman.*" Serge bolted for the door, but Jean Paul reached out an arm and snagged the boy by the waist.

"You're too filthy to go inside, and your mother needs rest."

"How else are we going to eat? Victor's going to be hungry soon, and then he won't stop crying until he gets food." Danielle wiped the fresh smear of mud from her cheek. Or tried to. She only succeeded in spreading the glob down to her chin.

Was life with children always so trying? Perhaps it was good that he and Corinne hadn't...

The thought stilled in his head. No. There was nothing good about what had happened with Corinne—and the man he had become in his grief. He'd give anything to have his own set of younglings one day, but no woman would want to marry him now.

"Let me go. I want to see *Maman*." Serge sent him a look so belligerent he could only have learned it from his sister.

"You can't. I...uh..." He scratched his head. What did one say to a boy who wanted his mother but couldn't have her?

The babe squealed and smeared another blob of mud across Danielle's face.

"I'm done with this." Danielle plopped Victor down onto the ground. "He can crawl if he wants to go somewhere."

Victor's face bunched up into an angry little mask, and he let out an ear-piercing wail.

Brigitte would never be able to rest with all this commotion, and the children needed to get cleaned up before darkness descended. Then there was the matter of supper.

He had little choice but to take them home, wash them up and feed them. He stuck a finger in his collar and tugged. How was he going to manage all that when he couldn't even keep them quiet outside their mother's window?

Chapter Eleven

Brigitte glanced out the window as she stacked plates into a pile on the table. Were she in the little house in the woods, she could see nothing but fir boughs through the windows. But with the position of Jean Paul's house on its little knoll, the sun's rays filtered through the window as the gilded orb dipped closer and closer toward the trees.

She wiped her forehead, where sweat beaded along her hairline, and carried the plates to the washtub. She should have served dinner earlier. She was going to be late if she didn't hurry, and after missing last week's rendezvous with the gendarme, she could hardly afford to compromise this one.

She only hoped he hadn't sent word to Alphonse. If she missed this week's appointment, as well, her father-in-law would likely send a battalion of men to Abbeville in search of her.

She picked up the first plate and scrubbed.

Thwack! Thwack! Thwack!

A thudding sounded at evenly spaced intervals from the yard.

She glanced toward the window again as she reached for

another plate. She could well guess what the sound was, though she couldn't see the activity from where she stood.

Thwack! Thwack!

She reached for the third plate. What had ever possessed Jean Paul to teach Danielle how to throw knives? The girl should be in here helping, not outside learning a man's skill.

Then again, Danielle would have found some other way to avoid doing the dishes.

Thwack! Thwack!

Brigitte raised her eyes to the ceiling. She only hoped the skill proved useful to Danielle rather than serving as another means for trouble.

Muted voices replaced the thudding sounds, while Brigitte scrubbed furiously at the last plate. She need only wash the mugs and utensils, and then she could dash off to her meeting. Of course, making her excuses for leaving the farmstead would be rather challenging, but she didn't have much choice.

The door opened, casting slanted beams of orange over her and the dishes, then closed as Jean Paul's heavy footfalls thudded against the dirt floor. "Are you almost finished?"

She nodded and grabbed another cup.

"Good, the younglings want us to go fishing."

"Fishing?" She dropped the mug. Why did they want to go fishing now of all times?

"I promised we'd take them once you were well."

A soft warmth warred with the trembling fear inside her. Here stood this gruff man with a perpetual scowl on his face, yet he taught her daughter to throw knives and offered to take her children fishing. Henri had never done such things.

"Can we go tomorrow?"

Jean Paul ran his eyes sharply over her. "Why? Has your fever returned? Are you feeling poorly?"

"Non," she blurted, then bit the inside of her lip.

He touched his hand to her forehead. "You look drawn, and your brow is warm. Go home and lie down. I'll take the children myself."

That might work, provided she could escape to her meeting with the gendarme and return before Jean Paul and the children finished fishing.

"And you'll stay abed tomorrow. I won't have you falling ill again."

She jerked her gaze up to meet his. She wasn't *that* ill. Her fever had broken nearly a week ago, yet she'd started working only yesterday. Being cooped up in that tiny hut and treated like an invalid again was about as appealing as being dunked in the Somme River in February.

Jean Paul shifted closer, his concerned eyes not leaving her face. *"Oui.* You must go home. Can you manage the walk alone?"

A sickening dread filled her stomach. She either proclaimed herself well and went fishing or condemned herself to bed again.

"I'm hot from being so near the hearth, not from fever." She plunged her hands back into the wash water and grabbed the mug she'd dropped. "In fact, I'm feeling well enough I might take a trip into town on the morrow. I need thread for the shoulder on Danielle's dress, and Serge's trousers are a dozen centimeters too short."

Plus if she went into town, she could find the gendarme, tell him why she'd missed the meeting two weeks in a row and explain that she was now in a better position to find information on Jean Paul.

Information that would prove his innocence, of course.

Jean Paul settled himself into the chair nearest her. "I don't think you're well enough to go to town."

Of all the things for the man to be stubborn about. "I promise I'm fine."

"Then I'll take you when I make my vegetable delivery tomorrow afternoon, but I won't have you making the trip alone. Mayhap you can find yourself material for a new dress while you're there."

Her cheeks heated, and she glanced down at the dress hanging loosely on her frame, the frayed material threadbare in places. Anyone would notice such an old gown.

So why did her entire body feel flushed, and her eyes refuse to meet his?

She fumbled about in the wash water for a handful of forks and started scrubbing. This conversation was not going as planned. Now she was not only stuck going fishing, but going to town with an escort, as well. 'Twould make speaking with the gendarme even more difficult than sneaking off to meet him tonight.

Jean Paul leaned back in his chair. "Perhaps we can also look for another post for you, one more suited than having you work here and live in a hovel."

Her back snapped as straight as the wooden timbers in the walls. "*Non.* I'm quite happy with my position here."

He cocked his head to the side. "I've not been able to put it together. If you needed to leave Calais, why come here, to me, for work?"

Silence hung thick in the air between them, and she licked her suddenly dry lips, her mind scrambling for something, anything to say. "I…I hadn't much choice."

"Did you hear stories of me? Of how I employed Pierre despite his loss of a hand, and how I gave food to widows?"

She opened her mouth to answer, but no sound came

out for several moments. "I knew I needed help, and you were the only person who could give it."

It wasn't a lie. Not completely.

"Surely you have family somewhere. Calais perhaps? Could they not have helped?"

"I'll never take help from the family in Calais." The words shot from her mouth like arrows from a bow.

"And you've not family in another town?"

She pressed her eyes shut. Did he suspect…?

What? That she was a spy sent to determine whether he was a horrible murderer or an honest farmer? Because truly, the answer had no middle ground. And as much as she wanted to proclaim him a farmer, wipe her hands of this messy business and leave for Reims, she still lacked proof.

"I have family in Reims, yes, but they know naught of my current situation. I'm planning to travel to them shortly, after I have more funds."

He stood and moved closer, then crouched down on the other side of the basin, making their eyes even and his gaze rather unavoidable. "And Abbeville is on the way?"

She nodded, praying he wouldn't think too hard about her reasoning. Abbeville was indeed on the way from Calais to Reims, but 'twas hardly the most direct route.

"So what prevents you from going to Reims now, besides your need to recover from the fever? Need you more money?"

She probably had enough funds, what with the two *livres* per day Jean Paul had given her and then Danielle for bread. Now that she worked as his housekeeper, he gave her three *livres* and ten *sous* per day.

But though she had money enough to complete her journey, Alphonse would never let her run. "'Tis not the money so much as the journey itself and fear of losing my older boys. Reims is a long way from the coast. I've left missives for them with the navy, but what if they don't receive them and can't find me? Abbeville may not be Calais, but I'm still near the coast."

She held her breath, waiting for his forehead to draw down into its familiar grooves and more questions to come. Waiting for him to see through her flimsy excuse.

But instead, his eyes met hers over the washbasin, his gaze roaming from her forehead to her cheeks down to her lips.

Her mouth turned instantly dry.

"Brigitte..." He reached out and tucked a strand of hair behind her ear. "If you ever need any—"

The door flew open and crashed against the wall. Jean Paul spun toward the noise, that familiar scowl back on his face.

Serge danced inside the room. "Fishing! Fishing! We're going fishing!"

"Are you coming, *Maman?*" Danielle asked from the doorway.

"I want to go now!"

Brigitte ducked her head as she washed the last of the knives and then dried her hands. Of course, they wanted to go and spend time with Jean Paul before the night grew too dark and they had to return to their cabin. Because her children were falling in love with this large, gruff man who treated them better than their father ever had.

If only she had the luxury of doing the same.

"Stay here. I'll be but a moment." Jean Paul pulled his wagon with its aging mare to a stop.

Jean Paul climbed down from the wagon, leaving Brigitte alone on the bench. To her left sat an old stone house that looked to have endured two centuries or more of use.

The yard was thick with weeds, with the door hung precariously on its hinges. The drapes visible from where she waited seemed soiled and old, and the windows appeared as though they'd not been scrubbed in a good long while. One of the top panes of glass had even been shattered.

Brigitte glanced around the quaint street lined with similar, if better cared for, houses. Then the dilapidated door to the first house flew open and a boy of about Danielle's age rushed down the steps. A girl—or perhaps she was a woman—sauntered behind the boy and batted her eyes at Jean Paul.

A woman, then. One who seemed barely old enough to look at a man. But that didn't stop her from sidling closer to Jean Paul as he unloaded the wagon and giggling when he asked how she fared.

Brigitte crossed her arms over her chest. Why did the siblings get to help unload while Jean Paul told her to stay in the wagon?

Not that the girl was helping him. Then again, she probably counted distracting Jean Paul a help.

"Are those raspberries for us?" The boy peeked in the back of the wagon.

"Oui." Jean Paul handed him the small crate. "And the leaf lettuce, turnips and carrots. Some flour, too."

He scrunched up his nose. "You should have brought more raspberries and left the turnips."

Jean Paul laughed. "Then I'd not have enough for my other stops. Go on and run those inside. If you help me unload, I'll pay you a *livre*."

The boy bolted inside with the raspberries and a sack of flour.

"Raspberries are my favorite, as well." The girl—because *girl* was precisely how Brigitte was going to think of her—edged closer to Jean Paul. "Perhaps we can share some with you if you've time to visit."

"That's a kind offer, Annalise, but I've got business to tend." Jean Paul scooted two more crates to the edge of the wagon. Then he hefted one and started up the walk.

The girl hurried after him, threading her hand through his arm before disappearing inside.

Brigitte rubbed at her temple. How long would Jean Paul be? She still had to find the gendarme. News of her trip into town would hardly reach him if Jean Paul stayed in quiet places such as this. Plus she needed to hurry back to prepare the evening meal and check on her children. Knowing Danielle, she'd decided to leave her brothers in Jean Paul's house and go rabbit hunting.

Brigitte shifted on the bench and looked up one end of the street and then down the other. Two children played in a yard farther down, but besides them, the road was deserted. And though the door to the house remained open, neither Jean Paul, nor the boy, nor that Annalise girl emerged. Yet one crate still sat apart from the others near the edge of the wagon.

Jean Paul was likely talking to the mother or father or whomever was inside, and it hardly seemed right to sit idle while there was work to be done. She was just as capable of helping as the others.

More capable than Annalise, surely.

She climbed down and grabbed the last crate, sliding the bulky box into her arms. My, but it was a bit heavy. Who knew turnips could weigh so much? She took a few wobbly steps toward the house. Perhaps Jean Paul was right and she'd yet to fully recover from her illness.

"Bonjour?" Voices emanated from inside the house, but no one greeted her at the door.

She moved inside and called louder. *"Bonjour."*

Jean Paul appeared in the corridor, that perpetual scowl planted on his face. "I told you to stay in the wagon."

He took the crate, and her arms screamed in relief. But she scowled right back at him. No reason to let him know he'd been right. The man was already arrogant enough. "I was trying to help, not earn a lecture."

He turned and stalked back down the corridor, disappearing into the room at the end. Brigitte glanced outside then back toward the door Jean Paul had vanished behind. Should she go back to the wagon, follow Jean Paul or simply remain here? The man hadn't told her what he wanted, yet if she did the wrong thing, she'd likely get another lecture.

She turned and took a step back toward the door. Best to wait in the wagon and hope he didn't talk for too much longer. Though if Annalise had her way, she was probably sitting atop Jean Paul's lap feeding him raspberries.

Brigitte clenched her teeth together. Had she ever been so young and foolish? So openly heartsick for a man?

Probably, when she'd first met Henri. She'd done many a silly thing that summer, including marrying the man and moving to Calais only to discover he was a smuggler. At least Jean Paul had character enough not to lie and take advantage of a girl the way Henri had with her.

"Please don't leave."

Brigitte looked up to find a woman moving down the corridor. The matriarch of the house, no doubt. Faint lines ringed her eyes, and she wore a faded gown and apron much like Brigitte's own. Most of the woman's graying hair had been tucked up beneath a mobcap, but stray strands fell about her face and neck.

A woman in threadbare clothes, aged beyond her years, with shoulders permanently slumped from the weight resting on them.

Brigitte touched a hand to her cheek. Was this what others saw when they looked at her?

No wonder Jean Paul plied her with food and rest and told her to purchase fabric for a new gown.

But Jean Paul saw her as more than a thin woman in worn clothes, didn't he? He'd visited her when she was ill, had touched her softly after her fever had broken, stared at her lips yesterday's eve… A flood of warmth raced through her at the memory.

"*Bonjour,* I'm Citizen Arnaud." The woman dipped into a small courtesy. "And you are?"

"I'm—"

"Leaving." Jean Paul stalked back into the room. "She ought not have left the wagon."

The woman's eyes darted to Jean Paul then back, and she smiled. "Oh, I see."

Brigitte raised her chin at Jean Paul. Whatever it was Citizen Arnaud saw, maybe she'd share the information, because Brigitte was flummoxed. How could anyone understand Jean Paul ordering her about like a dog?

"Perhaps you can stop and visit again sometime?" Citizen Arnaud asked her. "Maybe next week when Jean Paul brings the vegetables?"

Brigitte opened her mouth to respond, but the boy from earlier bounded down the corridor.

"You forgot my *livre.*"

"A *livre?*" The smile left the woman's face. "Jean Paul Belanger, you are not paying my son a *livre* for carrying in a box of raspberries."

Jean Paul dug into his pocket and dropped the coin into the boy's hand. "Good help is hard to come by these days, or have you not noticed how many of our men are off at war? Besides, I've a delivery for Gaston to make to Mayor Narcise."

"Now wait a moment. Gaston can surely…"

But the woman's words faded as Jean Paul nudged Brigitte out the door and Gaston raced ahead of them both.

"Get in the wagon and stay put this time," he growled in her ear.

She climbed up onto the bench while he handed some raspberries and a missive to Gaston. The boy turned and took off down the street like a horse at full gallop.

"You should have stayed here." The wagon shifted subtly as Jean Paul seated himself beside her.

"'Twas nothing for me to do, and that last crate needed to go inside, did it not?"

"You looked ready to faint when I took it from you."

"I was nothing of the sort." She glared at him, but he stared right back, his dark eyes watching her too carefully. "Well, perhaps I was a little wobbly, but I'll not regain my strength if no one lets me work."

"And what do you call fixing breakfast and making bread? Dusting my house a dozen times per day?"

"You know what I meant."

"Stay put at our next stop. There'll be men aplenty to unload the wagon." He flicked the reins, and the mare tromped slowly forward.

"The woman back there, Madame Arnaud, she didn't pay you for the vegetables."

"Non."

"So you…you gave her the food?"

"Oui."

Just like he'd given her food then paid her an exorbitant amount for the bread she baked. She shifted and looked at the crates in the back of the wagon, filled with turnips, lettuce, flour and even a few green beans. "Will you give all of this away, too?"

"The next delivery is paid."

"How…why…?" It didn't make any sense. How did he earn money to live on if he gave away as much food as he sold?

He pulled back on the reins, letting the wagon roll to a stop as he stared at the street ahead. "My first wife, Corinne, starved to death and I could do nothing to stop it. Now I have food aplenty, so I attempt to keep others from that same fate."

His first wife had starved? Something hollow hit Brigitte in the chest. The overlarge man beside her might not be the most genteel person she'd ever met, but he'd loved his wife. Still loved her. She could see it in the soft sheen of his eyes whenever he spoke of Corinne, in the questions he asked about her and Henri and how she'd grieved her own husband's death.

"I'm sorry," she whispered into the muggy air between them, because really there was little else to say. She was sorry. So terribly sorry a strong man like Jean Paul had watched the woman he loved slowly die from lack of food.

"As am I." He swallowed thickly. "But she'll naught be hungry again eating at God's table. It's the people remaining in France that need the worrying."

"Which is why you plied me with food when first we met."

"Oui." His voice sounded rough, like rock crushed together and then ground into gravel.

"Your generosity has mattered much to me and my family." She leaned forward and touched her lips to his dark, stubble-roughened cheek. Not a romantic, passionate gesture, but a silent offer of comfort that lasted not a moment before she pulled back.

But the brevity of the touch didn't stop warmth from traveling through her body, the humming feeling that shot from her lips to her head to her toes, or the desire to scoot a bit closer and lay her head on his shoulder.

Jean Paul stared at Brigitte, her lips entirely too close to his, while something soft and sweet spiraled through him. She'd kissed him. In the middle of the street. In broad daylight. And he must be going mad, because he wanted her to do it again. Or mayhap he could be the one to start the kiss, but this time he wouldn't settle for a peck on the cheek. Oh, no, he wanted a taste of her lips.

He leaned forward, just a bit, only to have her jerk away.

"My, but it's growing late." She wrung her hands together and then fussed with something on her skirt. "I'll have to hurry if I'm going to make my stops and be back in time to fix supper."

"Sûrement." He straightened and flicked the reins—a bit harder than he'd intended. Sylvie jerked her head up and lurched forward.

What was wrong with him? What kind of man spoke of his late wife one moment and then wanted to kiss a different woman the next? Shouldn't he be dreaming of kissing Corinne?

Except Corinne wasn't the one sitting beside him. She was dead, and had been for seven years.

But Brigitte Moreau? She was alive and well and utterly delightful. And at the moment, his thoughts had nothing to do with his late wife or hurrying on to his next delivery, and everything to do with stopping the wagon and pressing his lips to Brigitte's.

Chapter Twelve

Brigitte stared at the set of four buildings ahead and the sign that clearly marked them. "The gendarmerie post? You deliver vegetables to the gendarmes?"

Jean Paul shifted beside her, his every muscle stiff. He'd not looked at her once since the kiss, though she knew not what she would have done if he had. Heat rushed her face anew. What had she been thinking to kiss him?

"*Oui,* this is the delivery that pays, remember? I've a need to make coin every now and then, so I can give *livres* to delivery boys and pay for my bread."

She wiped her damp palms on her skirt and surveyed the buildings. 'Twas foolish to be nervous. She'd wanted to come here—or at least, she'd thought she had. But now that the post loomed closer, explaining why she'd missed two meetings to Alphonse's gendarme hardly seemed an easy task.

But the man from the woods had already spotted her. He stood by the side of the road, his cold gray eyes riveted on the wagon.

The moisture leeched from her throat as they rolled to a stop, and she sucked in a deep breath. A little explanation was all she needed. Surely she could force the words out and stave off the man sending word to Alphonse.

Provided it wasn't too late.

Jean Paul hopped down from the wagon and frowned at the guard. "Didn't I tell you to make yourself scarce when next I came?"

The man smirked, his face defiant and arrogant. "Captain Monfort's orders."

"Then I'll have a word with your captain." Jean Paul started toward the largest of the four buildings.

"He got called into town. The chef wants to see you, though. Wasn't too happy about the weevils he found in the flour you dropped off last week."

Jean Paul stopped, the tips of his ears turning a dull red. "My flour doesn't have weevils unless you put them there."

The gendarme offered a lazy shrug. "Talk to the cook, then."

Jean Paul changed directions and headed toward the smallest of the four buildings, his long strides quickly covering the ground.

Brigitte glanced from Jean Paul's retreating body to the gendarme and back again. Well, she'd not have to worry about getting a word alone with the gendarme. Jean Paul seemed to think nothing of—

A strong hand wrapped around her ankle.

"Come down here."

She licked her lips. "But Jean Paul told me to stay—"

"Jean Paul, is it? Not *Citizen Belanger?*" The grip around her ankle tightened. "Get down now, or I fear a terrible accident might happen and you'll fall from the wagon. Wouldn't it be distressing if you were to hit your head on a rock?"

"I'll need you to release me, Citizen, if you expect me to move."

The iron band surrounding her ankle dropped away, but she could hardly be thankful considering she'd be face to face with the henchman in another moment.

She slowly climbed down the side of the wagon. The second her feet touched the packed earth, both hands locked onto her shoulders.

"You skipped our meeting last night."

She tried to shrink away, but his grip was like iron. She scanned the yard, but no other gendarmes appeared, and Jean Paul had yet to emerge from the kitchen.

"You think Citizen Belanger will save you?" the gendarme sneered. "He'll be plenty occupied denying his flour had any weevils."

The gendarme yanked her away from the wagon and toward the far side of the largest building, then thrust her against the wall. This side of the building edged a patch of dense woods and no one was likely to happen upon them.

"Where were you last night, and the week before that?" he demanded.

"I was ill the first week. I took a fever after our meeting. Ask Citizen Belanger if you don't believe me."

His eyes bored into hers, and he moved closer, placing his hands on the wall on either side of her. "And last night?"

She shrank back, but the action did little good. He'd trapped her against the hard stone. "I was detained."

He lowered his head, his breath fanning hot against her cheek. "I ought to cart you and your whelps back to Dubois."

She shoved at his chest, but he only leaned closer. So big. So large. So intimidating. "Jean Paul wanted to take the children fishing last night. If I'd have left to meet you instead of going to the creek, my absence would have caused questions. Do you want him to discover my mission?"

The gendarme shifted back a fraction. Not much, but enough for her to suck in a breath without sharing his air. He was listening, at least. And he hadn't slapped her. Or dragged her into the woods to bind and gag her before carting her off to Alphonse.

"You need to move the meetings later," she pressed. "After dark. It rushes the evening meal too much otherwise. Were I to run off immediately after we ate, Jean Paul would grow suspicious."

"I care not for your excuses. Have you proof?"

"I was sick for—"

He grabbed her hair, wrenching her neck so hard to the side her muscles screamed in protest. "I asked not for excuses."

"Jean Paul!" A frantic, feminine voice called from the yard. "Citizen Belanger?" Footsteps raced past the corner of the building. "Jean Paul!"

"Release me, or someone will notice I'm missing," Brigitte gritted.

"Meet tomorrow night, a half hour after dark. And you'd better have proof. Because if you show up with nothing, I'll return you to Calais." And with that, the gendarme shoved her around the front of the building.

She pressed a hand to the throbbing ache on her skull and searched the yard. The girl from Citizen Arnaud's house moved restlessly about, her cries for Jean Paul increasingly frantic.

"He went into the kitchen." Brigitte pointed toward the smallest building. "Perhaps I can help. What troubles you?"

Annalise didn't bother to answer, just ran toward the door.

She hastened over the uneven ground, still curiously

absent of gendarmes. Perhaps they'd all been called into town or were out on patrol. She pulled open the kitchen door only to come up against Annalise dragging Jean Paul forward, her hand clasped tightly around his arm.

"It's Gaston and that awful Widow Pagett. She's saying he stole that *livre* you gave him and wants him thrown in jail."

Jean Paul's dark gaze landed on Brigitte. "Come quickly." Tears glinted in Annalise's eyes as Jean Paul ushered her to the wagon. The gendarme sauntered out from the door of the largest building while Jean Paul unloaded crates from the back of the wagon and stacked them in the yard.

"Gilles, you'll have to carry these to the kitchen yourself. I must away."

The gendarme scowled but didn't argue, and within moments, Jean Paul was seated beside Annalise and turning the wagon toward the center of town.

"*Merci,* Jean Paul." Annalise sagged against him.

"I haven't done anything yet."

"But you can help my brother, can you not?" Worry ignited in the girl's eyes. "Gaston can't go to prison. *Maman* has a hard enough time even with the money she makes from the mending and wash and Gaston working for Mr. Sveltner. If he were thrown—"

"I'm sure things can be set right." He patted her hand absently, the way a father might his child's.

Annalise blinked up at him then nudged closer. "I knew you'd be able to help."

By the time the wagon turned down the main boulevard, people teemed on the hard-packed road, mothers with children and old men who probably spend their afternoons inside a tavern, merchants who had closed their shops due to the commotion and a handful of idle youth. All eyes riveted on the scene in front of a small store.

Jean Paul pulled the wagon to an abrupt halt and jumped out, wedging his way through the throng.

"What if Jean Paul can't save him?" Brigitte whispered, half to herself and half to Annalise. Or worse, what if the boy truly had stolen a *livre* from the lady and now had two?

"He can." Annalise's chin trembled, but her eyes glinted with a childlike faith as she watched Jean Paul, who now stood in the center of the crowd with Gaston and several others. "Come, we must get closer."

Annalise took her hand and tugged her into the press of suffocating bodies, the foul scents of animal and sweat mingling with the strong odor of ladies perfumes to rob clean air from her lungs. Some citizens stepped aside when they saw Gaston's sister while others seemed determined to stand in her way. Nevertheless, they wound their way blindly toward the center of the chaos.

"The rat stole my money, he did." A woman's voice rang out above the throng.

Brigitte wheedled her way through the last of the people until she glimpsed an old woman, her face an uncomely combination of prominent bones and sagging wrinkles.

The woman pointed a gnarled finger at Gaston. "Now I want him punished."

Gaston stared at the ground, shuffling his feet back and forth. "I already told you, I didn't take any money. Citizen Belanger gave the *livre* to me."

Brigitte slid into an open space at the front of the crowd.

"What's the meaning of this?" Jean Paul's voice boomed loud enough for half the town to hear.

"Isn't he magnificent?" Annalise nudged into the spot beside her and sniffed back a tear. "He can save anyone."

Indeed, Jean Paul did look rather magnificent, with his

broad shoulders and towering form giving him command over the situation. The same traits that had terrorized her when first they'd met now seemed a blessing. Even his scar made him appear experienced rather than frightening.

"Jean Paul." A balding man with a protruding belly and a look of importance laid a hand on Jean Paul's shoulder. "Good to see you, my friend. We were having a little dispute and sent Annalise to find you."

"That's Mayor Narcise. Citizen Belanger saved the mayor's sister and niece from a gang of army deserters last year. He's a hero." Annalise's voice ended on a sigh.

Yes, with the way every person in the crowd watched Jean Paul, it seemed he was quite the hero of Abbeville.

"Citizen Belanger," a gendarme proclaimed, the badges on his coat indicating he outranked Alphonse's gendarme. He might even be the captain Jean Paul had gone in search of. "Did you give this boy a *livre?*"

A muscle worked on the side of Jean Paul's jaw. He looked down at the boy, then at the men. "Indeed. He helped me unload food today and then made a delivery."

Gaston's eyes came up for the first time, and he offered Jean Paul a wobbly smile. "'Tis as I said. I earned that money."

The old woman crossed her arms over her chest. "Then what happened to my *livre?* No sooner do I discover I'm missing one, then this here urchin struts into my shop, wanting to buy a fichu for his *maman.* A new fichu when everyone knows they don't have two *sous* to rub together."

Gaston's eyes dropped back to the ground and he dug the toe of his shoe into the dirt. "I only wanted to surprise her."

"Wanting to buy a scrap of cloth doesn't make Gaston a criminal," Jean Paul growled at the woman.

"Right. Right. And now we have the truth of things.

Sorry for disturbing your afternoon, Jean Paul." The mayor smiled brightly.

Annalise was correct. He truly was magnificent. Jean Paul had barged into the situation, taking control despite the crowd of onlookers, and gotten the mayor and gendarmerie official to take his side. How many men could manage such a thing?

"So that's to be the end, is it?" The older woman turned to the gendarme. "Citizen Belanger arrives and swears he gave the boy money and everyone believes him?"

The gendarme scratched his brow beneath the brim of his hat. "If Gaston can prove he came by his coin honestly—and he has—then I've no grounds to hold him."

The old woman glared at Jean Paul. "Well mayhap I don't trust Citizen Belanger's word."

A thick silence descended, all fidgeting and whispers ceased. Brigitte looked toward Jean Paul, waiting for him to declare the old woman a liar. Waiting for him to proclaim his honesty and uprightness before half the town.

But he didn't speak, only held the woman's stare with dark, haunted eyes.

Brigitte stepped forward. The mayor and gendarme turned their eyes to her, and a faint heat stole over her body, along with the desire to dart back into the throng and disappear. But 'twasn't right the way this woman maligned Jean Paul.

"I was with Citizen Belanger and Gaston earlier." She raised her voice, trying to make it loud enough for every last person in the crowd to hear, trying to eliminate its childish tremble. "I saw him give Gaston the *livre*."

A faint smile tipped the corner of Jean Paul's mouth, and her body grew warm yet again, but this warmth had nothing to do with the eyes of the crowd and everything to do with the approval written across one particular man's face.

"And who are you?" the woman snapped.

"Brigitte Moreau."

"My housekeeper," Jean Paul boomed in a voice meant to frighten off further argument.

"How dare you slander Jean Paul and interrogate his workers?" The mayor's face turned a deep red. "Surely you see the good he's done since he's returned. Why he saved my sister and niece from those deserters."

"Deserters who happened to deserve the prison cell I threw them into," the gendarme official added.

"And he brings us food," the boy interjected.

"Oui." Annalise stepped from the crowd to stand beside her brother while she glared furiously at the older woman. "You've no business making accusations against a man who devotes himself to caring for this town. Unlike you, who walks around pointing fingers at innocent people."

The crowd erupted with cheers and shouts.

"You've no right to speak ill of Citizen Belanger."

"Oui. See if we visit your shop again, Citizen Pagett."

"He's brought us food and money before. Are you going to accuse me of stealing, too?"

Brigitte slunk back amid the people as the cries continued. She now knew what Alponse's man had meant when he'd said a person couldn't simply kill Jean Paul. Too many people liked him. Too many people paid attention to his deeds. The haggard widow had only questioned whether he was trustworthy and people were threatening to protest her business. But if Jean Paul was found murdered in his bed one morn, this crowd would likely form a mob of vigilantes.

She glanced around the intent faces riveted to every word Jean Paul spoke. What would these people do to her if they knew the reason she was in Abbeville? Why she'd been so adamant about working for Jean Paul? Or about the proof she had to provide by tomorrow night? The air grew hot and thick around her, the press of bodies stifling and intolerable. She had to get away. Now.

"That's enough." The words rasped against Jean Paul's throat. He shifted away from a group of women at the front of the crowd, only to find a man standing close behind him. Sweat beaded on the back of his neck, a drop trailing down between his shoulder blades.

These people didn't understand. They looked at him with awe-filled eyes and hailed him as some gift from the Heavenly Father, when his past rivaled that of the vilest murderer. "I don't do more than anyone else. If I see a need, I fill it, that's all."

Citizen Pagett harrumphed, her wrinkled, aging arms still crossed about her chest. "Maybe I don't believe you were in Paris making furniture all those years you were gone. Maybe I think you were up to something else. Furniture doesn't make a man enough money to come back home and buy up all the land you did. Furniture doesn't give a man with a strong back enough coin to pay little urchins like Gaston a *livre* for work you could do yourself."

Something thick rose in his throat. So Citizen Pagett suspected his lie. He shouldn't be surprised. The flimsy tales of making furniture during the *Révolution* had held up too long as it was.

He glanced about the crowd of people, all so happy to see him come to Gaston's defense. What would the townsfolk say if they knew the truth? What would they *do?* He deserved to be in a prison cell more than anyone else in this town. Oh, the Convention in Paris might look at his past actions as legal, as helping to maintain order during a turbulent time. But he knew the truth, and so did God.

He didn't deserve to be alive after the crimes he'd committed.

"That's quite enough." The mayor waddled between him and Citizen Pagett, coming to his defense.

Always coming to his defense.

He'd done no more than any other man would have when he'd heard the screams of women and raced into the chateau after returning to Abbeville last year. Had given no thought to the importance of the women he'd saved. He'd have done the same for any street girl.

But those women hadn't turned out to be street girls. They were the mayor's relatives, and for the past year, he could do no wrong in the mayor's eyes. Then when he'd let land to Pierre and taken that first load of vegetables to Widow Arnaud, the entire town had hailed him as a hero.

A killer turned hero.

His gut twisted, but he shoved away the sickening sensation and surveyed the faces surrounding him. Some old, some young, nearly all familiar and—with the exception of Widow Pagett—every last one elated with his actions. Then his gaze rested not on a face, but on a back. Brigitte Moreau need not turn for him to recognize her. He knew her by the subtle sway of her hips as she walked, by the tresses of auburn hair dangling from her cap to tickle the back of her neck. She headed toward the wagon behind the crowd, her arms wrapped around herself and her shoulders hunched.

What did she think of this spectacle? Of him?

And why did her thoughts matter? Because of the kiss she'd given him naught but an hour ago?

The feel of her soft lips against his cheek still lingered in his mind.

"Au revoir," he whispered to Gaston and then started through the crowd. He had to get away from these people,

away from the hero worship and looks of adoration. And Brigitte gave him the perfect excuse.

If only she didn't intend to leave for Reims once she earned more money. Then he'd be alone again, bereft of her bright eyes and happy smile in the morn, bereft of children's laughter echoing through the yard.

But then, he deserved a life of loneliness after the horrors he'd committed.

Chapter Thirteen

Jean Paul wiped the sweat from the back of his neck and opened the door to his house. His muscles ached, his head throbbed and his throat felt parched as a dry and crumbling well. A wall of heat hit him as he stepped inside, the warmth from the fire making the two-room dwelling nearly unbearable, but with the heat came the scents of fresh-baked bread and chicken.

He inhaled slowly, drawing the homey aromas deep into his lungs. He'd made bread and soup and fowl aplenty since he'd returned to Abbeville. But nothing he'd cooked—or that his mother had prepared before she'd passed—had smelled quite so good.

Why had he not hastened from the fields earlier? He well knew that no amount of back-straining work could rid his heart of the memories that plagued him, or he'd have worked the guilt off seven times over by now.

The children gathered around the table, Danielle and Serge talking quietly while Victor grinned and babbled. And there at the foot of the table stood Brigitte. Though her back was strong and proud as it had been that afternoon when she'd come to Gaston's defense, she had a quiet grace about her. A soft efficiency that made her beautiful even while she did something so mundane as slicing bread.

Is this what he might have had if Corinne had lived? The sight of his own family awaiting him every evening? His own wife busy about the kitchen?

"Can I have another, *Maman?*" Serge nudged his plate nearer Brigitte and the bread.

Jean Paul moved farther inside and closed the door.

Brigitte's eyes came up to meet his, her lips spreading into a soft smile. "You're here. When you didn't come inside after we returned from town, I thought…" Cheeks suddenly pink, she hurried to the hearth where she'd set a plate of chicken and turnips. "We'd have waited, but I assumed you meant to work through supper."

"Don't worry yourself. Just let me wash first." He headed to the bedchamber, where he gave himself a quick scrub in the washbasin before heading back into the outer room. His plate sat in its usual spot at the head of the table, and he slid into his chair, the mere action of sitting making his muscles ache all the more for the weeding and hoeing and harvesting he'd put them through that afternoon.

Brigitte put a second slice of bread on his plate, then sank onto the bench in front of her own half eaten food. "Danielle, clear the table once you finish, please. After that, go back to your studies. We've yet to look at that question from your English lesson."

He stared at Brigitte's lips as she spoke, the same lips that had touched his cheek that afternoon. So soft. So warm. So sweet. Evidently the hard labor had done little to drive such thoughts from his mind. What might happen if she sent the children on their way a bit early tonight and they spent some time—

"I'd rather not." Danielle speared a turnip with her fork.

Heat stained the back of his neck. What was he thinking? Brigitte had duties to see to, children to tend and little business kissing him again.

"The English or the table?" he asked Danielle, if for no other reason than to clear his mind of Brigitte's lips.

Which were busy chewing at the moment.

Not that he'd noticed.

Because he certainly wasn't staring at them again.

"The English," Danielle muttered around her bite of turnip. "The table will take but a few moments."

"Ah." He drew his gaze up from Brigitte's mouth and forced himself to meet her eyes. Unfortunately her eyes weren't much easier to look at, as soft and warm as her lips. The memory of their dazed gleam after the kiss crept into his mind. Of course, she'd pulled away a moment later and then refused to look at him for the rest of the ride to the gendarmerie post. He shoved some food into his mouth. "English is a rather ambitious subject for you to take on with your daughter, think you not?"

"She doesn't think anything's too ambitious." Danielle stood from the table and dumped her plate into the washbasin. "That's what happens when your mother used to be a governess."

Brigitte raised one of her eyebrows and gave Danielle a frosty glare. "Do not try me, daughter."

"A governess?" A new image of the woman stole across his mind, one of Brigitte standing beside a globe, spectacles perched on her nose as she lectured her charges on geography. "I'd never have guessed it."

"*Oui.* In Reims, before I met my husband and moved to Calais. For a time, my twins and Danielle attended the church school in Calais, but once the *Révolution* started and the schools closed, I brought out my old lesson books."

"Your former profession has proved rather useful then." He ate another forkful of juicy chicken.

"More like a means of torture," Danielle retorted.

Brigitte shot her daughter another quelling gaze. The girl looked away and scooped up Victor, wiping the breadcrumbs from his mouth.

"What's torture?" Serge asked, his mouth stuffed with food.

"English." Danielle shifted the babe on her hip. "I—"

"Enough," Brigitte snapped. Danielle's mouth clamped together, and Brigitte rubbed her temples before turning back toward him. "Sometimes it feels as though I've lived two separate lives. One as a child in Reims and another as an adult in Calais."

As had he, except his life didn't divide into time spent in two cities, but rather into time spent as a farmer and time spent submerged in darker activities. "Childhood and adulthood oft separate themselves on their own. One doesn't need a move to accomplish it."

At least he hadn't. His childhood dreams had come crashing down the day Corinne took sick.

"Have you lived here your whole life, then?" Brigitte picked up a slice of bread and spread a smear of butter on it. "In the crowd today, I thought I heard mention of you leaving Abbeville for a time."

Had she heard such a thing? He well remembered Citizen Pagett's voice ringing accusations in front of the town. *Maybe I don't believe you were in Paris making furniture all those years you were gone. Maybe I think you were up to something else.*

The mouthful of bread he'd been chewing stuck in his throat.

"I'm sorry. I didn't mean to upset you." Brigitte laid a hand over his for the briefest of instants before sliding it away. "I simply thought to make conversation."

He gulped in a breath and slid his chair back from the

table, no longer hungry despite only finishing half his plate. Innocent questions, that's all. She'd spoken of her past and now asked of his, all part of the normal give and take in a conversation.

Or maybe not. Had Citizen Pagett's accusations from earlier aroused Brigitte's suspicions, as well? Or mayhap she'd never heard Citizen Pagett's words but the murmurings of another townsperson. At what point had she left the crowd and returned to the wagon? She'd stepped into the clearing and defended him, but he hadn't noticed her again until she was nearly to the conveyance. Regardless of when she'd left, something about her trip into town had given her questions about his past.

Questions he dare not answer.

Then again, how could he lie when she asked him so directly? All the town already knew he'd left Abbeville after Corinne's death.

"Oui." His vocal cords ground against each other with the simple word. "I've spent time elsewhere, six years in Paris."

"Paris?" Danielle's eyes lit up, and she moved Victor's plate to the washtub while carrying the babe on her hip. "What was it like? I've never been."

"Dirty and crowded." Teeming with starving mobs that hated the aristocracy, and an aristocracy that ignored the masses and their needs.

"*Maman* had a book with paintings of Paris, but we left it in Calais. Did you see the *Cathédrale Notre Dame?*"

"Oui." As it was being sacked. He stuck a finger into his collar and tugged.

"And the *Palais-Royal?*"

"It's called the *Palais de l'égalité* now," he snapped a bit too quickly, then clamped his mouth shut.

Brigitte stilled, her fork clattering against her plate. "The revolutionaries renamed it?"

"Ah…" Indeed they had. France could hardly call such a famous Parisian landmark by the name *royal* now that the country was a republic controlled by the people. But how to explain such a thing without sounding like a radical?

Which was rather difficult considering he *was* a radical, just not a radical who stood for the blind slaughter of innocent people. "*Oui,* I believe it got renamed."

Believed it because he had seen it happen, round about the time the Duc d'Orléans had thrown off his hereditary title and started calling himself by the name, *Philippe Égalité.* And since *Égalité* had owned the palace, it was only fitting that the *Palais-Royal* be changed, as well.

"That's doltish." Danielle poked out her bottom lip, her face dark. "Why must everything get renamed? As if the changes in the calendar and holidays aren't bad enough, now they've got to start renaming places? I no more than had the months memorized when we switch to the revolutionary calendar, and now—"

"Watch yourself, child." He cast a glance toward the door, which was ridiculous since the Terror was well and truly over. People weren't being guillotined for such careless statements anymore. But a year ago…

No. He refused to think on it. The girl had meant nothing by her words. She didn't understand the need for the changes, the unarguable demand that every remembrance of the tyranny and oppression which had once dominated France be cut from the country's future. She was growing up in the First Republic and likely wouldn't remember the horrors and debt that had plagued the country under the reign of the Bourbon kings.

But the new France could hardly use a calendar designed by a church that had seen fit to tax peasants so its priests could grow rich and fat while people like Corinne starved. Though some priests had truly endeavored to help the needy, far too many clergymen had allowed greed to consume them, just as the aristocracy had.

"What shall Serge and Victor do if we ever change back to the old calendar?" Danielle asked. "They'll have to memorize two, as well."

"It's not coming back." It couldn't. That would mean the Republic failed and the old system of government had been reinstated. And if such a thing ever happened, the average French citizen would once again be stripped of food and land and liberty.

He cleared his throat and glanced around at the serious faces watching him. "I see your mother hasn't failed in her geography lessons. You know much of Paris for never having walked its streets."

The austere look left Danielle's face and she smiled brilliantly. "*Maman's* never been. But *Papa* went often. I used to beg him to take me. He had the most amazing stories."

"Mayhap you can go sometime, then. But I advise you to wait until the *Révolution* is over. You never know what the streets of Paris hold these days."

"You were there during the *Révolution?*" Brigitte whispered.

He lurched to his feet, the well-intentioned comment giving away far more than he'd intended.

"Did you see when the people stormed that prison?" Serge glanced at his sister. "What was it called again, Danielle?"

"The Bastille."

Serge climbed down from the bench and bounced up and down on the balls of his feet. "*Oui,* did you see that? *Maman* told us all about it."

Jean Paul swallowed and stared down at his hands,

hands that had meted out far more harm than should ever have been allowed. Hands that could have been used for good, but had been bent on destruction instead.

"I was there to make furniture," he rasped, the lie painful on his tongue. "When my wife died, I left to make furniture. Now if you'll excuse me."

He stormed across the chamber and burst through the door into the fading sun, any hope of a pleasant meal with a delightful family forever shattered. Better that he muck out the stables and eat salt pork after the Moreaus left. Because he couldn't go back into that house, look into those innocent faces and pretend he was a normal, honest farmer.

So he'd work. His farm, his animals, the dirt, the straw, the feed. Anything to make him forget.

"Why'd he storm off like that?" Danielle scraped the food from Jean Paul's half-eaten plate and plunked it into the washbasin.

"I know not." Brigitte stared at the door, the echo of its slam still reverberating through the room. "'Twas almost as though the memories of Paris were too wretched for him to bear. But if his memories were that awful, then that must mean—"

"Is he coming back?" Serge gripped the side of her arm. "He promised to take us fishing again."

She laid a hand over her son's. "I doubt that shall happen tonight."

Or ever again, if the suspicions churning in the back of her mind were true. What had Citizen Pagett said earlier that afternoon? Something about her doubting Jean Paul's word as truth. She'd taken the older woman for a fool, but what if the widow wasn't a fool at all? What if the woman was smarter than anyone in Abbeville knew?

Citizen Pagett sensed something amiss with Jean Paul's story, just as Alphonse and the gendarme had.

A cold chill crept over her, stealing the warmth from her cheeks and the breath from her lungs. Jean Paul couldn't be a murderer, not with how he fed the poor and cared for her and the children. 'Twas impossible to imagine.

But what if it was true nonetheless?

Chapter Fourteen

Jean Paul twisted and writhed on his bed, a state of half sleep and half wakefulness hazing his mind. The memories whirled and spiraled, a flowing river that raced across time and space, full of hidden eddies and deep pools, rocks and fallen logs and broken pieces of his life.

He stood again on the streets of Paris, hunkered against a building, his back pressed to the cool stone as he choked down the bit of cheese and bread he'd stuffed into his pocket. His stomach growled at the first taste of food he'd had in over a day, and he ripped a bigger chunk of bread off the loaf before shoving it into his mouth.

The food would hardly sustain him. He'd only the one loaf to last two days, and he'd had to wait in line outside the baker's for three hours before dawn to get it.

He'd thought they'd had little food in Abbeville, but he hadn't known the half of it. People might starve by the dozens in the provinces, but they starved by the droves in Paris. He glanced across the street toward the muddy, churning waters of the Seine, its dirty banks filled with fishermen and washerwomen loitering rather than working. Who had money to buy fish these days? Or pay someone to wash their clothing?

The nobility and clergy. They had funds for such luxuries, but they would never leave their lovely palace and grounds at *Versailles* to enter the crowded, coal-blackened city of Paris. And why should they, when they merely needed to ring a bell and three servants would appear to take away their soiled silk culottes and stockings?

Jean Paul glared down at his own rough linen trousers, stained from the coal he'd delivered to the *Palais-Royal* last night. Silk culottes or linen trousers? The men of all France could be divided into two groups based on what they wore.

He scarfed down another bite of cheese then dragged in a ragged breath, heavy with the scent of coal and fish and muddy waters. The air was another thing no one had warned him about. Abbeville had more clean air than its inhabitants could use, but half the Parisians likely suffered from some foul lung disease after daily breathing this air.

"Charron, there you are."

Jean Paul turned instinctively at the name, the one to which he'd been answering for five months. He couldn't say what had driven him to use a different surname when first arriving in Paris. Perhaps a desire to forget the cherished days he'd spent with his wife. Perhaps a desire to hide his anger and hatred.

But he'd little need to hide in Paris. People teemed in the streets and poured from the tenements. One got lost in the anonymity of it all, in the endless string of voices and faces and empty stomachs. And everyone was just as angry as he.

"Charron. Has your mind ceased functioning? I've been calling your name for the past block." Jacques Lavigne, Jean Paul's friend and fellow worker, approached, his hands and clothes smeared with so much coal one couldn't identify the color beneath the grime.

He swallowed another bite of bread—what would likely be his last morsel of food until the morrow. "I was thinking."

Jacque raised an eyebrow. "About the women at the *Palais-Royal?*"

"About home."

The smile disappeared. "And why would you think of home when there's much to do in Paris? Come, you're about to miss the speech."

"What speech?"

"Robespierre's. At the *Palais-Royal*. And have you seen this latest report from *Versailles?*" Jacques shoved a paper in front of him.

Jean Paul took the sheets from that morning's press and scanned the article, his blood burning hotter with each word he read. "She tells us to eat cake? *Cake?*" He crumpled the paper in his fist and stomped it beneath the heel of his shoe. "We have no bread, and our queen wants us to eat cake?"

Jacques grabbed his arm and tugged him down the street. "'Tis more than that. The king has called in soldiers from Flanders and Prussia and ordered them to surround the city. They'll kill us all in our sleep if we don't act."

"Kill us? Why? Because we haven't cake to eat?" Marie Antoinette should be stripped of her crown for such a statement. Did she think he liked being hungry, liked watching Corinne starve while the rich sat down to feast-laden tables every night?

"'Tis why we must rid France of the monarchy. Now make haste."

And he did. Jean Paul stuffed the remainder of his bread in his pocket and quickened his steps. A mob of people had indeed gathered at the *Palais-Royal,* and Robespierre stood atop a table in the center of it all, shouting, *"Liberty, equality, fraternity!"*

"Liberty, equality, fraternity," the crowd echoed back. "Liberty, equality, fraternity."

Jean Paul lent his own voice to the chant.

"And what shall we do about the Swiss Guard?" someone cried above the melee. "How shall we defend ourselves from the soldiers who would steal our liberty?"

"They would cut off our heads in the night before they let us be their equals," another voice shouted.

"We must act!"

The bodies grew restless and hot around him, fists pumping the air and unintelligible voices ringing out, but the mob was no longer just men. Now women and children surrounded him, and rather than shouting for liberty, they wailed and pleaded. Robespierre no longer stood at the front of the crowd. Instead, a guillotine loomed before the people, set up on its platform for all to see when the glaring blade fell.

"Save him. Save my husband."

"Citizen, my son is innocent. He doesn't deserve to die."

A hand landed on his forearm, the feminine fingers slim and gentle.

He need not look to know who the hand belonged to, but he raised his gaze nonetheless. Redness rimmed Brigitte's eyes and tears streaked her cheeks. Her hair fell in dark tangles down her back, and with her free arm, she hoisted Victor on her hip. "Jean Paul. Help us, please."

"What do you need?" His voice sounded hollow, the empty words reverberating back at him.

She blinked a fresh bead of moisture from her eyes. "You have to stop this."

Something tugged on his coat, and he looked down

to find Serge, tears streaming openly down his smooth cheeks. "They have *Papa*. They have *Papa*."

"Please save him."

Jean Paul bolted up from the bed, his chest heaving with images from the nightmare. Brigitte. Serge. Victor. The only Moreau he hadn't seen was Danielle. But then, she was probably off plotting a way to free her father rather than begging him to help.

He pressed a hand to the back of his neck and stared down at his quivering stomach. How had Brigitte's husband died? He'd assumed the man had been a soldier, but what if he hadn't? What if…?

No. His blood pulsed with the denial. Brigitte's late husband, Citizen Moreau, couldn't have been guillotined. Only criminals had been guillotined during the Reign of Terror, only people deserving of death.

Or at least that's what he'd been told. But how many people had been led to the guillotine's wooden platforms for some innocent reason? Some false charge of committing a "crime against liberty?"

Jean Paul threw off the covers and leaped out of bed. He needed fresh air, mouthfuls and mouthfuls of it. He stalked out of the bedchamber and through the house before bursting outside. The gray-tinged light of early dawn surrounded him, and he leaned against the house, sucking in heavy breaths.

How had his life come to this? How had a handful of revolutionary meetings six years ago led to the atrocities he'd committed during the Terror?

He'd hardly known what he was involving himself in when he'd started attending those gatherings. But one assembly had grown into two, and two into three, and eventually he'd lost count.

Somewhere amid all those meetings, the delegates to

the Estates-General had announced that France now had a National Assembly. This new Assembly was somehow supposed to represent people like him, make sure bread didn't cost a full day's income and that the common worker wasn't forced to pay exorbitant taxes that the nobility and clergy evaded. But while the delegates to the National Assembly made their elaborate speeches, people still starved and the king continued to move a hired army to surround the city. There had seemed only one option: to fight.

"Jean Paul?" a small voice questioned from the side of the yard. "What are you doing out here?"

He turned to find Brigitte, her forehead drawn into a subtle frown and her eyes dark with concern. The image from his dream flooded back. Her hair matted and tangled, dirt smeared across her face and eyes rimmed with tears as she begged him for her husband's life.

"Your husband." His voice rang loud and rough in the quiet morning air. "How did he die?"

"I beg your pardon?" She took a step back from him, her eyes darting about in confusion.

She should be confused, should move away. He was, after all, a murderer. "Was your husband a soldier?"

"*Non. Non.* He was a…" Her lips pressed together.

"A what?" He pushed off the side of the house and moved closer, but she took another step back.

"A merchant."

Dread curled in his stomach. "Did he take ill?"

She ducked her head and stared at the ground.

"The Terror?" he rasped.

The air stilled around them, no faint breeze to rustle along the grass, or birdsong to float through the morning; no crickets to chirp and frogs to gurgle. 'Twas as though nature itself held its breath and waited for Brigitte's reply.

But she didn't speak. She didn't need to. Her head came

up slowly, her eyes red and brimming with tears—just like in his dream.

"Non," he whispered. He wanted to shout it, bellow it, run into the fields and yell his denial until the word became true. Until the woman before him had her husband brought back. Until her precious children had a father once again.

"I'm sorry," he offered inanely. As if his trite words could restore her husband to life.

"Why are you apologizing?" She wrapped her arms around herself and stared hollowly up at him. "His death had naught to do with you...did it?"

He opened his mouth, then closed it again. His feet ached to step forward, arms longed to draw her body against his and hold her close. But he couldn't. 'Twas as though some invisible chasm stretched between them. Brigitte was from Calais, had told him so on numerous occasions. And if she was from Calais, if her husband had been there during the Terror...

His throat tightened. How could he answer her question? How could he stand here, meet her eyes and tell her he might well have taken part in her husband's death? But that he would never know for certain, because there'd been too many people, too many deaths, for him to remember them all.

He forced his shoulders into a straight line and stalked off toward the stable.

"Jean Paul?" Brigitte's wavering voice called to his back. "Where are you going?"

He didn't turn and look, couldn't bear the image of her standing there, eyes red and swollen as they discussed the husband he might have killed. "To the fields."

"What about breakfast?"

"I'm not hungry."

And after this morn, he doubted he'd be hungry ever again.

Brigitte stared at Jean Paul's retreating form. It wasn't true. It simply couldn't be. Perchance he was gruff at times, and he could certainly be menacing when he wanted to, but he was all soft mush beneath.

If Jean Paul had been involved with the Terror, why would he return to a town like Abbeville and live the life he now did? It made no sense. He'd just stood before the entire town yesterday and defended an innocent young boy. He could have let Gaston face Citizen Pagett and the mayor on his own. Why expose himself like that if he was some hiding criminal?

Gaston, the townsfolk. Yes, they must be upsetting him, not some involvement with her husband's death. Of course, Citizen Pagett's sharp words yesterday would have bothered him. Who wouldn't be ill-tempered after someone spouted false accusations about him before half the town? She'd ask him about it at the midday meal and they'd set everything to rights.

Because the alternative was too wretched to consider.

Chapter Fifteen

The sun dipped behind the trees as Jean Paul trod back to his house, his feet weary and back aching. 'Twas two days in a row he'd worked past supper, and all because of the woman keeping house for him.

A fresh pang of hunger gnawed at his stomach, and he scowled. He'd not worked without sustenance all day because he enjoyed being hungry, but somehow the hunger seemed better than facing her. He only hoped she'd left a plate of food on the table.

He pushed the door open and stepped into the dimly lit chamber.

"Are you unwell?"

His eyes followed the soft voice to where Brigitte stood drying the last of the dishes and placing them on the shelf. Why was she still here? After everything he'd said to her this morn, the way he'd walked out on her before breakfast and tarried in the fields an hour later than yesterday, she should have fled long before now.

Yet she'd waited for him. He ran his eyes down her willowy form, so familiar as she stood in his house, puttering about with homey movements. A warm sensation started in the center of his heart and spread outward.

Something was changing between them, upsetting the precarious balance he'd instituted after his return to Abbeville. In the days and weeks they'd known each other, she'd become more to him than a mere stranger. She'd become someone he trusted; someone he cared for.

Someone he loved?

No. He couldn't love her. He still loved Corinne.

Didn't he?

Of course he did, and he always would. But his heart wasn't full of only Corinne. 'Twas almost as though his heart had expanded and there was room for Brigitte, too.

"I'm glad you returned." She came forward, her hair falling in wavy strands from beneath her mobcap and pink tingeing her cheeks from warmth of the dying fire. She was so beautiful it hurt to simply look at her. "I was worried."

"I thought you'd be gone." They were the only words he managed before he turned for the door, but her slim hand on his arm prevented him from heading out of doors. "I, ah…forgot something in the stable. I might be a while. Mayhap you should go home."

"I waited for you. After you left this morn, I couldn't… couldn't…" She shrugged and looked about the house. "Please don't leave again. Not without telling me what troubles you."

What troubled him? The question brought memories of that morn flooding back. What was he doing standing alone with her, soaking in her company, enjoying her presence when he'd likely killed her husband? "'Tis best that I stay away."

"'Tis not for the best when you starve yourself all day and then try to run the moment you see me." Her worried brown eyes peered up into his face.

Did they see the horrors from his past? The evil things he'd done in the name of liberty?

"Come and sit." She tugged on his arm. "Let me at least warm your food."

No. She saw not the guilt, just his weariness and hunger.

He could well send her off and warm the food himself. But his feet throbbed, and sweat stuck to his back and face. His shoulders ached with the familiar pain of a day spent in the fields, and his head pounded.

What he wouldn't give for the comfort that had invaded him yesterday, when her breath had feathered over his skin and her lips had touched his cheek for the briefest of instants. "Let me wash before I sup."

A smile curved her lips. "Certainly."

She moved away, puttering about the table and hearth with comfortable, familiar movements. He tore his gaze from the subtle sway of her skirts and headed toward the washstand in the bedchamber. He scrubbed the sweat from his neck, arms and chest, then pulled on his extra shirt, clean and soft from Brigitte's laundering.

By the time he entered the common chamber, she had a warm plate of chicken, turnips, beans and bread waiting. He sank into his chair and pinned his eyes on the plate before him, lest they accidently drift to Brigitte and he start thinking about…well, things best left unthought.

"You must be famished." She slid onto the bench across the corner from him.

He was. "You needn't wait for me. Go home and see to your younglings."

"Danielle's putting them to bed, so I've a few minutes of time yet. I can wash your plate before I dump the water."

"I can wash my own plate." His words came out a little too rough, and he stuffed a bite of food into his mouth.

Her forehead drew down until those irresistible little wrinkles appeared in the center of her brow. He tightened his fingers around his fork lest he accidently reach forward and smooth the furrows away.

"Something's still bothering you." She tilted her head to the side. "Will you tell me?"

Yes. No. He knew not what to say or do with the confounded woman.

Well, that wasn't quite true. He glanced at her lips as she nibbled on a single slice of bread.

He wanted to kiss her. To hold her in his arms and melt his lips into hers until she couldn't breathe, to feel more of the warmth that had crept through him when he'd entered his house and seen her working there, waiting for him. To taste her mouth and discover whether it was sweet or salty, soft or firm, responsive or flat.

He'd bet his mare the kiss wouldn't be flat.

"You've been upset ever since we returned from town yesterday afternoon." She surveyed him with that puzzled expression on her face. "You didn't like everyone watching you while you helped Gaston."

He jerked his eyes away from her lips and shoved another bite into his mouth before he forgot why he shouldn't kiss her.

Because he had a reason for not kissing her. Truly he did.

If only he could remember it.

"Jean Paul?" She leaned closer and pressed her slender hand, roughened from work, to his brow.

The calluses felt like silk against his skin.

His gaze fell back to her lips, close enough now for her breath to fan his cheek. He need only lean forward a few centimeters and…

"Non." He jerked back.

Brigitte's frown widened. "You're certain you're well?"

He swallowed. He hadn't been saying no to that, but

the word still served his purposes. He was as well as a man could possibly be when in the presence of a beautiful woman he could never permit himself to touch—even though his eyes kept drifting to her lips and his mind kept imagining how they would taste.

She rested her elbows on the table and shifted forward, bringing her face close to his yet again.

Torture. The woman was pure, simple torture.

"So if you didn't like everyone in the crowd watching you, why did you barrel into the center of it?"

The crowd? Was she talking about yesterday and Gaston? He couldn't seem to remember much of anything save the way her lips glistened in the light from the hearth. "The boy needed my help, so I helped him."

Her eyes took on a shining look. The kind of look she'd likely give him right after being kissed.

He cleared his throat and scooted to the side, but that didn't stop her from reaching out to rest her hand on his arm.

If she kept touching him, he couldn't be held responsible for kissing her.

"The world needs more people like you." Her gently whispered words floated through the cottage.

It was a lie. The world didn't need anyone like him.

But Brigitte's eyes still held that tender look, her hand rested ever so slightly on his arm, and her lips…

Her lips…

He clamped his hand over hers and leaned forward, just a centimeter, a millimeter, nothing more than the width of a hair.

But it was enough. His lips touched hers and nothing mattered but the softness of her mouth against his. The alluring combination of salt and sweet, the warm fever from her lips that spiraled inside him until the kiss echoed through every last crevice of his body.

"Brigitte." He pulled back. "I can't…"

But he could. And so could she. She left her place on the bench, coming around the corner of the table to curl against his chest. Her lips brushed his cheek and trailed feather-soft kisses along his jaw. He wrapped his arms around her and lost himself in the comfort, in the warmth, in a place with no memories of the past and no horrors in the future. In a place where love erased all burdens and guilt.

He pulled her closer and felt the heat of her breath on his lips, smelled the scents of sunshine and bread in her hair, tasted their sweetness on her skin.

She sighed softly, and her hands stretched up to curl in the hair at the back of his neck.

The back of his neck.

The back of his *neck*.

The very place where the guillotine struck its victims.

Brigitte closed her eyes and melted into Jean Paul's arms. How long since she'd had a kiss like this?

Henri's kisses had always been hard and fast, wanting something of her that she'd struggled to give.

But not Jean Paul's. For a man so large and with such a forbidding scowl, one might expect his kisses to be harsh and forceful. But there was nothing demanding about his mouth on hers. His lips were soft and gentle, timid even. As though he was afraid she would shatter if he kissed her too hard.

But she wouldn't shatter. Not here. Not now. Not with his arms wrapped strong and secure about her back and his soft breath fanning her cheek and neck. She burrowed deeper into his solid chest and stretched her hands up to toy with the hair at the back of his neck...

And then she was on the floor, her bottom landing hard against the packed dirt and her back jarring with the impact. She leaned back on her elbows and blinked up at him.

He no longer sat in his chair but towered above her, his gaze dark while the scar around his eyebrow tightened into a furious knot.

"Go." He ground the single word through gritted teeth.

A hot wave of mortification swept through her. Go? He couldn't tell her to go. He'd just taken her in his arms and kissed her as though...as though...as though he loved her.

And then he'd dropped her on the floor.

She scrambled off the ground. "I refuse to leave until you explain yourself."

"I owe you no explanation. You can either remove yourself on your own, or I'll throw you out."

She stared into his face, the hard planes and austere lines, the dead, flat look in his eyes. Why was he so angry with her?

"Don't try me, Brigitte. Just leave. Now. And...and... don't come back tomorrow." His chest heaved as he spewed the words.

She whirled toward the door and ran, barreling into the dim evening light. Her stomach churned as she stumbled across the yard, racing for the first shelter she spotted— the stable. The doors stood shut up tight for the evening, but she shoved the massive handle aside. Near darkness wrapped around her, mingling with rich scents of straw and animal as she rushed past the stalls and flung herself on the pile of hay at the back of the outbuilding.

She'd merely wanted a kiss, the feelings of belonging and rightness that had niggled through her yesterday when she'd kissed his cheek. He'd look so tired and weary, so

W

e'd like to send you two free books from the series you are enjoying now. Your two books have a combined cover price of over $10, but are yours to keep absolutely FREE! We'll even send you two wonderful surprise gifts. You can't lose!

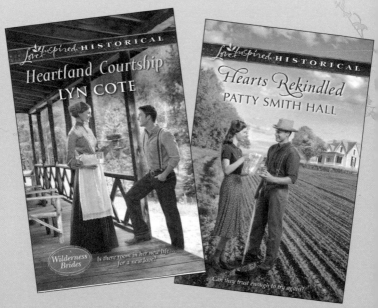

Each of your FREE books is filled with joy, faith and traditional values a and women open their hearts to each other and join together on a spirit journey.

GET 2 FREE BOOKS!

HURRY!
Return this card today to get 2 FREE Books and 2 FREE Bonus Gifts!

▲ DETACH AND MAIL CARD TODAY! ▼

YES! Please send me the **2 FREE books** and **2 FREE gifts** for which I qualify. I understand that I am under no obligation to purchase anything further, as explained on the back of this card.

PLACE FREE GIFTS SEAL HERE

102/302 IDL GEAK

FIRST NAME

LAST NAME

ADDRESS

APT.#

CITY

STATE/PROV.

ZIP/POSTAL CODE

LIH-314-IVY-13

needy sitting there shoveling food into his mouth. Was it that wrong to kiss him?

Evidently, seeing how he'd thrown her on the floor and told her to get out.

A cry welled in the back of her throat and moisture scalded her eyes. She pressed her hand to her mouth—the mouth Jean Paul had unapologetically claimed just moments ago—and attempted to stem the flood.

To no avail. A sob rose inside her, so deep and powerful neither her hands, her will nor her mind could stop it from bursting free. It tore from her chest in a deep, keening wail, and she buried her face in the hay.

She didn't fight the torrent but rather let it come. She hadn't cried like this when Henri died or when she'd sent her boys off to the navy or even after Alphonse had issued his ultimatum. She wasn't even sure why she wept. Maybe she cried for everything, or nothing, or the parts that hurt the worst. It hardly mattered. In a few moments, she would drag herself up and walk home to her children, where she couldn't cry, couldn't be sad, couldn't even state the reason she'd come to Abbeville.

So she burrowed deeper into the hay and let the tears flow until they dampened the bedding beneath her face. Until her head throbbed and her throat ached and her eyes were so swollen they could barely open. And then she lay there, still and exhausted in the sweet smelling hay.

The mare snorted from somewhere behind her, and a sow pawed at the ground of her stall. Night had nearly descended outside, making the stable almost dark. She rolled onto her back to stare up at the roof above, but her shoulder bumped against something hard. She shifted and frowned, turning toward the object. In the dim light she could barely make out the edge of a box as it poked through the strands of bedding.

She brushed some hay from the lid then sank back on her knees. It wasn't a box, and it certainly wasn't here by some accident or mistake. A trunk sat straight against the back wall of the stable, with a tight lock clasping the lid shut. When she tested the handle, she found it securely locked. She shoved more bedding away until it lay before her in its entirety, large and old and big enough to hold secrets from Jean Paul's past.

She gasped. The meeting with the gendarme. How could she have forgotten? She'd woken with thoughts of it this morn, but when she'd arrived at the house to find Jean Paul so upset, the rendezvous had slipped from her mind.

Even if she left now, she'd not be able to make the meeting.

Not that she wanted to meet the vile man. She was better off never laying eyes on him again.

She swiped a stray tear from her cheek. Perhaps Jean Paul did have secrets, but who was she to delve into them? The man Alphonse had told her to spy on was supposed to be cruel and vicious. A murderer bent on killing. But Jean Paul was nothing of the sort. Alphonse had the wrong person, even if Jean Paul did have suspicious memories of Paris and a body so large and burly the mere sight of it would frighten most sane people.

But none of that explained the presence of this trunk, so oddly hidden beneath mounds of hay. And locked.

Who locked a trunk already hidden?

She fingered the clasp and glanced back toward the door of the stable. Surely a lantern hung just inside. She only needed to light it and find a tool of some sort to open the lock. 'Twould be easy enough to break the iron bands.

To be sure, it wasn't her trunk, and whatever Jean Paul had hidden here certainly wasn't her business. But then, she'd been snooping all along, hadn't she? 'Twas the very reason she worked for him. And even though Jean Paul had told her to up and leave, she couldn't. Not without putting her children at risk and chancing that Alphonse would come for her.

She shuddered and tucked a strand of hair behind her ear. She had only one course of action: prove Jean Paul's innocence.

Because once she proved it, she could leave.

And if she was so certain of his innocence, why did she hesitate opening his trunk? After she had proof, she could visit the gendarme and then wash her hands of both the guard and Alphonse.

Yes. By this time tomorrow, she'd be free.

She scrambled to her feet and found the lantern, lighting it and searching around before her eyes landed on an ax leaning against the side of the stable. She took it up and hastened back to the trunk. One brisk swing, and the bands on the lock split open. She dropped to her knees and shoved the lid up.

No. It couldn't be true. It simply couldn't.

Her breath clogged in her throat and blood roared in her ears as she stared down at the items laid meticulously inside.

Chapter Sixteen

Jean Paul sank into the familiar rocker by the fire, the family Bible spread across his lap. Before her death, his mother had always taken this spot in the evenings. Now he filled it, reading the same book, page after page, night after night. He flipped through the crinkled pages, but the image of Brigitte and the soft, hazy look in her eyes right before they'd kissed tugged at his mind.

As did her hurt and disappointment afterward.

He rubbed the back of his neck and groaned. He hadn't been thinking. One look into her compassionate eyes, one touch of her lips to his, and he'd been lost. He couldn't afford to lose himself like that again with her. 'Twould bring only pain in the future.

No, not even in the future. She'd had tears in her eyes when he'd sent her away. His chest had ached as he'd wrenched the bitter command from his mouth, but what else was he to do? He couldn't keep her here, hadn't the slightest inkling how he could face her on the morrow, so he'd told her not to return.

Would she come back, anyway? 'Twould be easier, much easier, if she simply walked out of his life and never returned.

A man like him had no business having feelings for a woman like Brigitte. He should have put a stop to them sooner...except he hadn't any idea when they'd started. When she'd first approached him about a post? No, not that early. He'd merely felt sorry for her. But then she'd appeared the next day and again the following morn, until somehow, someway, she'd niggled into the place in his heart that had been hard and cold as stone since Corinne's death.

Into the place he'd intended to keep frozen for the rest of his life.

How dare he let himself become so attracted to her when her husband's blood might well be on his hands?

He shoved a hand through his hair and glanced down at the familiar verse of Scripture glaring back at him. *If we confess our sins, He is faithful and just to forgive us our sins, and to cleanse us from all unrighteousness.*

If only forgiveness was as simple as the Bible claimed. Then mayhap he could set his past behind him and move forward. But the verse didn't work. He knew. He'd read it, then prayed it every night since he'd returned to Abbeville.

Yet he closed his eyes and whispered the prayer again. "Father God, forgive me. For the Terror. For Brigitte. For everything."

But as usual, his words rose only to the ceiling before they fell back to taunt him, never reaching the ears of God.

Fresh tears blurred her vision as Brigitte stumbled up the little path leading to the hut. Her throat ached from keeping them pushed down for so long, and her head throbbed as the items of the trunk branded themselves repeatedly across her mind.

Jean Paul couldn't have killed Henri. He simply couldn't.

The things in the trunk didn't mean Alphonse was right. Surely they only proved…

But what if Alphonse was right? What if Jean Paul really had killed Henri?

It seemed impossible. How could such a kind, generous man like Jean Paul have a dark and murderous past?

Either way, she needed to learn the truth. Alphonse wanted information, and proving Jean Paul innocent now seemed nigh impossible. She'd no choice but to go to Jean Paul in the morning and ask him about the hidden things she'd found…

If he would talk to her after he'd already sent her away.

She wrapped her arms around her middle. Oh, goodness, she felt sick.

She should never have come here. She'd known it from the first, but as she'd sat across from Alphonse in that dimly lit warehouse, it seemed she hadn't a choice. *Be sure your sin will find you out.* The verse echoed back at her, a haunting memory in the darkness.

She'd had a choice all along. She could have chosen right. She could have chosen not to spy. She could have chosen to walk away from Alphonse and whatever twisted justice he'd devised for the man who'd killed Henri.

But she hadn't, and she was a vile, wretched person. Because now that she'd started down this dark road, how did she get out? This path of deceit hadn't freed her. If anything, she was more trapped now than she'd ever been in Calais.

Up ahead, a dim lantern cast its faint glow through the window of her little hut. She dragged her feet forward, the throbbing in her head pounding harder and the ache in her heart deepening with each step she took toward the little house Jean Paul had so generously lent her.

Her children should all be abed by now, hopefully sleeping soundly enough to not notice her swollen eyes or tear-streaked face. But she didn't have to dress for bed and lie down to know slumber and peace would elude her. She reached the door and groped for its handle in the darkness, but the rough wooden planks swung suddenly inward.

"You're late."

She jerked at the sound of the voice, irate and quiet, then trailed her eyes up the familiar blue and tan uniform filling the doorway. What was the gendarme doing here? In her home? With the children?

"You missed the meeting."

She pushed against him, hoping for the barest glimpse of Danielle or Serge or Victor. But he grabbed her arm and used his wide body to block her view of the bed where her children should be lying.

"Unhand me, or I'll…I'll…"

"You'll what?" he growled. "Tell Citizen Belanger I was here?"

A cold edge of fear skittered up her back. She tried to shove past him again, but only ended up trapped against his chest. "I said let me go."

"You're in no position to make demands. Not after you missed tonight's rendezvous." His fingers dug hard into her arm. "Where were you?"

"I'll tell you nothing until I know my children are safe."

"And what if they're not?"

The moisture leached from her mouth. She growled low in her throat and barreled into him. The gendarme's sturdy form stumbled back, just a step or two, but enough for her to reach the inside of the cottage and glimpse her children, all sleeping in the bed.

"They're fine," she stated, more to herself than him.

"They won't be if you continue dallying. I received word from Alphonse Dubois today. He feels the two of us have taken too long to complete our duties here. He's sending men."

"Men?"

Panic reignited in her belly. The arrival of more of Alphonse's men could only mean one thing: her father-in-law intended to drag her and the children back to Calais.

The gendarme frowned at her. "You didn't know."

"*Non.* How would I know?"

He took hold of her shoulders, his hands strong and tight. "I assumed that's why you skipped our meeting. That you'd found out about Alphonse's men and had left town."

She merely shook her head.

"Whether you knew or not changes nothing. I came for my proof. Where is it?"

In the trunk. A cold dread settled over her heart. "I told you before, I have no proof."

Because maybe there was a perfectly logical explanation for the items hidden in the stable. Maybe Jean Paul hadn't killed Henri but instead had—

"You're hiding something."

The breath froze in her lungs. Why, oh, why was she cursed with the inability to tell a lie?

His fingers dug harder into her shoulders. "What do you know?"

"N-nothing."

"You're lying again." He jerked her nearer, so close his breath fanned against her cheek and the stubble from his evening beard stood out against his skin despite the faint light from the lantern. "Alphonse's men are not a light threat. Tell me what you know, or you'll get both of us killed."

She raised her chin and clenched her jaw tightly.

"Do I have to hold a knife to the babe's throat to get you to speak?"

"Non!" She fought against his grip and reached out to rake her nails down his cheek.

He spun her around and clamped her hard against his chest, using one arm across the middle of her body to anchor both her body and her arms against him.

"Look at your younglings." He fisted a hand in her hair and jerked her head until she viewed the pallet where her three beautiful children lay. "Do you want them dead?"

She pressed her eyes shut. *"Non."*

"Then tell me what you know."

Father, forgive me, she cried silently to the heavens. How had she gotten here, to this place where she must choose between an honorable man or her own sweet children? She didn't want to choose one over the other. She wanted to protect both.

But she'd lost the chance to protect everyone the moment she agreed to Alphonse's plan.

"Well, what's it to be?" the gendarme growled in her ear.

Moisture blurred her vision as she stared at her children. "Citizen Belanger…"

She couldn't do it. Her shoulders slumped, and the air rushed from her lungs.

"Speak, wench."

"He…He…" Her tongue fumbled thick and clumsily in her mouth.

The gendarme's grip tightened around her middle, digging into her stomach until she could hardly draw breath. "I'll not give you another chance."

She swallowed and forced the words out. "He has a National Guard uniform hidden away."

"Ha! So he is the man!" The gendarme released her at once, leaving her gasping for air as she spun to face him. "I'll tell Alphonse to move forward."

"Move forward? You can't!"

A catlike smile twisted his face. "Can't what? We finally have the evidence we need."

"But…but…you have no proof Jean Paul is the man Alphonse seeks," she blurted.

"Don't be a fool. You saw the soldiers who travelled with the representatives-on-mission during the Terror. You know they wore the blue of the National Guard."

"Yes, but there are thousands of men who have worn such coats for one reason or another since the *Révolution* started. It only means that he was once in the National Guard, perhaps even while he was in Paris. It doesn't mean…doesn't mean…"

He killed Henri.

For once, there was no sneer upon the guard's lips, no cruel glint in his eyes. "Don't allow yourself to feel guilt. 'Tis easier that way. Meet me tomorrow in the woods after dark. All you need do is bring me his uniform's coat, and I'll give you your money. You've done your job, now let Alphonse do his."

"But you're going to kill Jean Paul!" Her throat felt as though a liter of sand had been forced down it.

"Oui."

"He doesn't deserve to die."

The gendarme took up a sack leaning against the wall by the door and swung it over his shoulder. "If Citizen Belanger had any part in the Terror, he deserves to die. You can hardly argue the point."

"But you don't know that he did. All I found was a uniform. Do your coat and breeches mean you were involved in the Terror?"

The gendarme's jaw hardened. "'Tis evidence enough that you found the uniform hidden when you add it to Citizen Belanger's disappearance from Abbeville, plus the exorbitant amounts of money he brought with him from

Paris and used to buy up land. He probably got that money looting the dead."

"*Non.* It's not enough evidence. Not at all. I need more time."

"For what? The coat buys your family its freedom to move to Reims."

"I don't want your filthy money, and I don't want…" *To move to Reims.*

The thought struck her, hard and cold and perhaps a bit life-altering. She hardly knew when that had changed, but as she stood here this night, facing a man who might well kill her children if it benefited himself, she wanted nothing more to do with him or Alphonse—regardless of the gold-tinged promises they made.

"Don't want what?" the gendarme prodded, one eyebrow cocked arrogantly high.

"Anything from you or Alphonse. Stop toying with my life. I'm a person, real flesh and blood. Not some puppet to be manipulated."

"That's where you're wrong. We're all puppets. Bring me the uniform at our usual location tomorrow night, and it might appease Alphonse enough so that his men won't come for you. Either that, or tell me where the uniform is hidden and I'll retrieve it myself."

She'd never betray Jean Paul in such a manner. "You can't make me do either."

"You haven't much choice. If I have to seek you out again, I won't leave your children to sleep so peacefully." He turned and stormed outside, the door slamming behind him with such force the entire house shook. Serge sighed and squirmed a bit at the noise before settling into stillness, Victor moaned, but Danielle sprang up from the bed far too quickly for a child who'd been sleeping.

"Citizen Belanger, *Maman?* You've been spying on him all this time? How could you?"

Brigitte sank to the floor, icy tremors racking her body. She'd just agreed to sacrifice the man she was falling in love with to keep Alphonse happy.

How could she indeed?

Chapter Seventeen

"Answer my question." Danielle tromped to where Brigitte slumped on the dirt floor, her back braced against the cottage's single chair. "How could you?"

"I hadn't a choice." She kept her gaze pinned on her hands, the very hands that had been running over Jean Paul's hidden National Guard uniform a mere hour ago.

"You lie. Everyone has a choice not to play traitor."

"You heard that man. He would have harmed you or your brothers."

Danielle's nostrils flared. "He only said it so you would comply."

She let out a short, bitter laugh. "Your lives are not something I'm willing to risk."

"Is that how you explain betraying Citizen Belanger?" Danielle tightened her fists into white-knuckled little balls at her sides.

Brigitte stared blankly at the packed dirt floor. 'Twas little point in hiding her doings now that the gendarme had appeared. "I've been on a mission for your grandfather, if you must know. He demanded I fulfill a task for him before we move to Reims."

"What kind of mission?"

Brigitte looked away. Admitting her misdeeds wasn't supposed to be so difficult, especially not to a girl of three and ten. But then, none of this was supposed to be difficult. Because when she first arrived at the farmstead two weeks ago, she should have found a hardened murderer, not a kind man with a gruff exterior. Not a man who gave them lodging and work. Not a man who cared for her children when she'd fallen ill and fed half of Abbeville's widows. Not a man the town loved and respected and might well elect to be their next mayor.

She pushed herself off the floor and moved to where her night dress sat on the shelf. "'Tis not important. It's nearly done, anyway, and then we'll leave."

Danielle stepped in front of her, the girl's back rigid in the dim glow of the lantern's light. "You just betrayed Citizen Belanger. I heard you! Is *Grand-père* why we're here? Why you asked Citizen Belanger for a post when he'd never sought a housekeeper?"

Brigitte pressed a hand to her pounding temple. "I told you not to worry yourself, and I meant it. No more questions."

"*Grand-père* wants Citizen Belanger because he thinks Citizen Belanger killed *Papa,* doesn't he?"

"'Tis complicated, Danielle. You wouldn't understand."

"I wouldn't?" Desperation crept into the girl's young voice. "What is *Grand-père* going to do? I want answers."

"And you're in no place to get them," she snapped, then reached around Danielle to grab her flimsy night rail off the shelf. "Now mind yourself, daughter. I'll not tolerate disrespect."

"*Non.* And you won't need to." Danielle reached up and yanked her own dress down. "Because I'm not going to stay here and help a mother who's decided to hurt a man like Citizen Belanger."

Before Brigitte could reply, Danielle turned and rushed out the door into the night.

Thump. Thump. Thump.

Jean Paul groaned and rolled over in his bed, then settled back into slumber.

Thump. Thump.

The annoying sound resonated through the house yet again.

He pried an eyelid open, glimpsed the gray light seeping in around the shutters then slammed his eye shut. Whatever the noise was, it could wait. He'd been up half the night, more than half the night, pondering what to do with Brigitte. Praying and praying only to have his words fall back around him like dried corn husks, useless and dead. He needed some sleep if he was going to face the fields in another hour or so.

If he was going to face Brigitte.

Thump. Thump. Thump. "Jean Paul?"

Brigitte. His eyes shot open and he propped himself up on his elbows. She alone could manage to say his name in that tone of voice. He'd half expected her to return and demand her old post back, but why was she here at this hour? The sky was barely light.

"Jean Paul!" The familiar voice shouted again, more panicked this time.

He jumped from the bed and yanked on his trousers.

"Just a moment." He left the bedchamber and padded to the front door, then pulled it open. "I'm glad you came. I was worried after I sent you…"

His mouth ceased working as he ran his eyes down her disheveled form. A jagged tear marred the hem of her dress and mud coated her skirts. No mobcap sat upon her head, and half her hair tumbled haphazardly down her back while the other half looked about to fall from where it had been pinned up. She pressed a sleeping Victor to her chest and blinked at him through eyes rimmed with red and smudged with shadows. Serge, just as weary and dirty as his mother, had plopped himself onto the ground, closed his eyes and was leaning his back against the outer wall of the house.

Had he done this to her? Had sending her away last night transformed her from a woman with soft smiles and kind words into the distraught person standing before him now? "Brigitte, I'm sor—"

"You have to help." She clasped his arm with her free hand. "Danielle ran off, and I can't find her."

Danielle had run off? The daughter who wanted to learn knife handling so she had a means of protecting her family had suddenly decided to desert them? "When?"

Brigitte's chin quivered. "Last night."

He reached out and took her hand between both of his, rubbing his thumb over her knuckles. "You've been wandering around in the dark looking for her?"

"What if she ran into trouble? What if someone found her and tried to…tried to…" Her eyes filled with tears, and the trembling returned to her chin.

"Come here." He opened his arms and gathered her close. She felt right there, curled into his arms with her body snug against his. Even the sleeping babe fit easily between the two of them.

Her sobs came in little waves, and she buried her face in his shoulder.

He stroked her hair. "Everything will be all right. I'll go search for her shortly. Just calm yourself first."

But she only cried harder. He kissed the top of her tangled hair and tilted her chin up until her moist eyes met his.

"Y-you'd do that for me? After last night, I…"

"Hush." He laid his finger over her cracked lips. "I was a fool last night. Forgive me."

"But…"

"I told you to hush. Here now, come inside and rest a spell." He led her to the rocker, and when she sank into the worn wooden chair, he pried the babe from her arms.

"It's my fault, all my fault. I drove her off, and now I can't find her." She shuddered before sniffing back another bout of tears. "She might be hurt or captured. She's probably scared and cold and hungry…"

He laid Victor on the bed nearest the door, then returned. "She's a bright girl with more than a bit of determination in her blood. No one's got reason to hurt or capture her. She's probably lost, is all." And she was hardly going to be cold with the heat they'd been having. But it seemed best to let Brigitte figure that out herself.

She stared straight ahead at the empty fireplace. "Of course."

"Let me lay Serge abed, then I'll head out. I know these woods, Brigitte. I'll find her within an hour or so."

She didn't look at him or smile at his reassurance, but merely kept rocking methodically back and forth, back and forth, and staring at the cold, gray hearth.

It took little more than an hour before he spotted the small curl of smoke against the spotless blue sky. 'Twas only a few minutes later when he strolled up to the crude campsite.

Danielle sat with her back to him, her hair long and free and matted like her mother's, but a dark, shiny ebony rather than the russet-and-red shades of Brigitte's tresses.

"Guessed you'd come as soon as I started the fire." Danielle didn't turn to face him. "I was hungry."

"Looks like a good meal." He squatted beside her. A

skinned squirrel lay impaled on a makeshift spit over the flames.

"It'll do."

"You get the squirrel with the knife I gave you?"

She nodded toward where the bloody blade lay on a rock. "*Oui.* I aimed between the eyes like you showed me, but I caught the tail instead. I got 'em between the eyes with my second knife, though."

"You've been practicing." Something thick and foreign swelled in his chest. Pride, mayhap? Or satisfaction? Hitting a moving animal was no small feat, and he'd taught the girl to throw. "You did good, Danielle. After you eat the critter, we can head—"

"I'm not going back, so don't waste your breath asking."

She wasn't going back? He shifted to better glimpse her profile. Fool that he was, he'd assumed finding the girl would be the hard part, not bringing her home.

Of course, he could always sling her over his shoulders and haul her away by force.

But then nothing would prevent her from running off the next time her mother turned her back. "Why won't you return home?"

"She didn't tell you, did she?" Danielle's blazing eyes flew to his, full of fire and vehemence. "Should have figured as much. She's going to bring you trouble, Citizen Belanger. Best to kick her off your land and wash your hands of her."

Kick Brigitte out? Had the girl gone daft? He couldn't send away a woman who bore the responsibility of housing and feeding three children. Let alone a woman who looked at him as though he had something to offer the world, as though he was somehow more than a murderer. "Whatever's going on between you and your mother, forcing her to leave won't solve anything."

And he wasn't about to announce that he'd already told Brigitte to leave. Last night. Right after he kissed her.

"You're wrong." Danielle toyed idly with a blade of grass at her side. "It would have solved everything. It's probably too late now, but you should still send her on."

"To Reims, you mean?"

Her shoulders rose and fell listlessly. "Doesn't matter. Wherever you send her, she's got trouble coming."

"Which makes me want to keep her close and help her."

"You'll end up dead."

A chill travelled up his back as he stared into Danielle's flat blue eyes. Was she serious about him ending up dead? What kind of trouble had Brigitte gotten herself into? "I'm a hard man to kill. Remember how I taught you to use that knife? Those types of skills are helpful if a man is attacked."

She pushed off the ground and paced before him. "I don't understand how she could do this to us. To you! What was she thinking? You're the kindest man we've ever met. You've given us food and shelter, care and—"

"Enough." He shoved a hand through his hair. He couldn't bear to hear such untruths. Not from Danielle. Not from the practical, sensible daughter of the woman he was coming to love. A man with his past deserved no compliments.

Danielle stopped pacing to stare at him, the familiar scowl etched back across her face. "My words are true, regardless of whether you like them."

"You don't know everything about me. Your mother might have her secrets, but I have mine, as well. And in this instance, you're wrong. Very, very wrong. I'm not kind. I'm the furthest a man can ever be from kind. Come now, let's eat this squirrel and get you back to the house."

She dug her heel into the dirt. "I told you I'm not going."

"*Non?* And what happens if I take your advice and send your mother on her way to Reims? Do you stay here and live off my land? Never to see your brothers or mother again, even after you've calmed? Even after you're ready to apologize? I know not why you're so angry with your mother, but are you willing to lose your family? If not, then you oughtn't say such things."

Her slender shoulders fell and she stared at the tips of her worn shoes. "I love them. I don't want to lose them like that, *non.*"

"Your mother was beside herself with worry when she sought me this morning. Did you know she woke the boys and spent the entire night looking for you?"

Danielle shook her head, her free mane of hair wild in the gentle breeze. "I just curled up and went to sleep in the woods. I wasn't even far from the cottage. She should have stayed and gone to bed, not taken the boys out and searched for me."

He stood and laid a hand on her shoulder. "She loves you and was worried you might have gotten hurt or met someone with ill intent. How could she not look for you?"

Danielle sniffled and swiped at her cheek with the back of her hand.

"Let's go show her you're well."

"All right." Danielle blinked up at him. "But you ought not trust her so easily."

"I'll not tolerate any more disrespect for your mother. If I have questions, I'll ask myself." And he would. Though she'd already given him answers about why she was in Abbeville and had approached him about a post. And he could hardly condemn Brigitte for any secrets she might be hiding in light of how he'd likely killed her husband.

Brigitte rolled her neck from side to side against the back of the rocker and yawned. She must have fallen asleep while waiting, and now she likely wouldn't be able to move her sore neck for the rest of the day.

She gazed wearily around the room, the soft light of morning filtering through the windows. Dawn had come and gone, but how long ago? How long had Jean Paul been out looking for her daughter? She stood and stretched, then checked on her boys. Both slept peacefully in the bed where Jean Paul had placed them, and both would likely be hungry when they woke. She should get some bread baking and head to the chicken coop for eggs. The least she could do was keep busy until—

The door to the house creaked open and she jerked her head up. One glance at the slim body with ebony tresses and she flew forward.

"Danielle!" She wrapped her arms about her daughter and squeezed. "Are you well? Did anything happen to you? Oh, love, I was so worried." She buried her face in Danielle's hair, clutching the girl even harder to her chest.

"She's well." A gentle hand landed on her shoulder, and the deep familiar timbre of Jean Paul's voice resonated through the room.

Jean Paul's dark eyes met hers over Danielle's head, the familiar angles and planes of his face somehow soft in the morning light.

She loved him. She wasn't sure when it had happened. Perhaps when he'd hauled the soup out of the well and sent her home with a full meal, or when he'd cared for the children during her illness. Or maybe she hadn't come to love him until later. Perchance the day they went to town and Jean Paul gave Gaston that *livre?*

But standing here, with her lost daughter safe in her arms and hazy sunlight pouring through the door to bathe the three of them, she need not know the exact moment.

Only that she loved him and couldn't fathom a life without him.

'Twas why she hadn't wanted to go to Reims last night, nor could she accept Alphonse's money in exchange for Jean Paul's coat. Her heart must have realized her feelings before her head understood them.

"You needn't hug me so tight, *Maman*." Danielle pushed against her chest. "I'm fine."

Danielle wriggled away, leaving her arms cold and empty, and perhaps a bit eager to embrace the tall man beside her.

"You look exhausted, Danielle. Go lie down with your brothers." Jean Paul gestured toward the bedchamber. "Your mother and I need to talk."

"All right." Danielle yawned and wandered toward the other room, her usually quick steps sluggish.

"Thank you for bringing her back." Brigitte took a step nearer Jean Paul. "I don't know what I would have done without you. I couldn't have lived with myself had something happened to Danielle. I'd searched all night and couldn't find her, and then—"

"You need not thank me."

"But you saved her. Of course, I need to—"

"Non." He ran a hand through his hair and stared up at the ceiling, then down at the floor, then toward the bedchamber once more before bringing his eyes back to meet hers. "Danielle's rather upset with you."

Shame crept into her chest, and she ducked her head.

"She wants me to ask why you came to Abbeville and sought me out for work."

This was it. The moment where she needed to confess all and explain how she'd come here to spy on him. The instant when she'd finally inquire about the National Guard uniform buried in the trunk in his stable. She sucked in a deep breath.

"Jean Paul…I…" But no further words would come. She opened and closed her mouth, once, then a second time. Everything seemed stuck, held fast by some thick, invisible barrier in her throat. Or maybe the barrier was in her chest, her heart. But either way, the words clumped together inside, and she knew not how to free them. How to even start her story.

Her hands turned hot, then cold, then hot again. But she had to say something, anything, no matter how painful. Perhaps he would send her away and never want to look at her again, but at least no more deceit would stand between them. Because if she truly loved him, she owed him the truth.

"Why don't we sit, and…and—" her tongue fumbled, but she pressed on "—I—I can tell you a story."

"We can sit, but you're not the only one with secrets, Brigitte. I have something to tell you, as well."

She took his hand and tried to smile. Perhaps if he had secrets, as well, they could forgive each other and move on. Find a way to cling together and forge ahead in this country wracked with revolution and blood.

Or so she hoped.

Until his next words shattered every illusion she held.

Chapter Eighteen

"I think I killed your husband." The words crashed through the small cottage, stark and irrevocable, drawing memories of blood and death and guillotines from the recesses of Jean Paul's mind.

And he lost her. Brigitte tugged her hand away from his, her eyes growing wide and her face suddenly pale. In that one instant, with those few little words, he lost the woman who had become so precious to him.

"What mean you?" she said.

Or at least he thought that's what she said, but her voice was too quiet to know for certain. He swallowed and reached for her hand, intending to lead her to the bench. But she only drew farther away.

He deserved it. He wasn't worthy to touch her or kiss her or love her. To have her in his life. To keep her with him forever.

So he rubbed the back of his neck, searching for some way to start his story, but 'twas no quick version of the tale. He plopped himself on the table bench and started at the beginning.

"I married Corinne when I was naught but eighteen, and I loved her. More than the sunshine and fields, more than this house or the rest of my family. More than anything else on this earth."

He blinked back a sudden burning moisture in his eyes. "She was like the rain. That's what I tell people. The spring rain that tinges everything in its path with gentleness, that gives life and color to all it touches."

And oh, had she brought gentleness and color and sweetness to his life.

Brigitte's throat worked slowly back and forth, though she still hovered near the door where he'd left her, too far for him to reach out and pull her near. "That's a beautiful way to remember your wife. I'm sure Henri never thought of me in such a way."

He moved his eyes over her, from her tangled hair to her hollow eyes to her trembling chin, down her worn dress and slender body. She stood in the same room as him, but she was separate somehow. All pulled into herself and planning to stay that way. Had no one ever told her she was special? Had no one ever likened her to the rain, or a delicate flower? The gentle, constant breeze that swept his fields?

Yes, that was Brigitte. Gentle, constant, always there. She might not be foremost in his mind when he went out to the fields or delivered food in town. But she was always present, and if she were to leave, something in his life would seem terribly wrong.

He held out his hand to her again. "Please Brigitte, come sit with me. 'Tis a long story."

But she didn't reach for his hand, and he didn't make her sit. "Corinne and I had been married two years when trouble came. 'Twas the winter of '89, and we'd lost our crop to hail, so we hadn't any food."

"I remember," she said quickly.

Of course she did. All of France remembered the brutal summer of 1788 and winter of 1789. The lack of wheat and bread had started the *Révolution*.

"That was when she…when she…" Brigitte's lip quivered, and her eyes came up to meet his. "Starved?"

"Oui." He'd forgotten how much he'd told her. 'Twas as though she already knew most of his past—except for the Terror. "She took ill, and at first, we hadn't money for a physician. She was too far gone before Physician Trudeau ever called. We sold one of our sows to pay for his services, and we followed his every last instruction. She started to improve, but she was so thin and we'd barely any food."

Something large and thick caught in his throat. "I gave her my food and went without. So did my brother, Michel, and Mother. But Corinne didn't…she couldn't…"

He pressed his eyes shut in an attempt to stem the unbidden tears. He was a man, a big man who could strike fear into the hearts of all that looked upon him, and here he was sitting in his house about to weep like a babe over an event that had happened over six years past.

But he'd loved Corinne. Truly, fully, completely. 'Twas no shame in that. "I went to *Seigneur* Montrose and asked for grain. He had an entire barn filled with wheat from the harvest two years earlier, more chickens than he could count, and hogs and cows. The *seigneur* laughed."

His blood surged hot with the memory of it, and he jerked his eyes open to find Brigitte no longer by the door but standing before him, her eyes soft and glistening, the blank expression that had settled over her face now replaced by understanding and compassion. "He asked if I knew how much a sack of grain was worth because of the famine, and I told him half the grain in the barn wasn't his, anyway. He hadn't worked for it. He'd stolen it from peasants and called it his land duty.

"The *seigneur* had me thrown out." Jean Paul's lips curved with bitterness.

"And she died." Brigitte whispered into the air between them. "I'm so sorry."

"Two mornings later, I woke, and Corinne was dead. All I could think was that *Seigneur* Montrose had laughed at me. Laughed. And Corinne had starved to death. After that, I couldn't stay here, couldn't bear to spot the *seigneur* in town or pass by his magnificent chateau with its full barns."

"I'd not have been able to stay, either." Brigitte took a step closer, but didn't sit. Instead, she looked down and twisted her hands in her skirt. "My uncle in Reims was a *seigneur,* though I know not how he would have handled a situation such as yours, or how he fared during the *Révolution.* Our families weren't close."

He reached out and took her hand, tugging her down beside him. "You sound as though you're apologizing, and there's no need. I understand now that not all *seigneurs* are like Montrose, though I didn't after Corinne's death. I went to Paris. My brother's a right good hand at making furniture. Made just about everything you see in the house." He slid his hand over the surface of Michel's table. "Michel and my father had taught me a bit of the trade, and I'd hoped to find work in the city. But no one in the furniture makers guild wanted to share their business with a farmer from an outlying province. I eventually found labor delivering coal.

"But I discovered something else, as well, something I hadn't anticipated. Not just work, but camaraderie, fraternity, brotherhood. People like me. Peasants who had nothing. Who had watched loved ones starve while the aristocrats dressed in silks, ate sumptuous feasts and ran our country into debt. Like me, they despised the highborn nobles who refused to pay taxes themselves but thought nothing of raising ours until we had naught to eat but our own fingernails. And we wanted something better. All of us. Was it so wrong to want more?"

Brigitte remained silent beside him, no answer to his questions on her lips. Still, his dreams and desires of seven years ago must have been wrong. Only something wrong could end in innocent people being dragged to the guillotine. Only something wrong could have led to the Terror.

"So when mobs formed in the *Palais-Royal* to cry for liberty, I was there. And when the Swiss Guard surrounded Paris and we feared they would slay us in the night, I stormed the Bastille with other Parisians to get the weapons stored inside. When traitors to liberty were guillotined, I attended the executions and cheered. I joined the National Guard, and everyone noticed my fervor. Then when the Convention needed soldiers to travel with the representatives-on-mission to help enforce order in the provinces, I volunteered."

He pressed his eyes shut against the grisly images invading his senses. The screams of women and children in the night when he dragged supposed traitors away, the scent of blood, the feel of limp bodies in his hands as he escorted men and women to their trials. "I didn't know there was going to be a Terror. I didn't think about the innocent people who were wrongly thrust beneath the guillotine's blade. I only thought of *Seigneur* Montrose and Corinne's death. I thought of the aristocrats who rode through Parisian streets in gilded berlins and silk stockings while I hadn't money for a second pair of trousers. I didn't think about people like your husband.

"I didn't think I would one day meet his wife," he whispered.

"But you did." The words echoed through the room. Short and simple, yet so terribly complicated.

Yes. He had most certainly met Brigitte Moreau, and he was just as certainly falling in love with her. But how could a man forge a future with a woman whose husband he'd killed? "You said he died in the Terror, did you not?"

She nodded dumbly.

"I was there, in Calais with Representative Joseph Le Bon. I may have even arrested your husband."

"I think you did."

Something sharp knifed through his heart. "How do you know?"

"I was there when you took him. The whole family was."

"Brigitte, *non*." She couldn't have been there. He'd have remembered. Or at least, he should have remembered. But there had been so many people, so many families.

He moved his hand to reach out and pull her against his chest, but she was already putting distance between them and staring blankly across the room rather than glancing his way.

"You came in the night to arrest him, yanked him out of bed where he slept beside me." A humorless smile twisted her lips. "'Twas rare that Henri was home at all rather than warming some tavern wench's bed. But he was there, and you came…"

Her words trailed off, but the implications saturated the air between them until he could hardly breathe. *And you came.* Those three words said more than he had in the past half hour.

"I remember your shadow against the moonlight from the window. A big hulking brute of a man. 'Twas what frightened me when I first approached you by the stable the other week. You were so large you reminded me of the soldier, and then you turned and moved toward me, your shadow blocking the sun, and I…I…grew ill."

"I'm sorry." He rested a hand on her shoulder, but her body stiffened beneath his touch. "I look back on those years of my life, and I feel naught but regret. Bitterness and grief controlled me, and I gave no thought for anyone save myself. 'Tis why I told you not to thank me for the food and shelter I've provided. 'Tis why I hate when the town lauds me for rescuing the mayor's sister or when Widow Arnaud and Annalise grovel because I bring them food. I'm a murderer. I don't deserve any gratitude. If I could go back to the Terror and sacrifice myself so that an innocent person might keep life, I would."

He stared blearily down at his lap. "But I can't."

Jean Paul hung his head, and moisture formed in Brigitte's eyes at the image of the strong, determined man slumped beside her.

Her worst fears were true. He had indeed killed Henri. He was the man Alphonse sought.

Could she tell the gendarme that he'd confessed? No. Never. Not even in return for her freedom. Because the listless man next to her wasn't cruel or vicious. He was humble, a hard worker who had left his violent history behind and dedicated his life to doing good. A strong person who couldn't rid himself of the guilt from his past.

A caring man she'd accidentally fallen in love with.

Her heart ached and her throat felt swollen and dry, her eyes gritty from tears that welled but refused to come. 'Twas as though Henri was being ripped away from her once more. Was Henri a criminal? Yes. A man deserving of death? Yes. But the hollowness that had consumed her as Jean Paul dragged her husband away against her children's cries and her own pleas returned to fill her now. She'd had such faith in Jean Paul. He'd seemed so good and honorable and right.

"What happened?" She suddenly had to know. "How did you change from the man who arrested Henri to the man who gives away food?" Because there had to be a story. Murderers didn't turn into benefactors on a whim.

"I passed through here while the Terror still raged." His voice was soft in the already-quiet room. "After Le Bon visited Calais he came to this region of France. While travelling through Abbeville my men and I happened upon a girl one night. Isabelle de La Rouchecauld, second daughter of the Duc de La Rouchecauld—though I didn't know it at the time. I suspected she was noble, though, so we beat her and left her for dead and I moved on to the next town. After all, I was too busy serving the new France and accusing people for crimes against liberty to spend much time on one forgettable girl."

Bitterness dripped from his words, and he drew in a huge, heaving breath. "But she wasn't dead, and Michel found her."

"Your brother?" She nearly choked. "Did he know that you'd…you'd…"

"*Non.* He didn't even know I worked for Le Bon. He thought I was in Paris making furniture. All of Abbeville still thinks that's what I did while I was away."

Which explained the rumors about his past. He'd left the little town for that exact reason. No one would know his life had turned into anything different unless he told them, or someone bore witness to the contrary.

"Michel took the girl in, nursed her until she was well and fell in love with her along the way. But when the Terror came to Abbeville, I returned home and found her with Michel. By then I'd heard of a duc's daughter who had escaped capture in Arras, and I'd wondered if it had been the defiant girl we'd found on the road. But I'd left her for dead. I never thought, never would have dreamed that…that…that…"

His voice cracked, and he pressed his eyes shut. But he need not speak of the memories or the pain they evoked for her to understand. The emotions etched across his face in harsh, regretful lines.

"I was so angry, and when I saw her standing in this very house, rage filled me anew. We fought, my brother and I. 'Twas the first time I'd ever gone to blows with him."

He blew out a breath and raked his hand through his hair. "And somewhere in all that, the girl ran off and headed to Saint-Valery to find passage to England. My men and I followed, but there were… ah…well, difficulties between me and one of the men. I ended up shot in the shoulder."

He touched his palm to his left shoulder as though the spot still pained him.

"I wasn't a kind superior to my men. I understand now why they wanted rid of me. And what better time to eliminate me than in a driving storm when no one was about? I deserved to die that day, and I would have, if not for Isabelle." He smiled then, just a small upturning of lips, but it was genuine rather than bitter. "She found me, and used the money she had kept for her passage to England to pay for a physician and a room in an inn where she could nurse me."

The air rushed out of Brigitte's lungs, and for a long moment, she could do naught but stare at him. "She saved your life? This woman you'd tried to kill?"

"'Tis what changed my heart, what forced me to see how much of a monster I'd become. I would have killed Isabelle without guilt. But even after I'd tried first to kill her and then later to drag her to prison, she wouldn't do the same to me. She *forgave* me. She reminded me of the

God I'd worshiped as a little boy, and she forgave me the way Christ had forgiven her for a past crime. What choice had I but to accept her forgiveness? She sacrificed everything to save me.

"But with that forgiveness, came all the responsibility of my former life. I could hardly go on killing. Before, I'd assumed all aristocrats wicked and selfish, like *Seigneur* Montrose. I felt no guilt in leading such people to the guillotine. But how would I know whether the person I now took was innocent or guilty? Noble birth was no proof of a wicked heart. Isabelle herself posed quite a problem. She was a duc's daughter and very much in love with my brother. 'Twas too dangerous for her to stay in France, and I had money…that which I'd gotten as pay, from looting those I arrested and from storming chateaux and hôtels in Paris. So I gave her and Michel money for their journey, and I took over the farm."

"It's a beautiful story," she spoke softly. And it was, not because of the things he'd done during the Terror, but because of the person God had changed him into. How could she do anything but forgive him for the role he'd had in Henri's death? "I had no idea."

She reached for his hand, but he stood before she could slip her fingers between his.

"You must have missed the portion where I mentioned taking part in your husband's death."

"But you overcame that. You turned—"

"No more, Brigitte." He stalked to the door and yanked it open. Bright sunlight flooded inside, sorely out of place as it poured over the dark man with an even darker past.

She followed him outside. "Where are you going?"

"To the fields. Where else?"

"Wait." He couldn't go. Not after the way she'd betrayed him last night. She needed to tell him the truth about why she was here; then maybe they could find some way through this. Jean Paul had committed some terrible crimes, yes, but she was hardly any better after last night.

He looked at her with a dark, haunted gaze.

What she wouldn't do to erase the tortured look from his eyes. Or to feel his arms around her, press her lips to his again. "Why don't you sit? I can make up a meal and we'll—"

"Not now." He turned toward the fields then paused and looked back. "Wait for the younglings to rise, and go back to your cottage. I'm not in need of your services today."

Something painful thudded in her chest. "And tomorrow?"

"I've yet to decide that." With those words, he stalked across the yard and toward the turnip-laden field nearest the house.

But I love you! The voice inside her heart cried after him.

She couldn't simply command the ache in her heart to disappear, not when he meant so much to her. *Father, what have I done?* She'd found the man that had killed her husband, and yet she hadn't found him at all. Because the man who had sat beside her and bared his agonizing story wasn't the same person who had stormed into her house and taken Henri. Oh, he might go by the same Christian name, might have the same large, powerful body.

But his heart was different.

'Twas almost as though he'd died and then come back to life, a new man.

If only Jean Paul's changed heart would appease Alphonse. Why, oh, why could she not have realized how much Jean Paul meant to her yesterday, before her meeting with the gendarme?

But then, what good would that have done? The gendarme had threatened her children, and the only way she could put off that threat was to turn traitor on the man she loved.

Chapter Nineteen

The summer air hung thick and heavy about her, but Brigitte wrapped her arms tightly around herself nonetheless, warding off an inner, bone-deep chill as she hurried across the yard to the stable. She glanced quickly back toward the house, where her children still slept, and then let herself inside. The scents of hay and animal swirled around her, tangy and comforting despite the way her heart pounded against her ribs.

She headed straight to the back of the building where the trunk lay buried. In a matter of moments, she had the rectangular box uncovered and the lid raised. If only she knew what to do with the items inside.

The uniform coat lay on top, warn and tattered with its unmistakable shade of blue. She ran her hand over the rough fabric. She couldn't turn this coat in and claim money from Alphonse, couldn't turn traitor on the man she loved—a man the entire town loved.

But if she didn't give the coat to Alphonse's henchman, what else was she to do? *Father God, how can I right this mess?*

She waited, eyes closed, face pressed up toward the heavens, but no resounding answer thundered from above, nor did any new thought appear in her mind. Not even a whisper of an idea flitted through her spirit. She reached farther inside the trunk, hoping, praying, willing some brilliant solution to spring into her head. Instead, she ended up with dark, leatherbound book full of blank pages.

She frowned. Why would Jean Paul keep an empty journal here? She buried her hands deeper in the chest and pulled out a bicorn hat, boots and breeches, all part of the National Guard uniform. A pouch full of money and gold buttons—evidently he hadn't spent all his money on the land. And another book, the leather cover soft with use and its sides dented and scarred. Dark, brash handwriting filling every last page.

She turned to the first page and smoothed it flat.

April 3, 1789.

Before the *Révolution* started.

I miss you, Corinne. People tell me I shouldn't. That it's been three months. That many others died during the winter considering how the crops failed. But I can't stop myself. Sometimes my pain is so real my stomach cramps as I fall asleep, or I'll find my eyes wet when shoveling coal. I tell my friends it's the smell of the coal, but they suspect the tears nonetheless. So I'm going to try journaling for a spell. Mayhap if I write things down, it might help me remember you when I should, and think about other things when I need my mind elsewhere.

I'm in Paris now. Couldn't abide to stay home after…well, after. I got a job hauling coal about a month back, and people call me Charron. I can't say why, but I don't want them to know me by Belanger. I

thought mayhap if I changed my name and became a
different man on the outside, I might be able to let go
on the inside, as well. But you still visit my dreams
every night, and some mornings when I wake, the
memories of you are so real I struggle to get out of
bed. I'd much rather fall back asleep, where I can
see you and hear your voice. If only I could stay in
that dream for days and weeks and months, never
waking up again.

The entry ended just as abruptly as that. No mention of
whether Jean Paul got out of bed the next morn. Though
surely he must have dragged himself off his tick eventually, as he was still around today.

She flipped farther into the book, a single word glaring
back at her numerous times from each and every entry.
Corinne, Corinne, Corinne, Corinne.

When she came to the page marked 14 July 1789, she
stopped and ran her fingers down it. She'd taught her children of the events of this day, but Jean Paul had evidently
lived them.

We stormed the *Hôtel des Invalides* last night to
gather guns and cannons, but found no ammuni-
tion. So we moved on to the Bastille for the gunpowder. Its stone walls hulked before us, solid and
strong and unbreakable. But we used the cannons on
the gates and demanded entry. Now we are armed,
the king's soldiers won't be able to slaughter us, the
prisoners are liberated, and that bastion of tyranny
will no longer tower over Paris.

The journalists and pamphleteers are beside themselves with cheer. All of Paris lauds us, and I had part

in it. Everyone is saying this is the beginning. Now that we have broken the Bastille, perhaps we can break the monarchy and aristocracy. Perhaps we can create for ourselves a New France. One where liberty rules rather than tyranny. One where everyone has bread on their tables and meat in their larders.

For the first time since your death, Corinne, I feel that I am doing something important. Something that matters. Just think of it. What if we can forge a France that has no more *Seigneur* Montroses?

Had our country been this way a year ago, you might still be alive.

Brigitte's stomach clenched as she pored over the words. Such dreams, such anger, such grief. 'Twas little wonder he'd ended up storming through the countryside, bent on forcing the French people to accept the National Convention's "liberty." Liberty and force had no place together, but it had taken a Terror before the country understood that. And the man from this journal, the image of Jean Paul Belanger that these words created, seemed sick and heartbroken, willing to do anything to right the grievances against his wife.

Just like the rest of the French people had been willing to kill the king and aristocrats in the belief that doing so would mean that they could have bread.

She flipped forward, her heart leaden as she searched for yet another memorable date.

21 January 1793.
The king is dead. I went to the execution and cheered. But will his death be enough? Robespierre says no, that all who stand in the way of liberty must die. I can't help but think of *Seigneur* Montrose and what

he did to you, Corinne, and I want him dead. I want them all dead.

Tears slid from her face to land on the worn page. What had happened to the man from the first page of the journal? The one who looked forward to dreams of his wife every night while he slept? How had four years changed him into someone who lusted for death instead?

She turned haphazardly through the pages, searching for something she couldn't quite name.

20 July 1793.
I shall be leaving Paris soon. The Committee of Public Safety is sending out representatives to carry liberty to the provinces. Rumors abound of citizens unwilling to bend their knees to liberty's law. I volunteered to go. I shall miss Paris, but how can I ignore the call of liberty?

And she had her answer, what had prodded him to leave Paris and return to northern France with a guillotine. There was more writing, pages and pages of the harsh, uneven words. But she couldn't keep reading, didn't want to see or know the cruel things he'd done during the Terror.

She shifted back, moving the heavy book from her lap onto the hay. The journal certainly hadn't given her any ideas about how to free Jean Paul. If anything, it incriminated him far more than the National Guard coat ever could. What was she to do?

Her eyes fell to the other items she'd pulled from the chest. And suddenly, the idea came. She had a way, one faint sliver of a chance, to protect both her children and Jean Paul.

If only she could manage it before her meeting tonight.

* * *

Jean Paul reached into the dirt and yanked up another weed, tossing it into a pail. The turnip field spread before him, wide and large, nearly amber in the setting sun, and full of weeds he should have dug last week. Except he'd been too distracted by Brigitte and her illness to remember his turnip field.

Brigitte. He closed his eyes. He had no business even thinking her name, let alone conjuring her image in his mind. Not after what he'd done to her husband.

He bent over, resting his arms on his knees. His back ached from twelve hours spent digging and pulling, and the knees of his trousers were so stained and damp they'd never come completely clean. He needed a quick dip in the stream, a hearty meal and a full night's rest.

He expected to have naught but nightmares.

He just hoped Brigitte had left his house when he'd told her to. The knowledge that he'd killed her husband should push her away, but he wouldn't approach the farmstead until well after dark. Better to not chance seeing her again. If she was smart, she'd gone back to the hut, packed her belongings and left Abbeville. She should have enough money to reach Reims now.

But how would he manage with her gone? Every moment he spent in her presence, he fell a little more in love with the brave woman that fought so hard for her children. That had approached a complete stranger in order to procure work. That didn't let raging fever or past heartache hinder the future she had planned for herself and her younglings.

None of which even included the feelings he had for the children who had wiggled their way into his heart.

He'd known his past would come back to haunt him. But to learn to love all over again only to discover his sins would forever keep him from making the family he cared for his own? 'Twas a cruel penance.

Forgiveness had seemed easy last year in Saint-Valery after Isabelle de La Rouchecauld forgave him for trying to kill her. A simple prayer and all was well. But if God had forgiven him, why did he still carry the shame of his past, memories of the Terror, and guilt that bound his chest so tightly he could hardly breathe at times?

He'd merely sought justice for his wife. Or at least, that's what he'd told himself. But it hadn't been justice, at all. He'd wanted retribution, and he'd gotten it…

More than he wished.

Father forgive me, he whispered to the sky, but to no avail. Just as last time, the wretched words fell back to litter the ground surrounding him, never making their way to God.

God probably had little desire to listen to prayers from a man like him, anyway.

The shadows at the edge of the field shifted, and a flash of white glinted in the dying sun. Jean Paul blinked then furrowed his brow. Sure enough, a figure walked along the edge of his field. Just a glance at the auburn tresses hanging down beneath her mobcap and the creamy hue of her skin, and he knew her.

What was Brigitte doing in his fields as darkness descended? He dropped the hoe where he stood and opened his mouth to call out, then stopped. Perhaps it was the fierceness in Danielle's gaze earlier when she'd warned him to send Brigitte away. Or maybe it was the ice in the girl's voice when she'd proclaimed he would end up dead. But either way, Brigitte heading away from both the farmstead and the hidden cottage hardly made sense.

So he followed.

She left his property and moved on to his neighbor's,

her footsteps quick and sure. A white bundle lay wedged beneath her arm, and she held her back rigidly straight. Again he nearly called out but some unnamable hunch made him stop. Instead, he moved into the forest where trees shrouded him and continued across the springy ground with quiet steps. Her white cap and apron stood out as the sun's final rays left the sky, but not until darkness had nearly swallowed her did she veer into the woods.

A sickening awareness twined through him. He scanned the forest, quiet and still at this time of night. But someone else was there, an unknown presence lurking just out of sight. He hunkered down and squinted at the bed of soft soil beneath his feet. Sure enough, a second set of footprints lay indented in the dirt, and too large to be a woman's shoe. Brigitte was meeting someone. A man. Alone. At night. In a secluded place.

His stomach twisted as he inched forward.

"*Bonne.* You're here."

Brigitte frowned at the unfamiliar voice and blinked into the darkness, but as usual only shadows greeted her. Did her nerves make her hear things that weren't so? Or perhaps the gendarme had taken on a cold, making his voice unrecognizable. She was at the designated rendezvous place at the appointed time, and the guard stayed hidden in the trees. Everything was normal.

But the air held a thick, foreboding sensation. A chill skittered up her spine, and she glanced around. Maybe if she could determine where the gendarme hid...

But no human shadow hunkered among the dark, towering trees—at least none that she could discern.

She smoothed her damp hands against the folds of her skirt. The voice likely seemed strange because her nerves were overtaking her. She clutched the journal tighter beneath her arm and swallowed. She could do this. All she needed was to hand over the book and claim she'd found it with Jean Paul's coat. He had no reason to accuse her of lying.

Unless he could see the sweat beading on her forehead or hear the rapid thump of her pulse.

But no. He couldn't sense those things, especially in the dark. And she had to appear strong. In control. Aloof.

"Have you my money?" She managed to form the words without her voice trembling. "I brought Citizen Belanger's journal, but I want the money first."

A sneering chuckle echoed from the woods. "You're not in control. I am."

She turned to look behind her, her heart quickening yet again. 'Twas definitely not the gendarme's voice that time. "Who are you? Show yourself."

"Show me the evidence first."

"Where's the gendarme I met last night?"

A louder laugh this time, cruel and unfettered. "Detained. Alphonse expects efficiency from his men. Neither you nor Gilles have been efficient."

Her hand tightened on the journal despite the moisture saturating her grip. What was she going to do? Would he be harder to fool than the gendarme? More cruel? What if he took one look at the journal and knew what she'd done?

But the man behind the trees was right. She had no control. If she did, she wouldn't be in Abbeville at all, spying on the man she loved. Tempted to betray him in order to save her children.

She straightened her spine and raised her chin. She only had to be strong one more time, only had to pass along this one falsehood, and she would be done forever. "I want the money first."

"And I want to see the evidence you've brought me."

She extended the journal in her quivering hands. "Fine. You can have it, but understand that Citizen Belanger is—"

Innocent. A crashing sounded from the forest behind her, and the word froze on her tongue. She whirled toward the noise, glimpsed a towering body and broad, unmistakable shoulders beneath a faint beam of moonlight trickling though the trees.

"Jean Paul." Dread curdled her stomach. Had he learned of her meeting somehow? Did he know everything?

He paid her no heed but rushed past and leaped into the shadows on the other side of the clearing. Two bodies crashed to the forest floor and rolled into the light until they collided with the trunk of a centuries-old tree. Then one form raised himself up over the other, and a grotesque crack echoed through the forest.

"I should kill you." Jean Paul's voice rang out over a moan of pain.

Another crack rent the air, followed by thumps and scuffles and groans.

She tucked the journal back under her arm and stepped closer to the tangled men, only to jump back when they rolled her direction. The thin slices of moonlight slanting through the trees cast a trail of light on the two men, but not enough to tell who was besting the other. Then again, she hardly needed light to know who would win. Jean Paul was too large and strong for another man to pose him much threat.

A third crack sounded, and the form with the overlarge shoulders slowly rose to his feet, leaving another shadow prostrate and still beside the tree trunk.

"I trusted you." Jean Paul turned toward her, wiping the side of his face with his sleeve.

She ran her eyes up his familiar body etched against the moonlight, then looked away.

She was never supposed to fall in love with him, but she had. She was never supposed to care whether her actions hurt him, but she did. If only she'd come to care a little sooner, had understood the feelings coursing through her body before this morning. Instead, she'd spent the entire day trying to protect him, trying to keep this moment from happening.

And she'd failed.

What was there to say—besides the bald, horrid truth. "Jean Paul, I—"

"I was a fool." He spat the bitter words. "Do you know how I felt about you, Brigitte? I thought I could love you. For six years, I've not been able to look upon a woman and see a future. Women were no different from children and old men, just more bodies needing bread, likely to starve at the hands of the aristocrats if no one fought for them. No woman has made me smile or laugh or cry. Not since Corinne have I bothered to imagine the way a woman would feel in my arms...

"Until you." His voice turned quiet, a gravelly rasp against the warm night air. "But it was all a lie, wasn't it? Every kiss, every subtle glance and worried look was one giant falsehood so you could get—get—" He threw up his hand in a frustrated gesture. "What did you come here for? Money? Revenge?"

She licked her painfully dry lips. "'Tis not how it appears."

"Not how it appears? Let me tell you how it *appears*. It *appears* you had suspicions about me before you came to Abbeville. It *appears* you traveled here for the sole purpose of getting close to me. Is that why you were so determined to work as my housekeeper?" His jaw moved back and forth in furious little jerks. "Fool that I was, I believed it. Believed you. Who are you truly? Are those children even yours? Or did you find them and—"

"Yes, they're mine!"

"And you expect me to trust you?"

"Non." Hot, searing moisture flooded her eyes, and the journal weighed heavy as a bushel of wheat as she extended it toward him. "But at least take this. It shows—"

"I know what it shows." He yanked the book out of her hand and sent it crashing into the nearest tree. It slid to the ground, the pages fluttering and tearing on the rough bark before it landed in a mangled heap. "The question is, why were you giving it to this man?"

"I was trying to show you innocent."

He scoffed. "Me? Innocent? Even now, after I caught you trying to destroy me, you offer more lies?"

"It's not a lie! Look at—"

"Not a lie? Then tell me, Brigitte, why did you first approach me? Why did you weasel your way into my house? Because you believed me innocent? I think not."

She closed her eyes and ducked her head at the mercilessly raw tone to his voice.

"Those days I went to the field and left you about the house, did you spend them snooping? Scouring every centimeter of my home until you found what you were looking for?"

"Jean Paul, please, you have to believe me. I wasn't turning you in."

"Save your words for someone who wants to listen." He stalked away, putting a good four or five paces between them before he whirled back. "So what happens now? Is someone going to come for my head? Is this man here going to shoot me in the heart one night while I lay abed?"

"Non! Nothing's going to happen. It's what I've been trying to tell you."

But he wasn't listening. She could spend all night pleading with him, and nothing would change. He stood before her too furious to hear what she said, too furious to care that she was sorry, too furious to understand she'd changed her mind about working for Alphonse. The man before her held no semblance to the gruff but kind farmer she'd first met, possessed no patience to listen to whatever explanation she might have.

"Return to the cottage and pack your things." His words shattered the silence. "I'll visit at dawn, and if you're still there, I'll...I'll..."

His voice broke, and he turned his back to her yet again.

"Just look at the journal. Please. It's—"

"It's private. Not something you should have ever touched. Something you'd not have found were you not snooping around my property."

"It's not what you think. I changed it." The words wrenched from her mouth. She stared at his back, willing him to listen, to care, to understand that though she may have been working against him for the past two weeks, today she'd been working *for* him.

He held up his hand. "Enough. You have until dawn to leave. I suggest you make haste if you don't wish to be dragged before the magistrate."

She glanced at the journal laying mangled on the forest floor and pressed her lips together. Perhaps he would take it with him and look at it come morning, then he might understand.

But she'd be gone by morning. He'd given her no other choice.

Or rather, she'd given herself no other choice from the moment she'd first agreed to work for Alphonse.

Chapter Twenty

Brigitte wiped the tears from her face as she moved through the tall trees toward home. Or more accurately, toward the place that *had been* her home.

If only Jean Paul had let her explain, or if, even now, he would just open the journal and realize she'd been trying to protect him, that she'd fallen in love with him despite what she'd done. Then he could come to the house and claim her before she left for Reims.

And she was dreaming the dreams of an errant schoolgirl. She'd spent the past two weeks working against the one man who had been kind and generous to her family. Why would he now come claim her?

She rubbed more tears from her cheeks and sniffled to stem the ceaseless stream. She would leave and go to some other city. It couldn't be Reims now, for Alphonse would surely search for her there. But she could start a new life with the money she'd earned from Jean Paul. It would be hard at first, but she could make do. And when memories of Jean Paul and his kindness visited her in the night, she'd push them away much like she did her longing to see her twin boys.

She gulped in a breath and moved swiftly over the uneven ground toward the cottage ahead, the familiar shadow of trees looming above despite the already dark night. Not even the flicker of a faint candle shown through the windows. Her children were all abed and now she'd have to wake them.

She opened the door and stepped inside. "Danielle, Serge, I'm sorry to wake you, but we must—"

An arm curled around her throat, yanking her back against a hard chest. She screamed, but another hand clamped over her mouth.

"Don't waste your breath screaming. There's no one around to hear."

Her heart pounded against her rib cage, and she sucked in a panicked gulp of air before shaking her head wildly. Her struggle did little good. The massive hand tightened its grip over her mouth, and the man yanked back on her neck, her chin jerking upward toward the roof of the cottage.

"The children," she rasped. She moved her eyes frantically toward the bed, trying to discern their small bodies beneath the covers.

"The children, you ask?" Scalding breath feathered over her ear. "They're already in the wagon, waiting."

Waiting for what? To go where? Why was this strange man here, in her house during the darkest hours of the night?

But she knew why. Indeed there could only be one answer to all of this: Alphonse. His men hadn't just interrupted her meeting with the gendarme, they'd also come to her home.

A burst of terror ignited in her stomach, tearing across her chest, her mind.

Her heart.

She'd been close. So very close to…

To what? A lump that had nothing to do with the forearm across her neck rose in her throat. What did she even want anymore? She wanted her children safe and away from Alphonse. But she didn't want to leave the man she loved.

He'd killed her husband. Some part of her should want to run to Alphonse with the news. But Jean Paul had been so sick and stricken with grief at the beginning of the *Révolution*. He was a different man now, one who filled needs rather than created them.

But it mattered not whether she longed to stay with Jean Paul, to throw herself on his mercy and beg to be his housekeeper for the rest of her life so that she might glimpse his face every morn. She'd be forced to go with this guard back to Calais and face Alphonse instead.

Though she had little choice in seeing her father-in-law, she didn't have to share her findings with him. If nothing else, she would see that he never learned the truth about Citizen Belanger.

"If you scream, I'll hit you," the gruff voice snarled against the back of her head, then the hand left her mouth.

"Are the children well? Tell me you didn't hurt them." She couldn't stop the tremble in her voice. Danielle was strong, but how must Serge and Victor have felt to awake at the hands of this man?

"Well indeed. They sleep like babes."

"They sleep?"

"*Oui.* As will you."

He yanked back on her hair, thrusting her chin up again. Before she could sputter a response, a clay mug pressed to her lips and bitter liquid poured down her throat until she was forced to either swallow or choke.

Betrayed. Utterly, thoroughly, completely.

Jean Paul rubbed a hand over his chin as he sat against

the base of the tree. The first gray fingers of dawn tinged the early morning sky, visible only through breaks in the leafy canopy above.

But he didn't move.

Hadn't moved for hours.

How was it he had strength enough to flatten a brute of a man and scare the man away a second time when he'd finally regained consciousness? How was it he had the strength to send away the woman he loved, but hadn't the strength to move from this tree for hours hence?

He raised his head and surveyed the little patch of forest floor once again. 'Twas obvious from the flattened earth and foliage this area had been used before last night. How many times had Brigitte met with that man and his comrades? How much information had she passed along before he discovered what she was about?

Did she know of his agreement with the Convention and the letters he wrote every month? Of the men he sometimes sheltered in his stable?

Or did she snoop because of his role in the Terror? Because he'd killed her husband?

He should have asked who she'd been working for before sending her off. Not that he expected her to tell him the truth. It could be some Girondist or Federalist. Any powerful person he'd happened to wrong while he was in the National Guard or working for Joseph Le Bon.

He'd likely discover her spymaster soon enough. Now that she had the information she sought, it wouldn't be long before his opponents showed themselves. Then again, mayhap they wouldn't show themselves at all. They could always sneak into his house while he slept and slit his throat.

He tilted his head up toward the heavens, the rough tree bark snagging the back of his hair. "Did You do it a'purpose, God? Did You know who she was and make me fall in love with her, anyway?"

Some sort of vengeance for his past sins?

Oui. Vengeance indeed. He'd been worried about that very thing when he'd looked upon Brigitte lying in her sick bed. Had figured God would give her to him for a time and then yank her away as He'd done with Corinne. But God had different plans in store this time.

He raked a hand through his hair. 'Twould almost have been easier to lose Brigitte in death rather than have her betray him in life. But betray him she had, and for some addled reason, he couldn't force himself up from the spot on the ground where he'd sunk after he sent her away.

"Citizen Belanger!" A familiar voice carried through the still morning air. "Jean Paul!"

He straightened against the tree and glared warily in the direction of the ruckus. What was Danielle doing here? She should be well on her way to Reims with the rest of her family—if they were truly her family.

He sighed and glanced around. It was too much to hope the girl wouldn't find him. He'd taught her to track, after all, and the path to this little clearing had been trodden enough that it hardly remained secret.

He raised himself up off the ground as Danielle's form bounded through the trees.

"You're supposed to be headed to Reims," he bit out.

She slid to a halt and scrunched her brow. "Reims? *Non*. 'Tis Calais."

"Reims, Calais. I care not, so long as the woman you call a mother goes away. Now why are you here?"

"You know, then." The girl's eyes turned dark and flat.

He crossed his arms over his chest. "*Oui,* I know. As you did yesterday morn, but you didn't tell me."

Her gaze dipped to her boots. "'Tis why I ran off. I

couldn't bear the sight of her once I learned her reasons for working here."

Well, at least they were agreed in wanting nothing to do with Brigitte—or they had been. How had he ever convinced Danielle to return home with him yesterday? "Your mother betrayed me. I never want to see her again."

She jerked her head up. "You can't say that, not after she sacrificed everything for you."

He gave a hard, bitter laugh. Brigitte hadn't sacrificed a flea for him. But Danielle's eyes locked with his, fierce honesty burning in her gaze.

Almost as though she spoke the truth.

He clamped his jaw together. She couldn't speak the truth. 'Twas impossible.

Yet the look in her eyes couldn't be falsified.

A memory of their first meeting flashed through his mind, Danielle standing proud over his stolen chicken, knowing she'd done wrong but refusing to cower or lie. Danielle Moreau might be strong and determined, but she'd tell him the truth and then throw punches to defend herself rather than spout falsehoods.

"Stop staring at me as though you think me dishonest. *Maman* needs your help, and we haven't time to lose." She turned and started down the little path.

Jean Paul dug the heels of his boots into the ground. "I don't help traitors."

Danielle whirled back and stalked toward him until the tips of her shoes met his. Then she tilted her proud little nose in the air and glared up at him. "She wasn't betraying you. She was trying to save you."

"Trying to save me? 'Tis laughable, child."

She jutted her chin toward the journal laying in the moist dirt. "Have you looked at it?"

Jean Paul glowered at the leatherbound book. "Why would I? I wrote the words. I well know what's in it."

Blood. Pain. Memories he tried to forget every night when he closed his eyes.

Danielle curled her bottom lip. "That's where you're wrong. It was written yesterday—and not by you."

The girl was befuddled, which wasn't terribly surprising given her conniving and manipulative mother. 'Twould be hard for any person to stay sane when forced to live with Brigitte Moreau.

"'Tis enough. I've work to do and haven't time to dally longer." He moved to retrieve the book then started down the path. First he needed to find a new hiding place for his journal—hopefully one that wouldn't be discovered so easily this time. Then he needed to stop by the second cottage and finish this business of forcing Brigitte off his land. After that he had breakfast to see to, since the woman no longer worked for him. Turnips lay waiting to be dug in the far field, and he needed to inspect Pierre's clovers. Then—

"Wait!" A small, hard body hit him from behind, causing his knees to buckle as he lurched forward.

"What are you doing?" He took the girl by her shoulders and held her out from him. "Go help your mother pack and leave me be, or I'll drag the lot of you before the magistrate."

"I know not what happened between you and *Maman* last night, though I can guess you found her meeting with one of *Grand-père*'s men." Danielle swiped a tangle of dark hair out of her face. "But I speak truth when I say she needs your help. Now. They've captured her and Serge and Victor. Every moment you tarry, they get farther away."

So someone had betrayed the traitor. 'Twas a fitting end. Mayhap now Brigitte would think harder before agreeing to carry out such dastardly tasks. "Who is this 'they' you speak of? Your mother's employer? I know not for whom she works."

"'Tis my father's father, and he doesn't give people choices about working for him. He forces it. Though I think he promised *Maman* we could leave Calais and move to Reims if she spied on you."

If nothing else, the girl was tenacious in defending her mother, though her reasoning made little sense. "Your mother could have left Calais on her own. She hardly needs to take on some ill-intended assignment from your grandfather."

"You don't understand who my *grand-père* is, or the power he wields." Danielle shook free of his hold. With her dress torn and dirt smudged on her cheeks, she should look like nothing more than a filthy urchin, yet somehow she was magnificent in her disarray. "His name is Alphonse Dubois, and he's both a *seigneur* and a smuggler."

Dubois.

Dubois.

Dubois.

The name rang like a bell through his head. He remembered it well, one of the few that stuck out from the Terror. There had been a Dubois in Calais, yes, a *seigneur*—not that the *Révolution* acknowledged such positions these days—who'd used his power to build a massive smuggling ring before the *Révolution* started. Though the Dubois family lands would have been lost with the rise of the *Révolution,* the man's smuggling power extended far.

Le Bon, the representative-on-mission from the Convention, had been set on bringing the smuggler down, but Calais closed up around them whenever they made inquiries. Jean Paul had only arrested one group of smugglers for an illegal import of wool, and the captured men had refused to speak one word of their leader, even though the arrest had landed them the smuggler's son. Henri Dubois.

Henri, the name of Brigitte's first husband. And not Moreau, but Dubois.

Jean Paul stilled, his pulse thrumming hard against his wrists and neck while silence descended over the forest. A man like Alphonse Dubois would want revenge for his son's death. A man like Alphonse Dubois, ruthless enough to strike fear into an entire town, would use his son's widow to get it. A man like Alphonse Dubois didn't care whom he hurt or why he hurt them, just as long as he got his way. And he was very used to getting his way.

His gaze slid to Danielle. Had Dubois threatened Brigitte's children? Is that why she'd come to spy on him?

"Well?" Danielle pinched her lips together. "Do you know my *grand-père?*"

"I know of him, and I…ah…I arrested your father."

She wrapped her arms around herself and shivered. "*Maman* told me yesterday when I helped with the journal. She had to give *Grand-père's* men proof of something, so rather than turn in the journal she found hidden, she wrote a new one that showed you innocent."

Innocent? Brigitte had been trying to prove his *innocence?* Blood roared in his ears and he struggled to suck in breath as he opened to the first page of the book. There the letters stood, bold and unmistakable in a poor imitation of his hand. He flipped through, page after page, certain words jumping out at him, like *furniture maker* and *apprentice, journeyman.* The entries were short and sparse but they covered from March 1789 until the time he'd been shot and Isabelle nursed him in Saint-Valery. The journal made no mention of his serving as a soldier or even setting foot in Calais.

"She didn't tell you last night?" Danielle asked quietly.

"I think she tried, but I didn't let her." He bowed his head. What had he done? He'd been so furious that he'd seen only her betrayal. If he'd have let her talk, simply trusted rather than turned his back... "I'm an oaf."

A small hand rested on his forearm. "We haven't time to waste. *Grand-père* sent men for us last night. They have *Maman* and the boys."

Dubois had already taken her and the children? He wasn't just an oaf, but a heartless, wretched one.

"Citizen Belanger," Danielle prodded.

He blew out a breath and looked up. The girl had the right of it. 'Twould be time to wallow later, but first, he had to find her. "Tell me everything of these men. What time did they come? How did they find you?"

"They came last night while *Maman* was still away. They made us drink a sleeping potion, bound us and threw us in the wagon, then laid a trap for *Maman*. It won't be good once *Grand-père* has hold of her.

No. He didn't imagine so. "And you escaped?"

A grin split her pretty little face. "Of course. I made it look like I choked on the potion, but really I spewed most of it out, and what I didn't spew out, I let dribble down the side of my mouth. "My neck and dress are sticky, see?"

She patted her slender neck and a stained spot at the top of her dress. "I've kept that knife you gave me strapped to my thigh. 'Twas a simple matter to feign sleep while they bound me, then cut the ties once the wagon began to move."

"I'm glad you escaped." If not for Danielle, he'd still be furious at Brigitte and ignorant as to the danger surrounding her. "Now come, we must makc haste."

Facing a smuggler might not be so terrible. But a smuggler whose son he'd killed during the Terror? A smuggler who now held the woman and children he loved captive?

If he did nothing else, he would go to Calais and free Brigitte and the younglings. She deserved little less after being used so terribly by Dubois. Then she could move to Reims and finally be with her family.

And what of his feelings for her? His heart gave a long, hard thump. He had no business loving a woman like Brigitte Dubois. He'd known it from the first. Because no matter how much he loved her, no matter how many men he fought to free her, he was still the murderer who'd killed her husband.

He could say he'd changed…but even the new man he'd become had let her down, let her come to harm when she should have been under his protection. He'd failed her, just as he'd failed Corinne.

Losing her from his life just as he'd lost his beloved wife was nothing more than what he deserved.

Chapter Twenty-One

Jean Paul burst through the door of the gendarmerie barracks then stopped to survey the room. The gendarme on the bunk closest to the door raised up on his elbow and squinted through sleepy eyes.

"Where's Gilles?"

The other man plopped back down on his bed. "Third bed on the right. Top bunk."

He turned back to Danielle, standing in the doorway. "Wait here."

Of course, the urchin didn't listen. She followed him down the aisle between the beds until he stopped at the bunk where Gilles lay peacefully turned on his side, slumbering as though he hadn't a worry in the world.

Well, that was about to change. He hauled Gilles up by his shoulder with one hand while wrapping his other around the man's throat.

The gendarme's eyes snapped open, instant panic flickering in their depths.

"Where are they?" Jean Paul growled. "Where are the guards taking them?"

Gilles opened his mouth then closed it before swallowing thickly beneath Jean Paul's hand.

Right. Strangling the man was rather prohibitive to talking. He released Gilles's neck and gripped the scoundrel's shoulder instead. "The truth, or my hand goes back on your throat."

"I know not of whom you speak."

With a single heave, he jerked Gilles halfway off the bed, their breaths tangling as he stared into the gendarme's frightened eyes. "Don't play daft with me. You were supposed to meet Brigitte Dubois last night, were you not?"

The man's face whitened at the mention of Brigitte's true surname. "So you know."

"Only that she's been taken. Danielle tells me you threatened her and the children two nights past. And I can surmise she was supposed to meet you last night, not the other man I found. Now speak. What know you?"

Gilles pressed his eyes shut. "They have her son, Julien. Dubois had men waiting for his grandson in Le Havre, and they captured him when his ship arrived. Dubois must have grown impatient with how long Brigitte was taking here. I had naught but a day's warning before the men arrived. They asked where Brigitte stayed and when our next meeting was."

"And you told them." He tightened his grip on the gendarme's shoulder. One more answer such as that, and he'd not be able to stop his hand from wrapping back around the other man's throat. "How dare you turn vile men like that on her?"

"I hadn't a choice. They'd have…"

The man's mouth clamped shut, but his thoughts lay written across his face. Men like Alphonse Dubois based their empires on fear, not loyalty. Dubois's henchmen would have killed Gilles had he not been truthful—or made him wish he were dead.

"Were they angered that you didn't have more information on me?"

"Oui."

"But they left you here alive." And they'd taken Brigitte. His heart twisted. Why could they not have taken the clod in front of him and left the woman he loved alone?

"They gave me another task with which to prove myself." His eyes were flat and lifeless as the words fell from his mouth.

"What kind of task?"

"I'm to go to your property and kill you, burning your remains in your house before I set fire to your land."

Jean Paul pulled back. Kill him and burn his fields? Alphonse Dubois didn't waste time. "You tell me this rather easily."

Gilles's eyes drifted down to where Jean Paul's hands fisted in his nightclothes. "They'll kill me if I fail. But it seems you've a mind to kill me first."

"Oui. I should snap your neck." Yet somehow he couldn't stomach it. He had every reason to drag this man before Captain Monfort, the mayor and the magistrate to see him guillotined.

But enough death already stained his hands to last three lifetimes over. He released the man and crossed his arms over his chest. "I'm feeling a bit merciful this morn. I might be convinced to barter your life for information— and a promise not to burn down my home and fields. Tell me more of what happened with Brigitte, and start at the beginning."

Gilles pushed himself up on the bed until he sat, then glanced about the room. One man stirred in the far corner, but otherwise the chamber remained still, most guards sleeping for another hour yet. "Dubois hired me some years back. I usually just…ignore certain signs of his smugglers' doings as I carry out my duties."

He was paid to ignore Dubois's smuggling activities? They'd likely been working against each other from the start, with Jean Paul reporting suspicious activities to the Convention once every month, and Gilles trying to cover them up.

"But when his daughter-in-law came to town, I was tasked with seeing she followed Dubois's orders." The man avoided meeting Jean Paul's eyes, but his face contorted with jealousy and pettiness. Hardly a surprise, given the man's sneering animosity toward him and his dealings with the gendarmerie. With an opportunity such as this, to see the local hero come to harm or at least be publically disgraced—the scoundrel had probably volunteered.

"She'd a full fortnight to perform her duties, yet she moved slow from the beginning. I tried to get her to work faster, but she fell ill and took a fancy to you. 'Twas plain to see my…uh, encouragement had little effect."

An image of Brigitte rose in his mind, sick and scared, and that wretched fever slowly overtaking her as this gendarme forced her to choose between her principles and her children. Why hadn't he discovered her situation sooner? Why hadn't he demanded she tell him more of her time in Calais?

"I heard naught from Dubois when she went past the fortnight, but I knew he must grow impatient. So two nights ago, when she missed our rendezvous, I searched out her house and waited. 'Twas obvious she'd found something of import before she'd returned. The woman is a poor liar. But she didn't want to talk so I did some persuading of my own." Gilles's chin rose defiantly.

Did the man feel no shame over terrifying a woman

and her younglings? "What did you do?" Jean Paul all but snarled the words.

"He threatened us," Danielle piped up from where she stood at the end of the bed.

Jean Paul narrowed his eyes until blackness blocked out everything in his vision save Gilles. "How?"

The man swallowed, color draining from his face. "Ah…I…um…" Gilles gripped his hands together and then looked away. "I said I'd hold a knife to the babe's throat if she didn't speak."

"How dare you!" He lunged at the bed.

Gilles rolled to his side, well anticipating the move, and shifting just enough to avoid being caught. "Have you a wish to hear the rest or not?"

"If you think you've a choice, perhaps I wasn't clear enough when I made my own threat," Jean Paul spat.

"'Tis not what you think. She pleaded for you, anyway, the heartsick fool," the gendarme grumbled, jumping off the other end of the bed, putting a good meter between them.

"She what?"

"She said she found a hidden National Guard uniform, but she argued the uniform meant nothing, that many a man had worn such a coat and it didn't make them murderers." Gilles's sullen words were little more than a whisper in the quiet barracks. "I insisted she meet me yesterday's eve with the uniform, anyway. But Dubois's men arrived."

She'd pleaded for him? Had defended him to this vile man? If so, then he'd played a bigger role in Brigitte's deceit than he thought. If she'd found his trunk two nights ago, 'twould have been right after the kiss he'd ended so brutally. Right after he told her to leave and not return. He'd watched her run into the stable then. Was that when she'd found his trunk?

It must have been. And after Gilles gave her an ultimatum between producing evidence or seeing harm done to her children, she'd still pleaded on his behalf.

How had the woman survived this endeavor? How had she managed to walk the line between protecting her children and not betraying him? When he'd found her with the journal last night, he'd assumed the worst. But he'd been wrong. Terribly, terribly wrong. She'd faced impossible circumstances and still found a way to protect both her children and himself.

But she'd needed protecting, as well, and he'd failed her.

Jean Paul met Gilles's eyes over the top of the bed. "Gather your things. I won't turn you in to the magistrate, but only if you come with me to Calais. You'll help undo this wrong."

The gendarme laughed, a harsh, hollow sound. "'Twill do you no good, save getting you killed sooner. I've never been to Calais, nor know I where Dubois stays. My father was indebted to him, and Dubois's men approached me after he passed. 'Tis that obligation I seek to work off."

"All the more reason for you to come and see that Dubois's smuggling ring is stopped."

"You suggest the impossible. Dubois's strength is vast."

Mayhap he underestimated Alphonse Dubois's strength, but he understood right and wrong, justice and injustice. The smuggler needed to be thwarted, and Jean Paul didn't plan to stop until one of them lay cold in a grave— hopefully after Brigitte and her children were free.

"I have a means of fighting back." Indeed, his letter from Fouché gave him such capabilities, though he wasn't about to proclaim his relationship with Paris to a filthy criminal like Gilles.

Gilles smirked, his overlarge nose tilting arrogantly in the air. "You understand little. You'll have to take the force into Calais with you. No one in that town will side against the one who employs nearly all the men to one extent or another. And even if you can muster the men to fight, you still know not where to find Dubois."

"I know." A quiet voice echoed into the otherwise silent room.

Jean Paul turned toward Danielle.

She took a step forward, her chin jutting in that familiar, determined angle so similar to her mother. "I know where *Grand-père* stays, and I'll help you get him."

Dark. Everything was dark. And bumpy. Something jolted her, sending her already throbbing head to crash against a hard surface.

Brigitte blinked her eyes open and groaned, though neither action did much good. Her mouth didn't work quite right, and a blurry darkness still surrounded her.

Water. She needed a whole liter of it, and a soft bed, not this hard, jostling…

The surface on which she lay listed to the right, and she rolled.

"Whoa there," an unfamiliar masculine voice called out. "Watch that rut."

"Don't tell me how to handle a wagon."

A wagon. That certainly explained the movement, and the hard surface beneath her side. She moved to push herself up, but her hands didn't work, either. They were stuck behind her back and…and… She gave another tug on her arms, and a biting sensation pinched the skin around her wrists.

They were tied.

She attempted to move her feet, but stiff bands of rope dug into her ankles. She moved her lips to call out, only to find a thick cloth on her tongue and a pinching sensation at the corners of her mouth. She'd been gagged, as well.

No wonder her mouth hadn't seemed to work right. But why was she bound and gagged and lying in the back of a wagon? And why had it taken her so long to figure out she was tied?

An unbidden tear slipped down her cheek. What was wrong with her? How did she get here, and why did her head ache? She fought back through her memories for an answer, but a thick, murky fog shrouded her mind. Something important had happened yesterday. What was it?

She drew her forehead down and stared into the darkness. It shouldn't be so hard to remember. There was something important... Something... Danielle! She'd run off and Brigitte had spent the entire night searching with...

The children.

She craned her head around and peered into the darkness. Were they in the back of the wagon with her? She blinked, but the black only turned more blurry with the action. *Non.* They couldn't be with her. They wouldn't be so quiet...

Unless they slept. Or were also gagged.

And she had no way of finding out unless she crept along the wagon bed. Using her shoulder to slide forward and her feet to push, she inched along the wooden planks like a slug. Heat stained her cheeks and more tears crept into her eyes, but she slid forward despite her humiliating position. Her children were more important than being forced to crawl like a bug.

She bumped into a soft, warm body. A small one. Victor. Was he well? She listened through the creaking of the wagon and grinding of the wheels against the road until his shallow breaths resonated in her ears. If one child was here and well, then the others must be also.

Or so she hoped.

She crept on. Just behind Victor, she nudged into Serge's still, breathing form, but not Danielle's.

Danielle, being the largest, should be the easiest to find. Where could she be?

Brigitte inched her way to the back of the wagon, then rolled and started her search again. Panic burned hotter and brighter with each moment. She passed by Victor and Serge once more, their little bodies unmistakable, but she reached the front of the wagon without any sign of her daughter.

Where was Danielle? Had she somehow escaped, or had the men who'd captured the rest of them done something terrible to her daughter? She tried to move her tongue around the gag, tried to force sound from her mouth and words from her lips, but only a loud groan emerged.

The wagon slowed and the canvas fell back to reveal a dark form towering above her. "She's awake. Douse the cloth."

Brigitte scooted herself up higher. "My daughter."

Or at least, she tried to say my daughter, but one sound was indistinguishable from the other with the gag constricting her speech. Though it did not stop her from trying again. "Where is she?"

"Stop moaning, wench. You'll wake the countryside."

A damp cloth pressed against her nose and mouth.

She inhaled the sickeningly sweet smell and nearly gagged, then the edges of her vision faded and her world went dark again.

Chapter Twenty-Two

The cold woke her, harsh and biting. Brigitte blinked and raised her head from the hard floor to look slowly about the bleak stone room.

Alone, with no sign of her children.

Her body shook with a bone-jarring shiver, and her head pounded as relentlessly as the nearby surf. But despite her brain's sluggish churnings, she knew she could only be one place.

Calais, and not in the warehouse, but in Alphonse's castle.

She pushed up until she sat against the wall, her head pounding fiercer with each movement, then she wrapped her arms about herself and rubbed. The warmth lasted naught more than a moment, and as soon as her hands stilled, the frigid dampness crept back.

She swallowed and her throat burned from dryness—which shouldn't be possible given how cold the rest of her body was. The small, high slat of a window near the ceiling let in the only light, and the corners of the room remained shrouded in shadow.

She should rise and bang on the thick wooden door, or at least call for someone. But the incessant throbbing in her head barely allowed her to sit, let alone stand, without throwing her stomach into turmoil, and her throat felt too swollen to speak. She narrowed her eyes at the open slit in the door. Alphonse would know she was awake, anyway. The guards had likely informed him the instant she began to stir.

So she waited. Head throbbing, throat aching, stomach churning. She huddled against the wall as a fresh bout of shivers racked her body. If only the guards had left a blanket, or a mug of water. A little straw tick on which she could lie. But even those bare comforts had been denied.

Alphonse must be angry indeed. He'd relish that he stood above her when he deigned to visit, as powerful and immortal as ever, while she huddled at his feet. What other tortures would she suffer at his hands? 'Twas only the beginning, this bare cell.

The door banged open, and she sucked in a breath.

But Alphonse's sharp voice didn't resonate through the room. A younger, softer one did. *"Mère."*

She jerked her head up. "Julien?"

"What have they done to you?" He surged across the room and sank to his knees beside her.

She shook her head—a mistake. It spun so badly she clamped down the urge to retch.

"Put your head between your knees, like this." Julien cupped a hand to the back of her neck and guided it down. "Slow, deep breaths. That's it. 'Tis from the drugs, whatever they gave you."

Tears blurred her eyes as she worked to steady her breathing and calm her sick head and stomach. Her son was here, beside her after over a year of absence. How she'd missed the familiar blue eyes, so similar to Henri's and Danielle's. How she'd longed for the quiet comfort of his presence, the quizzical looks he gave her when unsure of something, the silent responsibility he'd taken upon his shoulders whenever his father was gone.

"I'll have words with *Grand-père* over this." His hand stroked through her matted hair. "He ought not treat you such."

"He ought not treat many people as he does. Yet no one stops him."

"Hush." He bent his head close enough to whisper. "A guard stands just outside the door. He'll surely repeat such words to *Grand-père* should he overhear us."

"Why are you here?" She stared into his young face, the proud nose and high cheekbones, the disheveled hair a few shades darker than her own auburn tresses. His skin was tan now, doubtless resulting from the year spent at sea, and his body was stronger, broader of shoulder and thicker of chest. Yet he still carried the air of youth about him, that fragile demeanor of hope that life slowly stole from the young. "I didn't want you in Calais."

Because Julien's presence here could only mean one thing: Alphonse intended to train her son as his successor.

"*Grand-père* sent men for me when my frigate docked. I hadn't much choice in returning, only in how I went."

"But I wanted… Julien, you have to promise…" A fresh bout of tears welled in her already swollen throat. She gripped his hand. "You must—"

"A family reunion. How lovely." Alphonse stood in the doorway, as pale and gray as death itself, his body thin as a walking corpse. "Julien, I never gave you permission to be here. François will be punished for letting you in."

"*Non.* François will not be punished." Julien rose from his hunched position and met Alphonse's gaze. He was taller than his grandfather now, his new muscles painfully obvious beside Alphonse's weak body. "François well understands the precarious state of your health. He'll be working for me in a matter of months, and he wishes to retain his position after you leave us. You see, *Grand-père,* you can drag me from my post in the navy and name me as your heir, but not without consequences."

Brigitte drew in a ragged breath. So Alphonse had indeed brought Julien back here to take his place.

"Leave us." Alphonse barked at her son, his voice loud and thin.

"Non." Julien drew himself taller, a muscle working back and forth in his jaw. "She's my mother. I'll see her whenever I wish, and I'll not ask your permission. Anything you have to say to her can be said in front of me."

Alphonse's eyes turned as cold as ice-encrusted iron, but he held his tongue, his gaze locked in a silent battle with Julien.

Hope unfurled in her belly. She'd always assumed that if Julien or Laurent took over the smuggling enterprise, they'd be like their father, sucked in by greed, hardened to cruelty and fully subservient to Alphonse's will. But what if Julien was strong enough to break the cycle? What if the ages-old lures of power and wealth didn't sway her son? Maybe, just maybe, she'd raised a child with principles enough to defy Alphonse.

"Do you need water, *Mère?* Or food?" Though Julien spoke to her, he didn't take his eyes from Alphonse. "It seems *Grand-père* has been remiss in offering hospitality."

Alphonse darted a look her direction, and a cruel gleam flickered in his eyes. *"Non.* Traveling doesn't agree with you, *mon petit chou.*"

His little owl. If he called her that again, she might well retch on his shoes. "Because you drugged me."

"If you cooperate better next time, I'll not have need to drug you."

"There should have never been a first time, and there

certainly won't be a next time." Of that she was positive. She would never again use deceit to betray an honorable person like Jean Paul.

"Enough of this foolishness," Alphonse snapped. "Where's your daughter?"

Her heart quickened inside her chest and she cast a glance about the bare stone room. "She's not here?"

"Don't play me for a fool." Alphonse's boots echoed against the floor as he approached.

"I'm not. I'd assumed..." The flicker of a memory haunted the corners of her mind, her hands and feet bound as she inched along a wagon bed in the dark and searched for Danielle. She glanced down at her wrists, bruised and chafed from a rope. Had Alphonse's men bound her after they drugged her? They must have, and at some point she'd woken and realized Danielle was missing.

"If she's gone, I know naught of it."

A foul word flew from Alphonse's mouth.

Brigitte swallowed despite her painfully dry throat. If Alphonse and his men didn't have Danielle, was she safe? Had she gone for help or done something to warn others about Alphonse?

But then, where could Danielle have gone except to Jean Paul? And he wanted naught to do with her now. Besides, Danielle's disappearance didn't mean she was unharmed. Some other ill could have easily befallen her, and Alphonse doubtless had men out combing the countryside for her even now.

"Enough questions." Julien squatted down and wrapped a solid arm around Brigitte's shoulder. "*Mère* needs to go upstairs where she can sup and bathe and rest."

"Your mother stays here."

Julien's body tensed, muscles coiling tightly like a wolf

about to pounce. "She'll not be treated like some criminal, locked in your prison and deprived of sustenance."

Something dark and cruel flickered in Alphonse's eyes.

"Just go," she whispered. "I'll fare fine."

His arm tightened around her shoulders. *"Non."*

Alphonse cocked his head to the side, his thoughts obviously spinning, though she couldn't begin to guess what dastardly thing he'd settle on. "Very well. She can come upstairs, but only if she swears not to attempt escape."

"I swear it." She wasn't a fool. Escape would be futile with how well guarded Alphonse kept his lair. And no one in Calais would shelter her against his will.

But her father-in-law had something planned—the look in his eye gave him away. Though Julien had defended her for now, Alphonse was hardly finished. The next time they spoke, Julien wouldn't be interfering.

"I need men. Fast." Jean Paul slammed the letter down.

Captain Archambault, the commanding officer at Guînes's gendarmerie post, uncrossed his legs and leaned over the desk, frowning as he surveyed the letter. "This is from the Convention in Paris."

Jean Paul attempted not to grit his teeth. Did the man have to waste time with obvious statements? Brigitte had been gone four days. Four! 'Twas enough to drive a man crazy with grief and worry.

Hopefully Brigitte's journey from Abbeville had been slow. Hopefully the brutes who'd carried her and the children in the old fruit wagon Danielle had described had taken a wrong turn and ended up lost. Hopefully something, anything, had happened to keep Brigitte away from Alphonse Dubois for a few hours longer.

"Why, exactly, do you need my men?" The captain

leaned back in his chair and tapped the ends of his fingers together. Slowly. Far too slowly.

"Convention business." It wasn't a lie. Not that the Convention had envisioned his current situation when he'd agreed to write monthly reports last fall. The missive had merely been a precaution in case he ever needed assistance, though capturing a notorious smuggler was surely need enough to justify the use of soldiers.

"Last time the Convention sent men to our town, it ended in a bloody massacre at the guillotine."

Jean Paul coughed and reached up to tug at his collar. Must the man speak of the Terror?

The captain furrowed his brow and studied him. "Paris is a long way off. If I refused to lend you men, 'twould be weeks before the Convention found out. Provided this letter isn't a forgery."

Brigitte slipped farther into Dubois's clutches with each second he lingered in Captain Archambault's office, and the man wanted to thwart him? He could hardly face a smuggler as powerful as Alphonse Dubois with merely himself, a wayward gendarme and a thirteen-year-old girl.

Not unless he wanted to get them all killed in under a quarter hour. "The letter is as authentic as they come. Signed by Fouché himself."

The captain peered down at the missive once more. "I see that, but you've yet to tell me what you plan to do with my men once you take them."

Jean Paul worked his jaw back and forth. If Dubois had weaseled informants into the gendarmerie post in Abbeville, the smuggler would certainly have ears and eyes in a town that lay only a half day's journey from Calais. The captain himself might even be on Dubois's payroll.

Yet, if he kept silent, the man might well refuse the command issued in the letter. He hadn't the time to spend days convincing Captain Archambault to give him gendarmes. He needed to depart with enough men to fight Dubois, and he needed to leave now.

He reached down and rested his hand on the hilt of his knife. "There is a large smuggling ring in Calais run by a man named Alphonse Dubois. I mean to break that ring and bring in Dubois."

The captain's face turned white, his lips pinched. "His men have wreaked havoc in Guînes."

"I'm sorry." And he was. No group of men should be allowed to operate above the law. The Terror had taught him that, if nothing else.

Captain Archambault gripped the edge of his desk until his knuckles trembled. "They wanted my compliance in overlooking their activities."

Jean Paul tightened his hold on his knife. "Did you give it?"

"Not at first, but Dubois can be rather persuasive." The man's gaze dropped to the desk.

"What means of persuasion did he use?"

"His men raped my sister, then told me if I still refused to comply, it would happen again. And again. And again." Captain Archambault swallowed, the muscles in his throat working tightly against each other. "I have another sister in town, as well as my mother."

Jean Paul released his knife and came nearer the desk. "Look at me."

The man raised bleak eyes to meet his.

"If we bring Dubois down, he won't be able to force others to his will ever again."

The captain blew out a breath and slumped farther into his chair. "I can give you all the men under my command, but they won't be sufficient. Dubois is well protected. Few know where he lives or hides his wares, and those who have such knowledge refuse to talk."

"Mayhap, but his granddaughter travels with me, and she's talking freely."

"The girl in your party? That's Dubois's granddaughter?"

If only the other man knew. "Your family isn't the only one that man tries to manipulate."

The captain jumped to his feet, placing a hand on the hilt of his sword. "You may not only have my men, but my service, as well."

"Then make haste." Jean Paul turned and strode through the door. He was one step closer to rescuing Brigitte, and yet his stomach churned as he strode out into the sunshine. Surely she'd arrived in Calais by now, and he was still hours away. What if he was too late to save her?

Chapter Twenty-Three

They came in the darkest hours of the night. Meaty hands that wrenched her out of the bed where she slept with Serge and Victor, strong bodies that dragged her down two sets of stairs and across a great hall before propelling her back into the cold stone cell. Her head slammed against the floor as they tossed her inside. She righted herself and scrambled to the door, giving it a hard yank. It didn't budge.

"Let me go, Alphonse!" She pounded on the door. "You promised Julien."

She wasn't the sick, weak woman from a few hours ago. She was clean and fed and somewhat rested. She'd not cower in the corner and wait for Alphonse to appear while she huddled at his feet.

She raised her fist to pound again, but the massive door swung open.

Alphonse stepped inside, a solitary lantern hanging from his hand. His presence crackled in the room despite the dark shadows that shrouded his gray form.

"Julien said I'm to stay above stairs."

"Julien has been called away on an unexpected mission." His voice was flat and unamused, as though he spoke of the weather rather than illegal deeds. "Quite sudden, that. But needful."

A mission that Alphonse had no doubt contrived the second he'd brought her above stairs that afternoon. She only prayed the task hardened Julien to the smuggling business rather than lured him.

"And now we have time to talk uninterrupted."

"I'd hardly call being interrogated in a prison cell 'talking.'"

He crossed thin arms over his chest, the lantern swaying subtly with his movements. "I understand you have information regarding Citizen Belanger."

Please God, not this. Anything but this. "He's a good man, one you ought not bother."

She glanced toward the door. Why couldn't Julien barge through the thick wood, interrupting their conversation and saving her from the mess she'd created when she'd first agreed to spy for Alphonse? But the door stayed solidly closed, the small cell eerily silent as Alphonse waited for more information. "He feeds the hungry and protects the innocent. The entire town reveres and loves him, and with good reason."

"He killed Henri."

'Twas a statement, not a question. Alphonse already knew. The moisture leached from her mouth and she took a step backward. She couldn't do this. Not again. Jean Paul may have sent her away, may want naught to do with her, but she'd never again betray him. "He's changed."

Alphonse laughed, a cruel, taunting sound that echoed off the bare stone walls. "Men like me and him don't change."

"You're wrong." She raised her chin and glared, and if she looked a bit like Danielle in one of her defiant moods, then good. "You can change, just as he did. You don't have to hurt people anymore."

"Poor Brigitte. Has time spent in the presence of a murderer softened your heart?" His mocking tone held an icy cruelness behind the words. "Do you no longer want justice for Henri?"

"You never sought justice. You sought revenge. There's a difference between the two. Perhaps Citizen Belanger killed Henri, but Henri deserved death for his smuggling. As do you. What you're doing is illegal, Alphonse, and dangerous. Henri is hardly the first of your men to die."

The slap came so quickly she didn't see it. A hard strike against her cheek, setting her skin afire.

She gasped and shrank back.

"If one strike to your face causes such pain, you'll not want to spend time with my guards. I assure you." Alphonse leaned in close, his rancid breath feathering over her face.

She straightened, though her stance put her within mere centimeters of Alphonse's loathsome form. "I fulfilled your task and gathered information on Jean Paul Belanger. Now I demand you let me and my children go. 'Twas our bargain. You had no right to come into Abbeville and take me, or to take Julien from Le Havre. You owe me money and a journey to Reims."

"You foolish twit. Did you truly think I'd let you take my grandchildren to parts unknown when they can be of such use to me here?"

"But you said—"

He slapped her across the face again, the strike so harsh it would surely mar her skin. But she didn't flinch away this time, no. She kept her eyes riveted on his instead.

"I lied." His eyes turned hard in the dim light. "You'll

not leave here, unless it's in a shroud. Understand that now."

"I'll never let you control me or my children," she snarled into his face.

"Ah, yes, the familiar pronouncement of every impassioned mother. But you forget how much power I have." He took a step back from her. "I will indeed take your children and mold them, teach them. I'll have jobs for you, as well, of course, and if you behave, I shall allow you to see them every so often. This next assignment, for example, is in England, and I'm afraid you shan't be able to take your children. They'll have to remain here. With me."

"No!"

The side of his mouth curved halfway into a sneer, as though he hadn't the inclination to expend even a full smile upon her. "Very well, I shall kill you and offer the work to someone else." He turned toward the door. "Gerard."

The guard she'd met at the warehouse on that fateful night so long ago stepped through the door. His muscles shone big and thick beneath the lantern he carried in one hand, while his other hand gripped a large club.

She licked her parched lips and shifted her gaze back to Alphonse. "Think of what Julien will do when he discovers you've killed me. He'll never work for you then."

"Julien is away for several days." He walked backward toward the doorway. "He'll be told you had an accident and will never know the difference."

"He'll suspect."

"*Oui.* But he won't *know.* And that shall make all the difference. You see, Julien thinks I'm rather ill. It's not hard to fake an illness. A cough here, a shiver there, a feigned shortness of breath. Your son's actions are obvious. He intends to play along with me, biding his time until I die and relinquish control of my business. But I shall live longer than he expects, molding Julien to my wishes. And when I die, he will make a masterful smuggler, even better than Henri would have made. 'Twas the reason I brought Julien here rather than Laurent."

He stopped in the doorway, one mere step from leaving her alone with the guard. "Now then, if your questions are done, I'll let Gerard here get on with matters."

A twisted smile curved the guard's lips.

"Make it last two hours. At least."

"Wait," she croaked, her voice barely recognizable for its strangled sound. "I'll do as you say." She couldn't die, not here at Alphonse's hands, not with her daughter missing and her precious sons in his clutches. She had to at least live long enough to see them freed and safe—or Alphonse dead. Whichever came first.

Alphonse raised an eyebrow. "Are you certain? I tire of your wavering, Brigitte. Next time, I shall abide by your first answer."

She closed her eyes and nodded, unable to force a yes past her defiant tongue.

"Very well. You shall leave at dusk on the morrow. If you cooperate between now and then, I'll allow you to see Victor before you depart."

"And Serge. I must see him, too, and explain my absence."

Alphonse pressed his lips together into a thin white line. "Your time with Victor just got shortened by half. If you question me again, I'll take it away entirely."

Alphonse's footsteps echoed against the ancient floor, followed by the guard's heavier gait. Then the door swung shut, complete with the unmistakable sound of a lock clicking into place. Darkness surrounded her, stealing across the dank chamber until not even a flicker of light shone through the slot in the door. And with it descended the silence, so thick and eerie she nearly screamed just to fill the room with sound.

She wrapped her arms about herself and leaned against the wall. What had she just agreed to? How, oh, how, had she gone from the free woman who had met Alphonse in the warehouse two months ago to the person locked inside this room? How had she gone from a hopeful woman in love with a good man to a vile, deceitful being willing to break the law?

Alphonse's bargain in the warehouse had seemed like such a simple solution. Spy on the man who might have killed her husband, and everything would be done.

But Alphonse hadn't intended to ever let her return to Reims, and her mission hadn't stayed simple.

Be sure your sin will find you out.

Be not deceived; God is not mocked: for whatsoever a man soweth, that shall he also reap.

Deceit was sin, and wickedness had its consequences. One couldn't hold hands with evil and remain untouched. She'd known as much from the beginning, but her choices weren't supposed to cost her so dearly. She'd been trying to fight for her family, but instead of gaining their freedom, she was about to lose all she held dear.

A desperate loneliness enveloped her, the dampness cloaking the corners of the room crept up beneath her clothing until she trembled. She sank down against the wall and choked back the sob that welled in her chest.

Alphonse had said little of Jean Paul. Did Alphonse still plan to kill him?

Of course. Alphonse killed everyone who didn't behave as he wished.

And her daughter was missing, as well. Perhaps she lay dead or injured in a field somewhere, a cruel toy for a band of army deserters. Or maybe Alphonse's men had found her and she was inside his stone monstrosity at this very moment.

"I'm sorry, Father," she cried, clutching her knees to her chest. "I was wrong, so terribly wrong."

Why hadn't she trusted God to set her and the children free in His time? Why had she taken matters into her own hands and forged her own path?

"I know I'm doomed." Her raspy prayer echoed against the hard stone walls. "That I deserve no mercy or justice. But I beg of You, Father, even if You spare me not, save my children. Protect Danielle, wherever she may be, and help Serge and Victor. Give Julien clarity to see through Alphonse's lies and the strength to stand against them, and keep Laurent safe, wherever he is on the sea.

"And be with...be with..."

She could hardly push Jean Paul's name over her tongue. She'd done so much to harm him, so much to strip away the life he'd labored endlessly to change. She had no business ever forming his name on her lips again. But she would, if for no other reason than to pray God's protection on him.

She cleared her throat. "Be with Jean Paul. Give him another chance at marriage, allow him to forge a new life for himself. Reward him..."

Her words fell away as the tears came harder and stronger. She didn't fight them or pretend to be strong, didn't force herself to think on something else. Instead, she gave in. For her children. For Jean Paul. And for the life all of them might have shared had she been upright from the beginning.

"We should..."

The whisper of wind through the tall grass carried away Captain Archambault's next words. From his hunched position in the patch of amber marsh, Jean Paul leaned closer to the burly man. "What say you?"

The captain crouched closer to the ground. The slightest unnatural movement and they might well give their position away. "We should return after dark. It's too dangerous to attack in daylight. I had expected a well-guarded house, but this place is a fortress."

Jean Paul ran his eyes over the towering stone structure. Fortress was about right. Danielle had called it an old castle, and by the look of the crumbling stone, the edifice had long been abandoned to ruin and decay. But the tall walls, crumbling or not, still served as an insurmountable barrier between him and Brigitte.

"We can't wait until dark. Dubois has a woman and two children captive. There's no telling what he might do in the hours between now and then."

"Danielle," Captain Archambault whispered.

The girl scrambled back toward them from...well, who could guess why she'd been crawling through the grass?

"You're sure this is the place?"

Jean Paul could hardly blame the captain for asking. Dubois's perfectly hidden, undetectable headquarters was a fortified castle? 'Twas unfathomable. The man hid his illegal empire right under the noses of the French soldiers stationed in the forts outside the city walls, and he had never yet been caught.

Or maybe the smugglers didn't operate hidden. Maybe the soldiers knew of the illegal activities, but traded their silence in exchange for *livres*—or their lives.

"Oui." Danielle whispered to Archambault, her eyes wide and solemn. "*Papa* used to take me here, though *Maman* never knew. And I've worked for *Grand-père* before, delivering messages before *Papa* died."

The girl had yet to reach her maturity, and she'd already performed illegal tasks for the region's most powerful smuggler. 'Twas likely why Brigitte had grasped at any opportunity to get her children out of Calais.

"I still say we wait for dark," Archambault growled. "'Tis an unnecessary risk to approach in daylight. I want to ruin Dubois, not kill my men."

Dark would give them a better chance at surprise, but dark also meant leaving Brigitte, Serge and Victor at Dubois's mercy for nine more hours. Either way, he put people at risk.

"That's the best way in." Danielle pointed to a dark patch in the wavy grass. "It leads straight up to *Grand-père*'s chambers, and the guards will never see us coming."

Jean Paul rubbed the back of his neck. "How exactly do you expect grass to get us inside that castle?"

She rolled her eyes. "It's not grass. It's the entrance to a tunnel. That's why it's dark."

"And you know this how?"

She shrugged, two faint blotches of pink appearing high on her cheeks. "I told you I'd visited with *Papa*."

"And those visits taught you of a secret tunnel?"

"The door in *Grand-père*'s chamber hides behind a tapestry. It's not that hard to find."

"I see." He turned back to the castle. No men stood stationed as sentries atop the roof and no shadows moved in the windows. But somewhere inside those sun- and wind-buffeted walls, guards watched. Dubois hadn't built his smuggling empire by being careless. Getting inside would be nigh impossible without an army.

Unless he had access to an unguarded tunnel. "I don't suppose you know how many men your grandfather keeps inside there?"

Danielle shrugged again. "It depends. If he's got some

away on a mission, it could be as few as five plus himself. If everyone's there, perhaps twenty."

He raised his eyes to the heavens. "Father God, please let the men be on a mission."

"Amen," Archambault added.

Jean Paul stared at the opening to the tunnel for another moment. Even if he'd never be able to call Brigitte his or see her take his name, he couldn't leave her and the children with that monster a moment longer than necessary. "We go now. Me and the captain and four others will enter through the tunnel, leaving the rest to hide by the gates. Archambault, choose me four of your best."

A half hour later, he and five soldiers entered the packed-dirt corridor. Dark and damp, the pulsating earth swallowed his thin lantern beam and coiled dank, heavy air around them. He wiped a skin of feathery cobweb from his face and crept silently through the long-forgotten passageway. Sconces on the walls held torches ready to be lit, but he left them untouched lest the faint scent of flame filter into the fortress and alert the smugglers.

The castle had seemed near as they watched from the marsh, but the tunnel stretched endlessly before him, the trail of hard dirt seeming to lead him deeper and deeper into the earth instead of toward Dubois. Surely they'd passed the city of Calais and would soon reach—

"Oofff!" He bit back the curse that sprang to his lips as he stumbled over a crumbling stone step. Supportive hands reached out to steady him. He righted himself and glanced at the men. The dim lantern revealed little of their faces, yet a quiet enthusiasm emanated from their tense forms, even that of the gendarme Gilles. Sour toward Jean Paul he might be, but even he couldn't hide his pleasure at ending Dubois's reign.

"Not a sound once we ascend these steps." He whispered the final warning then started upward.

The wooden door loomed ahead, small and unassuming as Danielle had described. He hurried up the last of the stairs and reached out to clasp the rusted handle. The shuffles behind him stilled, and he sucked in a breath of foul air. 'Twould be no turning back once he lifted the handle. Whatever lay beyond this door, he'd have little chance to prepare. If he interrupted a meeting of Dubois's men, he and the others were dead. If he found the hardened smuggler taking an afternoon nap, their job was easy.

He turned back toward Captain Archambault, who stood between him and Gilles, then handed the lantern down the line of men.

Somewhere inside these ancient walls was the woman he loved.

Loved, but couldn't have.

Dear God, please let me be in time.

With one quick dip of his head toward the captain and Gilles, he took his pistol in hand and raised the latch.

Chapter Twenty-Four

Empty.

Jean Paul surveyed the massive stone bedchamber, devoid of any living body besides his and the captain's. He slowly rose from his crouched position next to the tapestry, then nodded to Archambault on the other side of the wall hanging. The man swept back the thick fabric, signaling the other gendarmes to spill quietly into the castle.

The room was large enough to hold a small army. A bed and various pieces of furniture were positioned near where they stood while a set of three steps led down to an open space below with table and chairs.

Where would Bridgette be in this monstrosity of a fortress? Tucked neatly near Dubois's chamber? Or locked away somewhere she'd never be able to escape?

His chest rose and fell with quick, heavy breaths, and he narrowed his eyes, senses open to any subtle sign that might reveal her whereabouts. But 'twas only one way to find her: search.

Calling up the image of the map Danielle had shown him outside, he pointed Captain Archambault and two of his men toward the large double doors along the far wall, the quickest way to get access to the front gates, according to Danielle.

"Gilles, Hugues, this way." He jerked his chin toward the smaller door near the bed. If Brigitte and the children were being kept in one of the bedchambers, then they should be down the corridor through this doorway.

He gripped his pistol tighter and used his free hand to feel for the knife tucked in his waistband. He had another blade at the small of his back, and another still in his boot. A man never knew when a knife would prove useful, and he aimed to be prepared.

"Make haste." He led the men through the door into a dimly lit corridor. Crumbling rock littered the dust-strewn floor, and the only light came from a window at the far end of the tunnel-like walls.

He eyed the ceiling, which looked to be flaking apart one stone chip at a time. Not the safest place in the castle to be standing.

A child cried from somewhere down the corridor. He knew that cry, could recognize Victor's ruckus anywhere. But from which room did the sound emanate?

"How many times must I tell you?" A loud female voice answered the babe, bearing no resemblance to Brigitte's soft cadence. "Stop crying. Now."

"He wants *Maman*. Not you." Serge's whine mixed with the ever-growing wails.

Jean Paul stared at the wooden door two rooms down. No guard stood in the corridor, but then, a guard might well be stationed just inside the door. He motioned to his men and crept silently through the shadows. Fifteen steps, then ten and five until he stood at the door. Was it locked? He glanced down at his pistol. One shot would break the bolt…

And alert the rest of the castle to his presence.

He reached for the latch and pushed. The door swung easily inward, and he rushed inside—only to have a sword prick the tender skin just beneath his jaw.

"Who are you?" a bearded man with aging skin and a weathered face barked.

He'd chosen the right room. Victor hollered in the corner, where a woman frantically bounced him on a plump hip, and Serge had grown still, his eyes wide as he stared at him and Dubois's guard. But Brigitte wasn't here.

A pistol cocked, and the smuggler's dark eyes travelled over his shoulder.

"Drop your sword, man," Gilles growled from behind him. "Unless you're wanting that pretty face blown off."

The gruff man's lips thinned, but he stepped back, his sword clattering to the floor. "Ain't no brats worth getting killed for."

Jean Paul picked up the sword. "He'll have at least one pistol and a knife, possibly more. Search him well before you tie and gag him."

"We should kill him and be done with it," Hugues said, his voice barely audible over the still-screaming Victor.

'Twas a time when he'd have killed the aging smuggler. But no more.

"We'll turn him over to the authorities." Which were likely corrupt, or this man would have been imprisoned long ago. "Better yet, you can transport him back to Guînes and deal with him there."

"Jean Paul?" Serge whispered.

He turned, and the boy ran forward to latch onto his legs. "I knew you'd come."

Victor seemed to disagree, as he wailed even louder.

He grunted but reached down to tousle the older boy's hair. "I could hardly leave you trapped here, now could I?"

"Hush now." The nurse hefted Victor over her shoulder and patted his back. "Help is here. Don't make such a commotion."

"Give him to Jean Paul." The boy beamed at him. "He can make Victor quiet."

A snicker sounded from where Hugues tied the smuggler's arms.

"Can you really calm a babe, Belanger?" Gilles sneered from his watch post at the door.

"I think he ought to give us a little demonstration."

"Aye, Belanger, take up the babe."

The back of his neck burned hot, and he scowled before looking down at Serge. "Where's your mother, boy? That's who the babe needs to stop crying. Not me."

Though he could likely calm the child, he wouldn't dare attempt it when he knew not what danger Brigitte faced.

Serge's smile plunged into a frown, and his eyes shot little daggers. "*Grand-père* won't let us see her. He took her away when we got here, then brought her back, then took her again last night."

Jean Paul rounded on the smuggler lying trussed on the floor. "Where does he keep her?"

The man spit.

Jean Paul stalked forward. "I said, where's the mother?"

Hugues nudged the smuggler with his boot. "Speak up, man."

The smuggler's eyes shifted around the room. He opened his mouth, closed, then opened it again. "Don't know who you're talking about. Got no woman here, save for the nurse."

"He's lying!" Serge shouted, loud enough to alert half the castle of their presence.

A commotion sounded from below and echoed up the stone walls, shouts of panic and the metallic clang of swords.

Gilles stuck his head out the door and surveyed the corridor. "The others must be here."

Jean Paul squatted beside the gnarled man. "You hear that ruckus? That's the sound of our men opening the gates and letting the rest of the gendarmes in. That's the sound of Alphonse Dubois losing."

Or so he hoped, because he really had no way of knowing if the gate had been opened yet, or who was trouncing whom.

He jerked the smuggler up by his shirt, their gazes colliding in a silent battle. "I'll give you this one last chance. Tell us where she is."

Something in his eyes must have warned the smuggler to comply, because the other man swallowed then blurted, "She's in the dungeon, she is."

"Dungeon?" Jean Paul dropped his hold, barely noticing the other man's head falling hard against the ancient stone floor. How dare Dubois put Brigitte in such a place? "Where is it?"

The smuggler gazed at him through pain-clouded eyes. "Follow the stairway at the end of the corridor down to the great hall. The entrance to the dungeon is in the south corner with a big iron door in front of it. Keeps the prisoners from escaping."

Alphonse Dubois was going to regret putting Brigitte in such a place.

"*Oui.* Hasten to the mother, if you would." The nurse bounced Victor on her hip, causing the babe's wails to subside into a more sedate mewling. "Dubois brought me here to tend the babe this morn, but he won't take no food from me nor from a spoon."

"I want *Maman,* too," Serge added, his chin trembling.

"And we'll get her. I promise. You wait here with Citizen…?" Jean Paul looked toward the woman.

"Renault," she supplied.

"Let me come, please!" Serge tugged on his shirt while shouts and clanging rang even louder from downstairs. "I can help find her."

"No, son." He cupped the boy's soft cheek. "You hear that noise from below? I can't take you into that."

Tears glinted in the young child's eyes. "You promise you'll find *Maman* and bring her back?"

"I promise on my life."

"Well, look at that, he can calm babes," Gilles mocked.

The tips of his ears heated anew. "Hugues, you stay and guard the children. Gilles, go make certain that front gate got opened. I'm heading to the dungeon. We've a fight to finish."

His boots clattered against the floor as he darted out the doorway, through the corridor and down the wide stone stairs. He hoped the voices and crashes were good sounds, hoped the other men had managed to open the front gates, hoped he ran toward his future rather than his death.

Because he hadn't told Serge the whole of it.

If he failed, then those precious boys weren't leaving this fortress, and neither was their mother.

Brigitte stared up at the cracked stone ceiling. Shouts and crashes echoed down the staircase and seeped in from beneath her door.

Something was amiss, but amiss in a good way? Had the law finally decided to capture Alphonse? Or dare she hope Jean Paul had learned what had happened and followed her here from Abbeville? That maybe she had a second chance to tell him the truth behind her actions and beg for his forgiveness?

Then again, maybe the ruckus wasn't due to the law or Jean Paul but another band of smugglers, ones who felt

Alphonse had wronged them in some way and now sought revenge—a revenge that would surely be shared by Alphonse's closest kin.

She swallowed tightly, a shiver working up her body. Meeting such a fate might well be worse than leaving for England tonight.

The sounds outside her door grew louder, closer. Perhaps someone fought on the stairs. She pushed herself up and moved to the entrance. The guard stationed on the other side had likely gone up to join the fighting by now. She tugged on the thick wood separating her from the rest of the castle, but the door didn't budge. Not that she expected it to be unlocked, but trying to escape hardly hurt anything.

She glanced around the chamber. It remained empty save for the single blanket Alphonse had allowed her and the one cup of stale water. Nothing she could use to break the...

Wait. There, in the farthest corner of the cell lay a little pile of rubble, likely crumbled from the wall above. She rushed forward and picked up the largest, most jagged piece of rock, then brought it back to the door. What better time to attempt escape than now?

She pounded the stone into the wood. A scratch marred the heavy door, but the lock didn't spring open. She set her jaw and gripped the rock tighter. Breaking the lock might take her half the day, but she had nothing better to occupy—

"Brigitte, are you in there?"

"Jean Paul?" Her heart thudded against her ribcage. Was it really him? Had he come? It seemed more a dream than a surety.

"Stand back. 'Twill take a musket ball to break this lock." His familiar, gruff voice rang through the door.

It could be no other. She shifted farther down the wall and stared at the door, waiting, waiting…

Boom! The unmistakable report of gunpowder and musket ball echoed inside the room, leaving a splintered hole in its wake. Then the massive wooden planks swung open, and Jean Paul's broad, unmistakable form filled the doorway.

He'd come. For her. All the way from Abbeville despite her betrayal. She threw herself into his embrace.

Strong arms wrapped about her back, and she buried her face against his solid chest. The scents of hay and sun and Jean Paul wound around her, while tears streamed down her cheeks and sobs wracked her body. She shouldn't feel his arms around her, shouldn't be standing against him at this moment. He should be far away from here, readying himself for whatever attack Alphonse had planned against his home. And yet he'd come, anyway, this strong, brave man that had stolen into her heart and captured it.

"I'm sorry," she whispered into his shirt. "How can you ever forgive me? I came to Abbeville only so that I could…so that I could…"

"Hush now." He coaxed her chin up with his large, gentle hand, then laid a finger across her lips. "I'm sorry, too, for not giving you a chance to explain when I followed you to that meeting. If I'd only been willing to listen—"

"I love you." She pushed his finger from her mouth and reached up to lay her hand on his cheek.

His throat worked tightly up and down, and he searched her face through eyes that seemed almost moist. "I killed your husband, Brigitte. Your husband, and many others. I don't deserve your love."

But he did. Didn't the man understand? She'd made the same mistake as he, choosing to do wrong for reasons that seemed right at the time, and if he could forgive her, why could she not do the same for him? But rather than tarry and reason with him, she simply rose to her tiptoes and pressed her mouth to his.

For one brief moment, an insanely wonderful instant, he drew her nearer. Ran his hand up her back to tangle in her hair, matched the fast pace of her frantic lips to his. She hadn't time for a slow sweet kiss, nor had she interest in giving him one. Instead, she put every word she'd left unspoken, every thought of her love for him into that one frenzied meeting of mouths and breaths.

Of hopes and dreams.

And then he jerked her away, chest heaving as he set her back from him. "Brigitte, we can't. Not now. Danielle is waiting, and the others—"

"Danielle?" Her fingers fisted in his shirtsleeves. "She's with you?"

"Hiding in the marsh outside the castle walls. Now are you hurt, or can you run?"

She couldn't help the tremble that raced through her body. Hurt? She'd come frighteningly close to being killed. Gerard had stood in this very spot just hours earlier, a thick club in his hand and a sneer of anticipation on his face.

"He hurt you." Jean Paul's jaw hardened into stone.

"Non."

"Tell me, and I'll make him pay."

"You came in time. He didn't hurt me, not yet."

Jean Paul touched his hand to her cheek one final time, then turned toward the door. "Come. We must make haste."

He poked his head into the corridor, then reached for her hand. The steps from the dungeon were narrow and uneven, crumbling like the rest of the castle. He drew her close and led her up before stopping at the top of the stairs. Shouts and footsteps resonated from the other side of the door as he looked through the small window slatted with iron bars.

"How did you ever find enough men to take on Alphonse?" she whispered.

He didn't bother to look at her but kept his eyes riveted on the events beyond the door. "I still have a bit of sway with the Convention in Paris, enough that I can rally men if needed. Now come, the men look to have things in hand."

He tugged on her arm and they stepped out into a massive room, likely a meeting place from centuries before, with its towering ceiling and arched windows. Men in gendarmerie uniforms grouped at the other end of the room, some conferring while others darted up staircases and into any number of the passageways leading from the great hall. But each carried a determined set to his jaw and an aura of importance and authority as he went about his business.

"André, have we caught him?" Jean Paul barked at one of the men racing past.

"Not yet. Archambault's convinced he's still inside, though."

Jean Paul merely grunted as he led her across the imposing room.

In the far corner beyond where the gendarmes stood sat a group of men trussed hand and foot, some familiar and some she'd never seen, but each glaring violently at their captors.

A pair of dark gray eyes met hers. She shivered and stared back at Gerard, his beefy muscles bound by such small ropes. What if he broke free?

Jean Paul wrapped an arm around her shoulder. "Give them no heed, love."

But she couldn't help one more backward glance. They were missing the most notorious prisoner. "Are you keeping Alphonse somewhere else?"

He quickened his pace toward a set of stairs in the corner. "That's who I just asked Hugues about. We haven't found him yet."

She watched the gendarmes, each coming back and reporting to a man with a decorated uniform and graying beard, likely the commander. "Is that why everyone's still busy?"

"*Oui.* We'll move the search out of doors if we don't get him soon."

"If he finds a way outside, you'll never catch him. He'll simply move his headquarters elsewhere and pay off the locals."

"I'll not let that happen, *ma chérie.*" He pulled her up another set of stairs, the same one Alphonse had taken her up when he'd allowed her out of her cell yesterday, and into a long, dimly lit corridor.

"The children's chamber is right…" He stilled, his every muscle tightening as he stared at the end of the passageway.

The faint tap of footsteps sounded, and was that a flash of gray?

Jean Paul dropped his arm from around her and raced forward, jerking his pistol out as he ran. She followed quickly behind, fear twisting her stomach.

He burst through the last doorway in the corridor. She flew through the opening behind him…

And stopped cold.

Her heart pounded in her chest and blood roared in her ears. She blinked her eyes once, then again. This couldn't be happening. Not now. Not when she and the children were so close to freedom. But all the blinking in the world wouldn't change the truth of the scene before her.

Jean Paul stood with gun already drawn, and Alphonse faced him from the center of an opulent bedchamber, a knife pressed to Serge's throat.

Chapter Twenty-Five

"Jean Paul Belanger, I presume." A hard, thin voice permeated the air while the man dressed in gray held the silver blade steadily to Serge's neck. "We meet at last."

"Alphonse Dubois." Jean Paul would have known the smuggler anywhere. The man carried an aura of danger and power that Robespierre himself would have envied.

Light footsteps echoed on the floor behind him, then a soft gasp. Brigitte. But he didn't turn. Instead, he kept his pistol aimed between Dubois's eyebrows, not that the musket ball would actually hit between the eyebrows at three meters. The old gun wasn't that accurate at one meter, let alone three. But Dubois would have no way of knowing how inaccurate the old gun truly was.

"Let the boy go."

"You killed my son, and now you've invaded my home and taken captive an enterprise that took decades to build. That's reason for me to hunt down every person you love and make them die a long, slow death." Alphonse repositioned his blade against Serge's neck, and the boy yelped.

Jean Paul flinched, meeting Serge's wide, terror-filled eyes.

"Ah, so you do love them." Alphonse's lips curved into a cruel smile. "And here I'd only guessed."

Had that single glance at Serge given him away? No doubt Dubois would now track the rest of the family were he to escape.

Which was why he wouldn't escape.

One good shot could stop him. "Release the boy, or die."

"Ah, I'm afraid we're at a bit of an impasse, as I have no intention of releasing the boy. And while it's true you could kill me with that pistol, the boy would die, as well. It only takes a slight jerk of my wrist, and his life is over." Alphonse moved the blade ever so slightly against Serge's throat, letting a trickle of red slide down his creamy skin.

"Don't harm him," Brigitte sobbed. "He's done nothing."

Alphonse's eyes gleamed with satisfaction. "Harm is exactly what will happen if your man here doesn't comply. You've a decision to make, Belanger. Either kill me and the boy, or slide me your pistol."

Jean Paul looked from Serge to Brigitte and back. What choice had he? He'd gladly forfeit his own life before letting Dubois kill Serge. Not that he'd give up so easily—he still had his knives, which he could throw more accurately than the gun could shoot. He drew in a long breath, then squatted down and placed the pistol on the floor. It didn't slide far across the uneven stone, but the little distance was enough.

"And your knives," Dubois commanded.

'Twas as if the man could decipher his very thoughts. He yanked the knife out of its place at his waist and laid it on the floor.

"And the other." Dubois glared down at him. "I'm sure you carry more than one."

Brigitte sucked in a loud breath, her desire to sob pulsing through the air like a tangible entity.

He clenched his jaw and grabbed the one at the small of his back, then slid that over the rough stone.

"And I'll take the one in your boot. I'm told you always carry one there."

This man had studied him too well. Jean Paul yanked the blade out of its hiding place and threw it across the floor, scarcely caring when the tip wedged between two uneven stones and broke. The blade wouldn't do him any good at present, anyway.

"Now you may rise." Something hard and feral glinted in Dubois's eyes as Jean Paul stood. "Finally, the man who killed my son stands weaponless before me. Such justice."

Idiocy is what it was. "Your son was a criminal. He deserved to be held accountable for his crimes."

"And you don't?"

Jean Paul worked his jaw back and forth and stared into eyes as cold and hard as granite. "Mayhap I deserve death, but your grandson doesn't. Your quarrel is with me. Let him go."

Frantic footsteps sounded from…

From where?

Not from behind him, and not from the massive open doors on the other end of the room. Then the tapestry on the wall moved, and Danielle sprinted out from behind the heavy fabric.

"Serge!"

"Halt!" Dubois's sharp command resonated against the ancient walls. "Or I'll slit your brother's throat."

Danielle stumbled forward another two paces before she managed to still. Her eyes moved from her grandfather to her mother to Jean Paul to the pistol and knives on the floor. "*Grand-père*, what are you doing?"

"I'm leaving. Belanger here is going to call off his men and let me walk out of this castle with your brother. But first I need you to take a few steps away from me, *mon petit chou.* Go stand beside Belanger there."

"*Oui,* move behind me." At least he could put himself between the crazed smuggler and one of Brigitte's children.

For the first—and likely only—time in her life, the girl obeyed without argument, coming to stand directly behind him.

Alphonse took a step backward toward the tapestry and hidden doorway, pulling Serge with him. A fresh panic lit the young boy's eyes, but Dubois kept inching steadily toward the hidden door.

Jean Paul bunched his hands into helpless fists at his sides. The smuggler was going to escape, and if he so much as called for the men, Dubois might use that knife. When he'd left Abbeville and gathered gendarmes, he'd meant to rescue Brigitte and her children. Now Serge stood in danger, and he'd no way to save the child. Was this his fault? It should be. Had he never involved himself in the *Révolution* or the Terror, then he wouldn't be watching a vile smuggler toy with an innocent boy's life.

Nor would he have the bloody nightmares that plagued him, or the guilt that fisted around his chest so tightly he struggled for breath at times. And he wouldn't—

Something cold and hard slid against the waist at the back of his pants.

A knife. And not just any knife, one of *his*. One whose weight and balance he knew. One he could throw with deadly accuracy.

He forced his cheek muscles to harden, lest they inadvertently smile and give him away. Of course, Danielle would think to give him his knife. Now he didn't have to stand helpless while a child paid for his mistakes. One throw, straight at the smuggler's head and...

No. He had no wish to kill again. And besides, hitting Dubois in the head with a knife posed the same problem that shooting him had. If he hit the smuggler in the forehead, the man would fall backward, his blade likely slicing Serge.

But Dubois must have a weak point somewhere. If only he could find it. He narrowed his eyes, scanning the thin old man. *The forearm.* 'Twas the perfect target. A good stab into the muscles that ran between the bones there, and the smuggler would drop his knife.

He tensed his arms at his sides, ready, waiting. But Dubois's eyes remained riveted on him. If he reached for the knife now, Serge's throat would be slit before the blade had left Jean Paul's fingers.

"In here!" a masculine voice cried.

Boots, an entire horde of them, clomped and echoed through the wide doorway at the other end of the room.

"Take another step, and the boy dies," Dubois cried out, but his gaze remained pinned to Jean Paul.

The clatter of boots on stone stopped, the men likely taking in the situation before them, but Jean Paul didn't dare pull his eyes from the smuggler and Serge.

The boy's fear-stricken eyes scanned the newcomers, and he swallowed.

Jean Paul held his breath and nearly cursed. Too big of a swallow, too quick of a movement, and Serge's life would be gone.

"Call the men off, Belanger," Dubois barked. "Tell them to wait in the corridor. Then I'll leave. If anyone follows, the child is dead."

"No," Brigitte whispered.

"Now, Belanger!"

Jean Paul opened his mouth. Did he have any choice but to obey? His men had invaded Dubois's crumbling structure, yet the smuggler still lived, prepared to sacrifice his grandson's life for his own freedom. How did one prevent that?

God, he prayed earnestly, frantically. Not that he expected God to listen when God had been ignoring him for six years' time, but in a situation this desperate, he had nowhere else to turn, nothing to cling to but the faith he'd learned as a child. *If You could send some sort of distraction. It can be anything. I only need an instant to reach the knife and throw.*

And then the most amazing thing happened. 'Twas almost as though God had heard his prayer, as though God cared enough about a filthy murderer like him to listen.

A lone set of footsteps clomped down the corridor behind him, entering through the door at his back, and Dubois's eyes darted toward the newcomer.

Just for a moment.

But Jean Paul needed only half a moment.

He whipped the knife from the back of his waist and threw. The breath stilled in his lungs as the blade flew through the air.

A thunk. A scream. A jerk. Who had cried out? Serge? Brigitte?

Dubois.

Pain etched the old man's face while Serge broke free of the hold and ran toward his mother.

Captain Archambault charged forward, leading the gendarmes to descend on Dubois while the smuggler sank to the floor, cradling his bleeding arm.

Danielle intercepted Serge halfway to Brigitte and threw her arms around him. Brigitte's eyes and cheeks streamed with tears as she rushed toward her children and wrapped them both in a fierce embrace.

Jean Paul surveyed the scene before him, his heart still thudding wildly against his ribs, as though his body had yet to realize danger had passed.

Something shifted in the corner of the room. He took a protective step toward Brigitte then stopped. The distraction had come from that very part of the chamber. Who had drawn Dubois's attention when half a gendarmerie post hadn't been able to help?

His eyes landed on a tall youth with tanned skin and unruly auburn hair slightly darker than Brigitte's. The lad lifted his gaze to meet Jean Paul's, and eyes as clear and blue as Danielle's stared back at him.

"Julien Dubois?" It could only be Julien. 'Twas no mistaking the family resemblance, and Laurent was still at sea.

The young man gave a curt nod. "You must be Jean Paul Belanger. Serge has much to say of you."

He crossed his arms over his chest. What did a man say to such things? That he didn't deserve Serge's praise? That he'd killed Julien's father?

"Thank you for saving my brother's life."

"I put him in danger," he growled. "It seemed only just I get him out of it."

The young man's gaze wandered to his family. "You didn't put Serge in any more danger than I. I knew I tread a treacherous path in attempting to appease *Grand-père* enough so he wouldn't harm my family. When he sent me away on a 'mission' last night, I understood what he was about, but I couldn't get back any sooner. I…I didn't think he'd hurt them." His voice shook, then he snapped his mouth shut.

Though Brigitte, Serge and Danielle huddled together not three meters away, the boy stood alone, blinking against his tears. A suspicious moisture filled Jean Paul's eyes, as well, and something hard tightened around his chest. But not the familiar guilt. No. He'd done right by this family. He'd come here and faced his past, and a part of him had been freed in the process. If he felt anything tight around his chest, 'twas love rather than regrets.

A love he knew not what to do with, since he wasn't worthy of Brigitte or her children.

"Go fetch Victor from the nurse down the hall and then see to your mother, boy," he gritted out. Then he turned and left, because if there was one place he didn't deserve to be, it was in Brigitte's arms, surrounded by her children.

Chapter Twenty-Six

"I've been looking for you."

Brigitte's fragile fragrance wrapped around Jean Paul as she sank into the long grass beside him. Rather than look at her, he stared out over the marsh toward the wall that cut off the fortified town of Calais from the sea.

"I grew concerned when no one could find you."

Why was Brigitte here? She should be within, surrounded by her children and basking in their love and safety—a love and safety he'd endangered not an hour earlier. "I wish to be left alone."

She slid her long, slender fingers beneath his palm. "Well, I don't wish to leave you. I wish to thank you."

He turned to her then, stared into her deep brown eyes and took in the defiant hair hanging free about her shoulders, the soft curve of her cheeks and moisture on her lips. He loved this woman, yet he'd killed her husband and then endangered her when he'd sent her away from Abbeville. She'd proclaimed she loved him in the dungeon, but those were words spoken in haste.

Now Brigitte was free. She could return to her home in Calais or move to Reims. The only thing she couldn't keep doing was loving him. "I've told you before not to thank me. I didn't do anything worthy of being thanked."

"You just freed my son from a man who would have slit his throat."

"Consider it repayment for having your husband killed."

"Non." She gripped his cheeks between her hands and pulled his head down so he had little choice but to look at her.

It was torture, the wild hair begging to be touched, the soft lips waiting to be kissed, the eyes full of love and trust and other emotions begging to be returned.

He could have none of it.

"You mustn't think that way. You were merely doing your job. As it was my job to spy on you for Alphonse. And I'm so terribly sorry. You didn't deserve what I did to you, but my husband deserved his punishment." She sunk her teeth into the side of her lip and glanced down. "You must hate me."

Hate her? Had she gone mad? "I once thought it right to kill others to revenge Corinne's death. I'm in no position to judge, and I hardly hate you." He swallowed, working his jaw back and forth before he blurted the rest. "I love you, Brigitte, but that doesn't change my past."

The air stilled, a crackling sensation filling the space between them. "You love me? Truly?"

He nearly rolled his eyes. Teach him not to better mind his tongue.

And yet, as he gazed into her sincere face, he could hardly lie. *"Oui,* I love you. I realized it about a quarter hour after I sent you away. Danielle found me sitting against one of the very trees where we had quarreled. I couldn't convince myself to move, only sat their thinking how much I loved you and…"

"And how deeply I'd betrayed you."

"You hadn't much choice. I didn't understand at the time, but I do now." He raked a hand through his hair. If only he'd let her explain when he'd found her and Alphonse's man in the woods, so much could have turned out differently.

"But I did have a choice. I could have walked away from Alphonse when he first gave me my task. Instead, I chose to bow to him and deceive you. Then even when I knew I owed you the truth, I put it off, making excuses until you discovered what I was about. I deserve what happened." She pressed her eyes shut and sucked in a ragged breath. "I almost lost everything. I would have—if you hadn't come. You claim you don't deserve me, but truly, 'tis the other way around. You're far too good a man for someone like me."

His hands shook, aching to reach up and smooth the matted hair from her face, to cause those lips to curve in a smile, to bring light back to her lifeless eyes. If only gentle words and tender touches could heal the wounds between them, but the festering sores of his past ran too deep, too painful. "No, Brigitte, I'm still not deserving of you."

Her mouth pressed into a firm white line and her eyes flashed. "Did you leave your sanity back in Abbeville, Jean Paul Belanger? You just travelled four days to save me. Four! You freed Serge from near death a half hour ago and captured one of the most sought-after men in our country. And if today's events aren't enough to prove your value, think of your endeavors in Abbeville. You give food to the hungry and work to the lame. You try every day to right the wrongs you committed a lifetime ago.

"Look at me." She got up onto her knees and stared him straight in the eyes. "I love you, and I'll not be able to stop loving because you wish it."

He dropped his gaze to his lap and the tall amber grass

crushed between his legs. "Perhaps you think you love me now, in this moment, after I just pulled you from a dungeon cell and saved Serge. But will you still love me in three years? After your life has settled, will you be able to look at me—the man who killed your husband and children's father—with love rather than hate?"

Her eyes glazed with tears. "I don't simply love you, Jean Paul, I forgive you. For what you've done both before I met you and after." She reached out and pressed her palm to his cheek, her skin cool and soft against his. "My love lets me forgive you, just like God's love for us lets Him forgive us."

He pulled back and sucked in deep gulps of air. Forgiveness again. Just like Isabelle had spoken of at the inn over a year ago.

He'd been cruel to his future sister-in-law in those days, still wishing her dead though she'd saved him, taunting her until she'd cried and fled the room. But she'd returned, sand from the beach ground into the knees of her skirt and fierce determination in her eyes.

I forgive you.

He'd wanted to spit fire. Had actually spit at her feet, if he recalled.

"I don't want your forgiveness. You deserve to die."

"I forgive you, anyway. What you do with it is your choice."

"Why are you rescuing me, forgiving me after I tried to kill you?"

She swallowed then, but she met his eyes. "Because it's what God wants. It's no less than He did for me."

No less than what God had already done. Jean Paul shuddered at the memory. Isabelle and Brigitte made forgiveness sound so easy, but 'twas as impossible as taking on an army with a band of four men.

He raised his eyes to Brigitte's. "You understand not how little I deserve God's love. Why should He forgive a person such as myself?"

She reached for his hand, the small connection flooding warmth through his body—a warmth from which he couldn't bear to pull away. "Because that's the beauty of God's love. None of us deserve it. Not I, nor you, nor Danielle and Julien, or even little Serge. But God bestows His love, anyway. And it isn't something you need to earn by giving away vegetables or renting land to armless tenants. It's just there. You only need reach out and take it. Surely you know this, Jean Paul. Surely you've heard it before."

He hung his head. *Oui.* He'd heard it. And perhaps he'd even known it somewhere deep inside. Maybe Isabelle had been right that day at the inn. Maybe all his mumbled prayers hadn't been barred from heaven. Maybe they'd gone straight to the ears of God, and he'd only imagined them stopping because he hadn't believed God would listen.

Because why would God want to love and forgive him if he didn't want to love and forgive himself?

His body turned cold, yet his eyes burned suspiciously. Could he have been wrong all this time? Could God have truly heard the prayers he'd uttered over the past year? Have offered forgiveness the first time he'd asked for it in that little room in Saint-Valery? He raised his eyes to the heavens, but instead of whispering yet another hopeless plea for forgiveness, he offered one of thanks. *Father, thank You for forgiving me. For loving me. For restoring my life and giving me a chance to correct my wrongs.*

The coldness left his body and warmth settled about him, creeping in to the darkest places of his heart, the places that had been cold for longer than he could remember. He drew in a deep, calming breath. Felt the touch of the sun on his face and whisper of the breeze against his skin.

"You were right." He squeezed Brigitte's hand, which somehow still rested beneath his. "It wasn't God who refused to forgive me. It was I who refused."

She leaned in and dropped a soft kiss on his lips. "Well, accept it now. And then forgive me."

He placed his hands on her sides beneath her arms and scooted her forward, grinning all the while. "Of course. Need you even ask? I mustered a gendarmerie full of men and came to Calais to save you." He lowered his head for another kiss. And this time, when his mouth met hers, no warnings screamed inside his brain declaring he didn't deserve her, no guilt haunted him as he wrapped his arms around her and tumbled her back into the grass. He was free now. God's love and forgiveness had made him so.

He pulled his lips away from hers for the barest of instants and whispered against her neck. "Marry me, Brigitte Dubois. Come back to Abbeville and be my wife."

She smiled up at him, her eyes alight with life and hope. "I wouldn't want anything else."

"Today. We'll see the magistrate before we leave Calais."

She giggled. His Brigitte, giggling like a schoolgirl.

He found her lips again, the tall grass tickling his neck and hands as he lay with her in the sunshine.

In many ways, he still wasn't worthy of her love. But then, what man was worthy of a woman like Brigitte? If he lived a thousand years, he'd never let go of her, the light and laughter she'd restored to his life, the feelings of forgiveness and understanding that twined through him.

From the rainy day he'd watched his first wife's body

lowered into the ground until this moment, he'd been on a long, hard journey. A journey in which he'd made a slew of poor choices and had caused unspeakable harm.

But God forgave him, anyway. And God loved him enough to offer him a chance to make right choices and love again. A chance to welcome the family he'd thought he'd lost after Corinne's death.

He buried his face in Brigitte's matted hair, dragged her familiar scent into his lungs, and pressed her tighter against him…because he wasn't going to let this new chance slip away.

Epilogue

One year later

*T*hwack!... *Thwack!*... *Thwack!*... *Thwack!*

Brigitte tucked a strand of hair beneath her mobcap and pulled open the door of the cottage, letting the sunlight flood inside.

Sure enough, Danielle stood with Jean Paul, her face fierce as she gripped a knife and scowled at an upright log already impaled with half a dozen blades.

"Your grip is too tight. You've got to hold the knife hard enough so it doesn't fall, but loose enough so it glides forward when you thrust. And don't flick your wrist."

Danielle glared at the log. "I'll get it, *Papa*."

Papa. Brigitte pressed a hand to her neck and swallowed. She never tired of hearing her children use that word. Even though Julien and Laurent were still away in the navy, she and the children had forged a true family with Jean Paul, so unlike the days of fear and loneliness that plagued her with Henri.

She rested a hand on her back, the ache there growing a little worse each day. Just a couple weeks, if her calculations were correct, and her heavy, protruding belly would give way to a babe. 'Twas a bit ridiculous to be having a baby with Jean Paul at her age. She'd already raised two boys to near men. But then, she wanted nothing more than to share a child with the man who loved her and shared his life with her, who gave her foot rubs at night and insisted Danielle—and sometimes even Serge—clean up supper rather than her.

Thwack!

Brigitte jumped with the sudden sound, just as Danielle let out a holler and threw herself into Jean Paul's arms.

"I did it, *Papa!* Did you see? Right in the center like you showed me."

Jean Paul wrapped his arms around Danielle, his face alight with pride. "I saw."

"I'm going to hit it again." She wriggled out of his arms and raced toward the log where the knives stuck.

Brigitte smiled from where she stood in the doorway. "Danielle's getting better."

Jean Paul turned, his lips curving into a soft smile as he ran his gaze over her distended body. "I didn't realize you were watching. Come here." He held his arms out, open and waiting.

She came forward. "Your eyes are tired. You should be napping, not playing with the children."

He enfolded her from behind and rested a hand on her belly. "I'm not the one with child, love."

"*Non.* You're the one with the nightmares that keep you up for hours in the darkness."

His body tensed behind her, and she could well imagine the contentment on his face growing into a serious mixture of hard lines and foreboding angles. "Just when I think they're starting to leave, they return with renewed force."

"They're not as bad as when we first wed."

"I owe that to having such a nice distraction when I wake."

She turned in his embrace and wrapped her arms around his neck, something she could barely manage now that her belly was big as a bushel of turnips. "Do you now? And what else do you owe to me, since we're on the subject?"

He pressed his forehead to hers. "I don't know. Is there something nicer than that?"

She released her arms from around his neck and shoved at his chest, but to no avail. His solid arms were looped too tightly about her back.

"Your meals," she spouted. "You owe your meals to me. And your mended clothes. And the dusting. I've tended the herbs this year, not you, and…"

Thwack!

"I did it again!" Danielle's voice, proud and elated, rang from behind them.

"*Maman,* come look, come look, Danielle got it!" Serge called from where he and Victor played in the side yard.

"Yelle get it," Victor mimicked in his sweet toddler voice.

She tried to turn, but Jean Paul still kept his arms locked around her, his eyes serious. "The children. I owe the children to you." His gaze dipped to her stomach. "Even the wee one. My happiness, joy and contentment. I owe that to you, as well."

"I can't give you happiness or joy. Only God can do that."

He hugged her tight. "Which is exactly why God gave me you."

She leaned against him, settling into the familiar strength of the man she loved, the man she didn't deserve, the man God had given her, anyway. The children's voices rang through the yard, accompanied by the steady *thwack,*

thwack, thwack of Danielle throwing her knives. Birds danced in the sky above, and a faint breeze whispered through the wheat in the nearby field.

She pressed her eyes shut and sank deeper into her husband's arms. She offered no sensual words or kiss of passion, and she didn't need to. Her husband's presence was merely enough.

The *Révolution* might still rage, leaving the government in turmoil. British warships might still stalk French vessels on the sea, and Austria might well take up arms against France once again.

Yet here she stood, wrapped in the arms of a man who didn't merely offer security, but love and forgiveness and understanding. Together, they had strength to face whatever the future held.

* * * * *

Dear Reader,

I'm so excited to finally get *The Soldier's Secrets* into your hands. When I wrote the first book in this series, *Sanctuary for a Lady,* two years ago, I never thought I'd continue the Belanger Family Saga and share Jean Paul's story with you. But here it is! I hope you enjoyed reading this novel and cheering for Jean Paul and Brigitte when they finally succeeded.

I enjoy writing stories set in revolutionary France because I sympathize greatly with the French people of the 1790s. They'd been abused for years by a government that used its citizens mercilessly. While I understand that a lot of bloody and unpleasant events took place during the French Revolution, the plight of the common people to be valued, treated fairly and recognized as citizens is something I wholeheartedly support. It's also something I wish the governments of today better understood. People are innately valuable because they're just that: people.

As I wrote *The Soldier's Secrets,* I endeavored to examine not just the events of the French Revolution, but also honesty and how important a trait truthfulness is.

In spite of past mistakes and dishonesty, God's forgiveness is always present and waiting to be bestowed on those who ask. When I sat down to write the ending of *The Soldier's Secrets,* I enjoyed revealing how both Jean Paul and Brigitte realize their mistakes and accept God's forgiveness. Then they get to turn around and extend that forgiveness to each other. I'm so thankful for God's forgiveness in our own, everyday lives. My prayer is that God uses this story in your life to illustrate the depth and breadth of God's forgiveness, as well as the importance of honesty in daily living.

Historically speaking, 1795 saw a bit of a lull in the French Revolution. France had won or was already winning most of their military campaigns, and with the fall of Robespierre and the end of the Reign of Terror nearly a year earlier, some of the political situations started to calm down for France. However, certain aspects of the revolution remained the same. The price of bread was still appallingly high for those in the cities, the poor concentrated in population centers often had little to no work and the paper money printed by the revolutionary government was dropping drastically in value. All of these things helped pave the way for Napoleon to take power in the next year. If you continue following the Belanger Family Saga as I write it, you'll soon see what France looks like with Napoleon in a prominent leadership position.

I'm calling the next book in this series "Danielle's Story" for now (though the title will certainly change by the time the book is printed), but "Danielle's Story" takes place at the beginning of the Napoleonic Wars and follows the character of Danielle from *The Soldier's Secrets*. If you liked *The Soldier's Secrets,* I hope you take the time to read the next book in the Belanger Family Saga when it becomes available.

If you enjoyed *The Soldier's Secrets,* I would love to hear from you. You can contact me via my website at www.naomirawlings.com or write to me at PO Box 134, Ontonagon, MI, 49953.

Thank you for taking time from your busy life to journey with me back to revolutionary France and read *The Soldier's Secrets!*

Blessings,
Naomi Rawlings

Questions for Discussion

1. Throughout *The Soldier's Secrets,* Brigitte makes numerous sacrifices to keep her children safe. If you are a parent, what kind of sacrifices have you made for your children? If you are not a parent, do you think you'd be willing to make similar sacrifices to those Brigitte makes? Why or why not?

2. When Brigitte first approaches Jean Paul, she's not completely honest about why she seeks him out. As the story progresses, it gets harder and harder for Brigitte to keep the truth from Jean Paul. Have you ever found yourself in a situation where it seems easier to lie than tell the truth? How did you get yourself out of the situation?

3. Jean Paul deeply regrets his past actions and spends a good part of the novel trying to overcome his past. Have you done anything in your past that you regret? In what ways have you tried to overcome those things?

4. One of the ways in which Jean Paul tries to overcome his past is by giving food to the needy, which he finds great personal satisfaction in doing. Our world today is full of similar charitable projects. What good do you see coming from charities in your local communities?

5. Have you ever been involved in a charity or ministry? If so, which ones? In what ways do you think people working in these ministries find their work rewarding?

6. Jean Paul struggles with being able to forgive himself and consequently, he doesn't understand the forgiveness God already offers him. Have you ever struggled to forgive yourself for a past wrong? In what ways did your personal struggle with forgiveness hinder your relationship with God?

7. Jean Paul struggles with wanting to accept Brigitte because he still grieves the loss of his first wife. In what ways do you think it would be hard to move on after losing a spouse?

8. One of the things Jean Paul regrets about his first marriage is that he never had any children. What trials do you think couples without children face?

9. Near the end of the novel, Brigitte needs to make a choice between either protecting Jean Paul or her children. How does Brigitte confront this problem? What does she do to try keeping both sides safe?

10. Alphonse Dubois is bent on revenge. What pain and heartache does Alphonse cause the other characters in this story? What kind of trouble do you think a person bent on revenge can cause in real life?

11. Near the end of the story, Jean Paul finally decides to share his past with Brigitte. How does Jean Paul struggle leading up to this point? How does Brigitte respond to Jean Paul's admission?

12. At the very end of the book, both Jean Paul and Brigitte asking each other for forgiveness. How does their willingness to forgive each other help their re-

lationship move forward? What types of problems do you think withholding forgiveness can cause in real situations?

FALLING FOR THE RANCHER FATHER
Cowboys of Eden Valley
by Linda Ford

Widow Abel Borgard has his hands full raising twins and establishing a homestead. Mercy Newell's offer to care for the children seems like the perfect solution. Will opposites attract when the wild-at-heart beauty helps a single father set on stability?

THE HORSEMAN'S FRONTIER FAMILY
Bridegroom Brothers
by Karen Kirst

The Oklahoma Land Rush is single mother Evelyn Montgomery's last chance at a new life. But Gideon Thornton insists the land her late husband claimed is *his!* Can two stubborn hearts find common ground?

HIS CHOSEN BRIDE
by Rhonda Gibson

Levi Westland has a year to find a bride and produce an heir— or risk losing his inheritance. But when his mail-order bride changes her mind about marriage, Levi must persuade her to give love a chance.

A RUMORED ENGAGEMENT
by Lily George

Years ago, Daniel Hale saved Susannah Siddons from her uncle's scheming with a betrothal—then disappeared. Finally reunited, Susannah has no intention of trusting Daniel again. But when scandal looms—she might not have a choice!

LIHCNM0414

REQUEST YOUR FREE BOOKS!

2 FREE INSPIRATIONAL NOVELS
PLUS 2
FREE
MYSTERY GIFTS

Love Inspired
HISTORICAL
INSPIRATIONAL HISTORICAL ROMANCE

YES! Please send me 2 FREE Love Inspired® Historical novels and my 2 FREE mystery gifts (gifts are worth about $10). After receiving them, if I don't wish to receive any more books, I can return the shipping statement marked "cancel." If I don't cancel, I will receive 4 brand-new novels every month and be billed just $4.74 per book in the U.S. or $5.24 per book in Canada. That's a saving of at least 21% off the cover price. It's quite a bargain! Shipping and handling is just 50¢ per book in the U.S. and 75¢ per book in Canada.* I understand that accepting the 2 free books and gifts places me under no obligation to buy anything. I can always return a shipment and cancel at any time. Even if I never buy another book, the two free books and gifts are mine to keep forever.

102/302 IDN F5CN

Name	(PLEASE PRINT)
Address	Apt. #
City	State/Prov.	Zip/Postal Code

Signature (if under 18, a parent or guardian must sign)

Mail to the Harlequin® Reader Service:
IN U.S.A.: P.O. Box 1867, Buffalo, NY 14240-1867
IN CANADA: P.O. Box 609, Fort Erie, Ontario L2A 5X3

Want to try two free books from another series?
Call 1-800-873-8635 or visit www.ReaderService.com.

* Terms and prices subject to change without notice. Prices do not include applicable taxes. Sales tax applicable in N.Y. Canadian residents will be charged applicable taxes. Offer not valid in Quebec. This offer is limited to one order per household. Not valid for current subscribers to Love Inspired Historical books. All orders subject to credit approval. Credit or debit balances in a customer's account(s) may be offset by any other outstanding balance owed by or to the customer. Please allow 4 to 6 weeks for delivery. Offer available while quantities last.

Your Privacy—The Harlequin® Reader Service is committed to protecting your privacy. Our Privacy Policy is available online at www.ReaderService.com or upon request from the Harlequin Reader Service.

We make a portion of our mailing list available to reputable third parties that offer products we believe may interest you. If you prefer that we not exchange your name with third parties, or if you wish to clarify or modify your communication preferences, please visit us at www.ReaderService.com/consumerschoice or write to us at Harlequin Reader Service Preference Service, P.O. Box 9062, Buffalo, NY 14269. Include your complete name and address.

LIHI3R

Can an estranged couple find a way to mend fences when they're forced into Witness Protection together?

Read on for a preview of FAMILY IN HIDING by Valerie Hansen, part of the WITNESS PROTECTION series from Love Inspired Suspense.

Grace parked in the shade across from the school and released her three-year-old from his booster seat and looked for her two children.

It wasn't hard to spot her eldest. His red hair stood out like a lit traffic flare at an accident scene when he left the main building and started in her direction. Then he paused, pivoted and ran right up to a total stranger.

The man crouched to embrace the boy, setting Grace's nerves on edge and causing her to react immediately.

"Hey! What do you think you're doing?"

The figure stood in response to her challenge. The brim of a cap and dark glasses masked his eyes, yet there was something very familiar about the way he moved.

Grace gaped. It couldn't be. But it was. "Dylan?"

He placed a finger against his lips. "Shush. Not here. We need to talk."

When he removed the glasses, Grace was startled to glimpse an unusual gleam in her estranged husband's eyes, as if he might be holding back tears—which, of course, was out of the question, knowing him.

"If you want to speak to me you can do it through my lawyer, the way we agreed."

"This has nothing to do with our divorce. It's much more important than that."

Grace's first reaction was disappointment, followed rapidly by resentment. "What can possibly be more important than our marriage and the future of our children?"

"I'm beginning to realize that my priorities need adjustment, but that's not why we have to talk. In private."

"What could you possibly have to say to me that can't be said right here?"

"Let me put it this way, Grace," Dylan said quietly, cupping her elbow and leaning closer. "You can either come with me and listen to what I have to say, or get ready to save a bunch of money, because you won't have to pay your divorce attorney."

"Why on earth not?"

Dylan scanned the crowd and clenched his jaw before he said, "Because you'll probably be a widow."

Will Grace and Dylan find a way to save
their marriage and their lives?
Pick up FAMILY IN HIDING to find out.
Available May 2014 wherever
Love Inspired® Suspense books are sold.